A Bad Place Alone

Tony Packer, Volume 1

JT Viner

Published by HSB Publishing, 2024.

This is a work of fiction. Similarities to real people, places, or events are entirely coincidental.

A BAD PLACE ALONE

First edition. May 5, 2024.

Copyright © 2024 JT Viner.

Written by JT Viner.

Table of Contents

A Bad Place Alone (Tony Packer, #1) 1
Chapter 1 2
Chapter 2 7
Chapter 3 16
Chapter 4 23
Chapter 5 30
Chapter 6 36
Chapter 7 41
Chapter 8 48
Chapter 9 53
Chapter 10 61
Chapter 11 67
Chapter 12 76
Chapter 13 84
Chapter 14 91
Chapter 15 98
Chapter 16 105
Chapter 17 112
Chapter 18 122
Chapter 19 128
Chapter 20 136
Chapter 21 144
Chapter 22 150
Chapter 23 158
Chapter 24 166
Chapter 25 175
Chapter 26 180
Chapter 27 186
Chapter 28 193
Chapter 29 200
Chapter 30 210
Chapter 31 217
Chapter 32 222

Chapter 33 231
Chapter 34 238
Chapter 35 245
Chapter 36 249
Epilogue 253

ALSO AVAILABLE FROM JT VINER

An Absence So Cruel

A Bitter Silence

To join my mailing list and receive news on work-in-progress and new releases, please e-mail me at james.viner.author@gmail.com. I will never provide your e-mail address to any third party.

Chapter 1

There was a blast of cold air along Aberdeen Street when they stepped down from the front entrance of the nightclub and onto the footpath. The bouncer ignored them. They were leaving the hotel, which made them someone else's problem.

Haylee stumbled at the bottom, her high heels falling off the edge of the concrete step and one of her ankles turning as she tried to maintain her balance.

Sadhi gripped her plump arm just below the shoulder, pulling her back upright.

"Steady there," he said, forcing a smile.

She stared at him, a drunken grin across her face. Her cheeks were pink from all the alcohol, her eyes heavy-lidded and unfocussed.

"Okay?" Sadhi asked.

She just grinned at him, too drunk to reply.

Inside the pub, where the light had been much dimmer, she had looked really hot. Here, under the harsh glare of the streetlight outside, he could see her better, and she looked much less pretty. She was a lot fatter than he had thought and her nose had a strange hook shape to it.

Sadhi didn't care, though. His erection was pushing against the inside of his jeans now.

Gripping hold of Haylee's arm, Sadhi steered her along the street past the edge of the club and around the corner.

There was a Chinese noodle shop along the street, its intense light spilling out onto the street. A man so heavily intoxicated that he was swaying was using a plastic spoon to dig clumsily in his cardboard box of takeaway noodles. He was dropping as much on the front of his shirt as he was getting in his mouth.

Someone was sitting on the street beside the shop, his head down. The front of his brightly-striped shirt was a mess of spilled alcohol and sweat. Someone was standing beside him, staggering slightly as he tried to light a cigarette, the wind blowing away the flame.

Sadhi looked around hurriedly. There had to be somewhere.

He pulled Haylee along the street. She was swaying a lot now, unable to stand up properly.

Hardly surprising, Sadhi thought. He had bought her twelve drinks to get her into that state.

Sadhi turned the corner, pulling Haylee behind him.

The headlights of a car flashed in his eyes, and he squinted against the glare. Haylee didn't even seem to notice.

Up ahead was another nightclub, a long line of patrons trying to persuade the two bouncers that they were sober enough to get in. Four or five of them sat on the ground outside, having failed in their mission and been told to sit outside for a while until they sobered up enough to come in.

Sadhi looked around, starting to get desperate. Shit. There had to be somewhere.

In his hurry to pull Haylee along the street, he almost missed it entirely.

Nestled back between two buildings was the narrow alleyway between them. The entrance was only about a metre across, with a couple of derelict boxes blocking it and graffiti plastering the walls on either side.

Sadhi stopped and looked more closely. It was hard to see, but it was dark and looked empty. It would do.

He turned towards the darkened space and pulled Haylee along behind him.

"Ooooh," she slurred, surprised by the change in direction. She stumbled again on her high heels, almost falling, and he had to hold her upright by her arm.

"Where are we going?" Haylee mumbled, her words almost unintelligible.

"Just over here," Sadhi said, "Just for a minute."

He kicked a broken cardboard box out of the way and walked into the darkened alleyway, dragging Haylee behind him. She followed numbly.

At the end of the alley, there was a narrow space about ten metres long. It reeked of urine and something much worse, making Sadhi wrinkle up his nose. He thought about trying somewhere else, but he didn't want to risk it. He had to do it now while Haylee was still compliant.

The space was so narrow that the walls brushed against his shoulders as he shuffled along, the ground slimy underfoot.

"Where are we going?" Haylee slurred again.

"Nearly there," he told her, tugging her forward.

In the near distance, he could see a patch of brighter light. The end of the alleyway opened into a much wider space. There was a rectangle of concrete about ten metres across that ran along the backs of all the nightclubs and shops on the other side. A couple of metal rubbish bins lay against the walls, together with broken boxes and a stack of metal beer kegs. There were no lights out here, but the top was open to the sky and the moonlight and lights from the surrounding buildings was bathing the place in a faint twilight. Just enough to see.

To his relief, nobody else was here.

Sadhi steered Haylee over to the one of the walls, then turned her around so that she had her back to the raw brickwork. She stumbled slightly, groaning and lurching to the side, until he propped her up.

Sadhi leaned forward, pressing against her large breasts and belly and pushed his mouth against hers.

As his tongue slipped between her puffy lips, she stood there unresponsive. There was a sickly-sweet taste of cocktails and cheap wine in her mouth.

After a moment, Haylee began to respond dully, her mouth opening to receive Sadhi's tongue, as he pushed it between her lips. Her hands slid along the sides of his shirt, fumbling at him.

Sadhi slid one hand up beneath the bottom of her short skirt and pushed it between her heavy thighs.

She groaned into his mouth and clumsily moved her legs apart for him.

His fingers rubbed across the front of her panties, touching her through the thin material.

He pushed hard against her with his hand, moving his tongue around inside her mouth as he roughly groped her.

Haylee's movements were slow and awkward, but she stroked his arms with her hands.

Still pushing against her with his mouth and his chest, Sadhi reached down for his belt buckle. Curving his arse out behind him, he managed to get his belt undone and tugged open the button on his flies. He pulled down the zip and yanked his erection out of his underpants. The night air felt chilly against his naked skin.

Sadhi straightened up, pulling his mouth away from Haylee's.

He put both hands on her shoulders and pushed her down to her knees in the grime. She staggered and fell onto the filthy ground with a slight thump.

She muttered something, but he couldn't understand what it was and didn't care anyway.

Gripping the base of his erection with one hand, he pushed it forward. He gripped Haylee's wavy, blonde hair with the other hand and pulled her head down.

"Ugh, fuck," he grunted, as the wet heat of her mouth washed over him.

Gripping her hair with both hands, he began to thrust, shoving himself into her mouth. She gave a muffled gag, but he ignored it and continued thrusting.

Grinning, Sadhi forced himself into Haylee's mouth, pushing deeper and deeper. One of her hands was on his thigh, trying to push him back, but he slapped it away and kept thrusting. She was far too drunk to stop him.

"Yeah," he grunted, "That's it."

As he thrust, Sadhi glanced to the side. There was a dark-green wheelie bin along the wall beside them, with a pile of boxes and other garbage spilling out of the top and onto the filthy floor beside it.

A pair of eyes was staring up at Sadhi.

Someone was lying on the ground amongst the rubbish looking at him.

"Ah, fuck!" Sadhi yelled out in shock.

He pushed Haylee's head away and stepped back.

Haylee gave a loud grunt of relief and wiped at her mouth with her hand.

"You fucking arsehole," she slurred drunkenly at him.

Sadhi turned away, as he hurriedly pushed his rapidly-softening penis back inside his underpants and pulled the edges of his jeans together.

In his haste to get his jeans done up, flesh caught in the zip.

"Fuck!" Sadhi screeched in pain. He fumbled with the zip, finally getting it done back up and began to buckle his belt once more.

Haylee was screaming abuse at him now, her words barely coherent.

Now dressed once more, Sadhi turned back to the rubbish near the bin.

He stepped forward.

"What the fuck are you doing?" he yelled, "Getting a fucking sneaky peak at us? You fucking perv."

Sadhi kicked at a broken box, sending it skimming across the dimly-lit space.

It was hard to see, but there was enough moonlight overhead for him to make out the face once more. Now he could also see a shoulder and part of an arm, chocolate-brown skin blending in with the patch of darkness beside the bin.

A hand stuck out from beneath the pile of boxes, fingers splayed out on the ground.

"Well?" Sadhi yelled, "I asked you a fucking question."

He kicked at the boxes again, but there was no response.

Belatedly, Sadhi realised the person on the ground wasn't moving. The eyes stared up at him, unblinking, the mouth hanging open slightly.

Sadhi stepped forward, his anger disappearing and something else taking its place.

He leaned down towards the ground.

Holding out a hand, he waved it in front of the face looking up at him.

There was no reaction at all.

"Oh, shit," Sadhi hissed, taking a hasty step backwards, "Shit! Shit!"

He stumbled over something on the ground and landed on his side, mud squelching against his jeans and something sharp sticking into the back of his thigh.

Hands sliding in the filth, he pushed himself back to his feet again.

Haylee was standing up now, drunkenly swaying as she watched him.

"What is it?" she slurred.

Sadhi looked up at her.

"It's a body," he yelled, "There's a fucking dead body over there."

Monday

Chapter 2

Tony Packer turned the car along Lake Street, heading deeper into Northbridge.

Up ahead, the dim flash of blue lights cut through the darkness. Two marked police cars were blocking the end of Aberdeen Street, a fence formed from traffic cones and fluorescent tape creating a barrier across the footpath. A group of uniformed officers were standing guard as a large crowd of onlookers stood a couple of metres from the makeshift barrier, trying to see what was going on.

A couple of the rubber-neckers were clearly drunk and had begun an argument with one of the officers who was shouting angrily at them and pointing down the street, trying to get them to leave.

Packer pulled up on to the footpath, parking half over the curb and turned off the engine.

One of the uniformed officers saw him and started shouting. He walked across to Packer, gesturing for Packer to move the car.

Packer walked towards him, pulling his identification out of the pocket of his jeans.

"It's alright, mate," Packer told him, "Detective Senior Sergeant Packer."

He held out the ID for the officer to read.

"Sorry, Sarge," the officer said, looking embarrassed, "You're the new bloke?"

Packer nodded, and the officer introduced himself.

"It's just that we're having trouble keeping the crowd contained," the officer continued, "There's a lot of drunk dickheads causing problems."

Packer nodded dismissively.

"Where is it?" he asked.

The officer pointed over towards another marked police car and a police van that were parked on a concrete area a couple of metres in from the road.

"See there's a laneway over there behind the car? Right down the end. Forensics are there already."

Packer nodded again and headed over towards the car.

He could see a uniformed officer standing near the wall, talking to a heavily-built man whose large belly pushed against the front of his shirt.

As Packer got closer, the big man turned towards him.

"Evening, boss," Detective Senior Constable George Thompson said. Twenty years of living in Australia had softened his Belfast accent, but only slightly.

Packer nodded a greeting.

"What's the story?" he asked.

Thompson nodded over towards the police van. "That prick over there."

Packer followed his gaze. A man in his mid-twenties was sitting in the back of the van, looking out through the grill over the window and staring daggers at the blonde girl who was sitting in the back of the patrol car. The door of the patrol car was open and a female officer in uniform was squatting on the ground beside her, making notes in her notebook as they spoke.

"Got that girl over there pissed as a parrot," Thompson went on, "then dragged her down the alleyway here for a blowjob. He was shoving his dick in her mouth when he suddenly realised they were standing next to the dead body."

"Jesus. That'd put you off your stroke," Packer said.

"Aye," Thompson agreed, "Two lads heard the screams and grabbed a couple of uniforms who were down the road on patrol."

"Who was screaming? Him or her?"

"Both, according to them."

"Have you spoken to either of them?"

Thompson nodded. "The girl's sobered up a bit, but she's still too pissed to have much idea what's going on. Says she was trying to push him off, then he fell over and started yelling that there was a body in there."

"What about him?"

"Says they were going back to his place for some 'consensual sex' - quote, unquote - but passion suddenly got the better of them. They couldn't wait until they got home, so headed down here to make a start. Just as they got started, he noticed someone was watching them, so they stopped. Then he discovered the peeping tom was no longer capable of doing any peeping. Next thing he knew, a couple of police officers arrived."

"Do we know who he is?"

"Sadiq Mehri," Thompson said, "I ran a check on him. There have been a couple of previous complaints of sexual assault, but not enough to charge him with. He knows the ropes. First thing he did when he calmed down was ask someone to contact his solicitor."

"How drunk's she?"

"Blew 0.23 on the breathalyzer."

"Shit," Packer said, "How's she still standing up?"

Thompson shrugged. "Robust constitution?"

Packer looked over at Sadiq Mehri sitting in the back of the police van. His hair was greased back and he had a sneer of arrogance on his face, angry at being detained by police.

"After the girl's given her statement, charge him with sexual assault," Packer said.

"It won't go anywhere," Thompson pointed out, "She's the only witness and she was far too pissed to be a reliable witness. Presumably, that was why he filled her up with booze first."

"You're right. But do it anyway. At the very least, the bail conditions will cramp his style for a while and he'll run up a few dollars in legal fees before the DPP drops the charge."

Thompson nodded. "Okay, boss."

"Where's the body?"

Thompson jerked his head towards the alleyway behind him.

"Down there. FME's down there with a team."

"Is it someone you know?"

Thompson shook his head. "Nobody I've seen before. Young Indian lass."

"Let's go and have a look. Have you got any shoe covers?"

Thompson produced two pairs of disposable paper shoe covers and a pair of blue gloves. Both men pulled the shoe covers on over their own shoes, then tugged on the blue gloves.

Thompson led the way, walking down the narrow alleyway. He had to move carefully to avoid his thick belly brushing against the walls on either side. Packer was broad shouldered and had to be just as careful.

The empty space at the end of the alleyway was now lit up by several powerful halogen lights on stands that were placed up against the walls. Three forensics officers in white paper suits and hoods were standing on either side of the wheelie bin. One was recording the examination with a video camera, the second was taking still photos with a large camera, and the third was recording samples on an exhibits sheet that was mounted on a wooden clipboard.

A fourth figure in a white jump suit and hood was squatting down beside the bin. The white suit clung to her figure, which was thin, but clearly female. A black plastic toolbox was open a metre away from her, the lid hinged back to form two trays that were covered with neatly arranged swabs and sample bags.

Thompson and Packer stood back a couple of metres to wait.

Cardboard boxes and rubbish had been moved from around the body. Some items had been sealed in large plastic sacks, while others had been moved into a neat pile away from the bin.

With the rubbish removed and the powerful beam of the halogen lights trained on the ground, Packer could clearly see the body.

It was a woman who appeared to be in her early twenties, or possibly even late teens. Her dark brown skin and facial features clearly showed her African heritage. Her hair was tied into tight braids that hung around her face in a tangle. She was narrow-waisted but wide-hipped and large-breasted.

Her eyes stared sightlessly up, her mouth hanging open over teeth that seemed shockingly white between her puffy lips.

A green plastic sheet, like the tarpaulin from the back of a ute had been wrapped around her, but one long edge had fallen away, exposing the side of her body. She was completely naked.

The woman squatting on the ground was running a cotton swab along the inside of the dead woman's mouth, gently easing back her lips with its tip. She pushed the swab into a plastic tube that she held in her free hand, then screwed its cap on.

She held it on its side and read the barcode on the label aloud, then waited while the officer with the clipboard wrote it down. She placed the tube in a plastic tub behind her.

As she turned towards the tub, she caught sight of Packer and Thompson standing a couple of metres away.

She straightened up and took a step towards them.

Her hair was hidden by the hood of the suit, although a few stray locks of brown hair fell down around its edges. The skin of her face was dark, in sharp contrast to the white suit. Packer thought she was probably forty or thereabouts. Her thin face was attractive but had an expression of faint annoyance at being disturbed.

"Hello," she said, her voice carrying the faint melody of an accent, "I'm Doctor Chandra."

"Senior Sergeant Packer," Packer said, looking over the doctor's shoulder at the dead body, "What can you tell us?"

"Female, aged about twenty years, in good physical condition. I'll confirm this with the autopsy, but she appears to have been strangled. And not using hands. She's been strangled with some kind of garrote."

Packer frowned. "Yeah?"

"Mmm. There are horizontal bruises around the throat where the skin has been caught. And there's a rectangular mark at the front where some kind of buckle or toggle has been tightened."

Doctor Chandra held a blue-gloved hand in front of her own throat, showing the positioning.

"The attacker was facing her?" Packer asked.

Doctor Chandra nodded.

"Yes. She has striations on her wrists and ankles, too. She was bound while she was strangled."

"Christ," Thompson mumbled behind Packer.

"When did she die?" Packer asked.

"Based on the rigor, I'd say at least twelve hours, but less than twenty-four."

Packer looked at his watch. It was just after 2:00am. Some time during the previous day.

"I don't think she was killed here," Doctor Chandra said, anticipating the next question, "You see the dried saliva down the side of her face? It's on the wrong side. She's been moved since that dried. I'd say killed somewhere else and then brought here later."

"Any idea how long she's been here?" Packer asked.

"Hard to say. It was raining yesterday, so the top layers of boxes were wet. The boxes closest to her were not, so she hasn't been there long enough for the rain to seep through. I'd say a few hours at the outside."

Which would mean she was killed somewhere else, kept there all day and then dumped here yesterday evening, Packer thought. Made sense. If she'd been brought here before the sun went down, then someone probably would have seen her being dumped.

"Was she raped?" Packer asked.

Chandra shook her head. "I don't know yet. No obvious signs, but I'll examine her at the hospital."

"Anything that looks like intimate samples from the attacker?"

Doctor Sinclair shook her head. "Not at this stage. I'll take some samples when I get her back to the lab, so we might get DNA on something. I wouldn't hold out much hope, though. There was mud on the ground and the rubbish around her will have contaminated the body."

"Has she got any ID on her?" Packer asked.

"She was wrapped in a plastic sheet, although it seems to have fallen open when she was placed here. There's a handbag and a plastic bag full of clothing tied at the top, both bundled in with the sheet. I don't know what's in them."

"Can you open them?" Packer asked.

A wrinkle of annoyance appeared between Chandra's eyebrows.

"My job is to examine the body," she said, "Scene-of-crime will process the effects when they get here."

"Right now, someone's wondering where she is," Packer said, "The sooner we know who she is, the sooner we can let them know."

"Will waiting for scene-of-crime to arrive make so much difference, officer?" Chandra snapped, the frown of annoyance deepening.

Packer looked impassively at her for a moment.

"Yes," he said, "It might."

Chandra glared at him a moment longer, and he expected her to argue. Instead, she nodded curtly.

She peeled off the blue gloves she was wearing, then pushed them into a plastic bag that was open on the ground beside the black toolbox. As her hands were exposed, Packer noted that her fingers were long and thin, the nails plain, but well-manicured.

Doctor Chandra took another pair of gloves from the bottom of the toolbox and pulled them on, tugging at the bottom of each pair to make them tighter.

She moved over to the body once more and squatted down on the ground beside the corner. She waited for the officer with the video camera to move closer and train the lens on her hands, and another of the officers to hold a hand-held torch over the top. Then she peeled back the edge of the green, plastic tarp.

A brown handbag was under the edge of the tarp, its cheap vinyl scuffed and peeling along the seams. The zip across the top was open, and Doctor Chandra gently pulled back the edges to expose the contents, then tilted it towards the harsh beam of light from the torch.

Inside the bag was a pair of cheap, plastic sunglasses that looked like they had come from a service station or a chemist, a non-descript case for glasses, and an aerosol deodorant container. Doctor Chandra pushed these aside, exposing a make-up compact, a tube of lipstick and couple of tampons.

Doctor Chandra's hands moved across the back of the handbag, and she found a pocket. She reached inside and retrieved a garish, pink purse with a heart marked out in sequins. She opened the purse and folded it back.

One side was made up of a plastic sleeve containing a photograph of a dark-skinned family, a middle-aged couple, the woman on the ground beside them and a boy who looked to be in his middle teens. A row of pockets for credit cards and identification cards was completely empty.

Doctor Chandra opened the back pocket of the wallet. It contained two ten-dollar notes. The wallet was otherwise empty.

Doctor Chandra turned it about in the light, so that it could be seen by the video camera.

"Nothing here, officer," she said, looking up at Packer, "Satisfied?"

He nodded. "Thanks."

Doctor Chandra returned the wallet to the pocket at the back of the handbag once more. She put the handbag back where it had come from and stood up.

As she peeled the blue gloves off, she looked at Packer, her face unreadable.

"Leave your details with Scott," she said, nodding towards the exhibits officer, who was holding the clipboard, "I'll e-mail my report once it's finished."

Without bothering with a farewell, Chandra turned back towards the toolbox for a fresh pair of gloves.

Packer took out a business card with his contact details and handed it to the exhibits officer, who slid it underneath the metal clip on the top of his clipboard.

He turned to the officer holding the camera.

"Have you got a clear picture of her face?" he asked.

"Yeah. Of course," the officer replied.

"Can you e-mail that to me? Just the face."

The officer nodded.

Thompson and Packer turned back towards the alleyway once more.

"Pretty nasty stuff," Thompson said, "Tying her up, then strangling her. And why do it from the front?"

"Maybe he wanted to watch her face while he was killing her."

"Christ," Thompson swore, "What kind of sick bastard does that?"

Packer shook his head.

He stopped at the beginning of the entranceway and looked back over at the body, a frown on his face. He stood there in silence for a moment.

"What is it?" Thompson asked.

Packer shook his head again.

"She was bound and strangled. Whoever did it had to get bindings and a garrote ready in advance, which takes planning.

"But dumping her here was stupid. She was bound to be found, and pretty quickly, too. It doesn't make sense. Someone planned ahead enough to organise the binding and the garrote but didn't plan how to get rid of the body afterwards."

"Maybe he panicked," Thompson suggested, "Had some other plan, but got interrupted."

"Maybe," Packer said, but clearly didn't sound convinced.

He looked over at the dead woman on the ground for a moment longer, with the forensic team moving around her, white paper suits rustling slightly as they moved.

Then he turned and led the way back up the alleyway.

Chapter 3

Packer and Thompson stood at the end of the alleyway, far enough away from the street that they were insulated from the noise of the crowd of onlookers and would not be overheard.

The van with Sadiq Merhi and the car with the girl had both gone, leaving only the officers guarding the cordon on the street.

They tugged off the shoe covers and gloves.

"You get home, George," Packer said, "Get some sleep while you can. I'll see you back at the station at six. Send a message to the rest of the team, too."

"It was my call-out," Thompson said, "I can wait for scene-of-crime."

"No, you go. I'll stay."

Thompson stood there a moment longer looking at Packer, whose eyes were elsewhere. Packer had only been at the station a couple of weeks and Thompson was still having trouble getting a handle on him. The man was distant and intense, making it difficult to get a feel for him. He had clearly made the decision to remain here, though, so there was no point discussing it further. Whatever thoughts Packer had were his for now.

"Right you are, boss," George said, "See you in the morning."

He left the alleyway and walked back out onto the street.

Packer remained standing in the alleyway.

Eventually, he turned and walked back out to the street.

The crowd had died down to about half the size it had been earlier, now that the novelty had worn off, but there was still about twenty or thirty hangers-on in various states of intoxication.

Packer looked at his watch. It was coming up on 2:40am. He stood by the entrance to the alleyway for a while, looking around. The alleyway was a long way back from the main street, maybe forty or fifty metres. The glare of streetlights and the bright lighting of the clubs and late-night eateries was a long way from here. The place was isolated.

He didn't want to miss the scene-of-crime unit when it arrived, but there was no sign of them at the moment. Wanting to see the surrounding area as it was right now, he headed along the street.

The same uniformed officer who had challenged him earlier gave him a nod and held the fluorescent tape up for him when he approached. Packer muttered a thanks as he ducked under the line.

A couple of bystanders watched him leave, and he half expected questions, but they watched him walk past in silence, before turning back towards the alleyway.

Packer wandered along the street, checking over the territory. He was new to the area, and knew Northbridge only by reputation, but that was something that worked in his favour; he wanted to see the place from someone else's perspective.

Someone who garroted a woman to death, then dumped her naked corpse in a back alley.

The footpaths here were dirty, the filth encrusted on the bitumen and clinging to the gutters. Rubbish crackled under his shoes.

It was an odd part of the city. Two blocks west was Perth's CBD, towering office blocks and trendy restaurants surrounding the twin malls and the train stations. The place was packed during the days and into the early evenings, but oddly quiet after about 9:00pm as business finished for the day.

Across the Horseshoe Bridge past Yagan Square lay the busy section of Northbridge. Nightclubs and hotels that opened in the late afternoon and stayed open until early morning, noodle bars and greasy spoons that catered to the patrons of the clubs who were loaded with overpriced alcohol and readily-available drugs.

There was a dirtier side to the place, too. Underground sex shops and brothels filled Northbridge, illegal but ignored and barely hidden from view. Prostitutes openly plied their trade on street corners and dealers sold their wares without making much effort to hide it.

But here on the periphery, where Packer was walking, it was like a wasteland. A few years ago, the couple of blocks that led along the train line away from the main street had housed Chinese restaurants, Italian pasta places and cafes that spoke of the odd mix of cultures that had once filled the place.

Now, it housed empty shops and derelict buildings. Faded 'For Lease' signs still hung in a few windows, but an equal number of them had plywood nailed across the smashed shop fronts and all of them were covered in graffiti.

The COVID pandemic had had less effect on Western Australia that it had on the rest of the country due to the state's steadfastly closed borders, and life in Perth had continued on more or less as normal for the first two years. But the tourist trade had disappeared. Many of the shops and restaurants that relied on tourist dollars felt the squeeze.

Then when the borders had come down, the virus had ripped through Perth infecting almost the entire population in weeks. The months of heavy restrictions that followed this had destroyed businesses that were barely clinging on without tourists.

The area had remained a graveyard ever since.

Packer crossed Mountain Terrace, the area dark beneath broken streetlights. The park loomed in the near distance, the rusting playground barely visible beside the decaying bushes and trees. Addicts and homeless slept rough there, so he avoided going too close.

He stopped and looked around the area where he was standing.

By night, the place was deserted. It was too far from the main street and the nightclubs for the light to reach and close enough to the exits from the freeway that anybody could come through here undetected.

He looked at the posts around him but saw none of the telltale domes of CCTV cameras. Some of the local businesses may have had them once, but there were none left now.

Turning, he began to walk back towards the alleyway and the police cordon. He pictured driving along here in the early evening, looking for a place to dump a body.

Was the killer familiar with the area? Or had he simply cruised past, knowing the area was derelict, and looked for somewhere quiet to use?

As Packer moved closer to the police cars and the silently flashing blue lights in the distance, he saw how easy it would have been to dump a body with nobody seeing.

The uniformed officer manning the plastic fence was a different officer to the one who had been there earlier. The shifts must have changed.

"Excuse me, sir," the officer said firmly, his English accent heavy, "This area is currently-"

Packer cut him off with a nod, holding out his identification once again.

The new officer mumbled an apology and Packer ducked back under the fence again.

Packer could not see the scene-of-crime van, but wasn't surprised. Resources were stretched thin, and Saturday was their busiest.

He returned to the alleyway and stood a few metres away by the wall to wait.

After about a half hour, there was movement from the alleyway. Two of the paper-suited officers stepped out, one carrying the black toolbox and the other carrying a plastic sack. They moved away from Packer and walked to an unmarked van parked behind one of the patrol cars.

Packer watched as the third officer left the alleyway, lugging a cardboard box in both arms, and followed the others.

A few paces behind them came Doctor Chandra.

She had the hood of the disposable suit pulled back. Her long, brown hair was pulled into a messy-looking knot behind her head and held in place with a band.

As she stepped out of the alleyway and into the light, there was the faint chime of her phone. She reached inside the suit and retrieved it.

She stood against the wall, looking at the screen of the phone, the dim light reflecting off her face.

After a moment, she looked up from the phone. Her eyes found Packer.

She put the phone back in her pocket and, to his surprise, walked towards him.

"Still here?" she asked, stopping a metre or so away from him.

"Waiting for scene-of-crime," he said.

"Can't you delegate that?" she asked, a hint of a smile playing at the corners of her lips.

Packer shrugged. "I had nowhere better to be."

She raised an eyebrow. "Home in bed?"

"Wouldn't have slept anyway."

She stood there a moment longer, as though she was going to say something more, but didn't.

"I'll send my report as soon as I can," she said, "Good night, Sergeant."

He nodded a goodnight and she turned to leave.

He watched her walking away, narrow hips swaying beneath the baggy suit, then turned back towards the barrier.

The crowd had largely drifted away now, and the uniformed officers had gathered in a huddle talking amongst themselves.

After another hour, there were headlights in the distance and the scene-of-crime van moved slowly along the street. A couple of the uniforms undid one end of the plastic fence and held it back for the van to drive up onto the footpath, then tied it back in place again.

The driver's door opened and a skeletally-thin man with a bald head got out. His police uniform was about three sizes too large and hung off him like a tent.

Seeing Packer, he gave a grin and walked over.

"Haven't you got a home to go to, ye miserable bastard?" he hissed in a thick Scottish drawl.

Packer gave him a faint smile. "Haven't you?"

"I dinnae need sleep any more," the officer replied, "I'm superhuman, lad."

Senior Constable Alistair Goodge had once been a hugely overweight man with a thick beard who looked vaguely like a bear. Months of chemotherapy was holding the cancer at bay but had taken all the meat off him and made the beard fall out. He insisted that he was still working because he was 'on the mend', but nobody believed that any more than Goodge did. He continued working because the grim reality was far too ugly to face.

Packer had met Goodge only once before, but Goodge acted like they were best friends, just as he did with everyone else he met.

"What have ye got back there?" Goodge asked, the humour disappearing.

"Girl of about twenty," Packer said, "Strangled. With some kind of garrote, the FME thinks."

"Christ A'mighty."

"Yeah. Naked and wrapped in a plastic tarp."

"Been there long?"

"FME doesn't think so. Few hours at the outside."

"Alright, then. Better get my kit on."

Packer followed Goodge back to the van. The tailgate was open and a younger officer was standing there. He gave Packer a nod and handed him a fresh set of shoe covers and gloves.

Packer waited while Goodge and the younger officer pulled on white disposeable suits and blue gloves, then gathered a toolbox, camera and plastic sack.

He led them down the alleyway to the back area. The halogen lights on stands were still blazing away, left behind by Doctor Chandra's team for the scene-of-crime unit and eventually, the undertaker. A single uniformed officer stood against the far wall, guarding the scene and looking bored.

"Oh, Christ," Goodge said, as he saw the dead woman lying by the bins, "What a horrible thing."

He placed his toolbox on the ground and folded back the lid. The younger officer waited with the camera ready in his hand, while Goodge moved around the edge of the green tarpaulin. Holding a torch beside his face, Goodge leaned over until he was inches away from the plastic surface and made his way around. A couple of times he stopped and sprayed black powder over the surface with a small spray bottle.

Within five minutes, he straightened up.

"Not a thing, my lad," he said, "Clean as a nun's pussy. I'd say your man's drop cloth came straight out of the packet from the hardware store before he wrapped her up in it. Must have had on gloves, 'cause he hasn't left a hint of a trace on the thing."

Packer nodded, unsurprised. He had noted the creases in the tarpaulin earlier, and assumed it was new.

"Might have more luck with the handbag or the clothes," Goodge said, "but I wouldn't bet ye pension on it."

Packer waited while the younger officer held out a plastic sack and Goodge eased the brown handbag inside it, then sealed the top with exhibits tape and placed a bar code sticker beside it. The younger officer photographed the bar code, then put the camera down.

Goodge changed his gloves and lifted up the plastic bag full of clothing. It was a semi-opaque plastic bag, like the kind used in a rubbish bin. The handles on top were tied into a tight knot, then knotted a second time.

Through the sides of the bag, Packer could just make out a dark blue colour and a paler one crumpled together.

The younger officer held out a second plastic bag, while Goodge placed the bag of clothing inside then sealed the top and placed a bar code on it. After it was photographed, he closed up his tool kit.

"That's us, then," Goodge said, cheerfully, "Be lucky."

"Thanks," Packer replied.

"Any time," Goodge said.

Packer followed them back up the alley and waited for the undertaker.

It was nearing 4:00am.

Chapter 4

Packer and his team were based in the police complex in East Perth near the WACA grounds. It was a semi-circular building that was built side-on to the river, obscuring any scenic view that it might otherwise have had. The building had been a monstrosity when it was constructed in the seventies, and age had not improved it.

Packer turned off Hay Street into the complex at about half-past five and stopped the car outside the security door. He leaned out the window and touched his security card against the reader, then entered his pin number.

The gate slid slowly open on creaking tracks and Packer drove into the dingy basement carpark.

He had not slept in nearly twenty-four hours, but that was not unusual.

Packer used the tiny elevator to make his way to the seventh floor.

The place was in darkness, lit only by the tiny tracks of lights that ran along the edges of the ceilings.

Packer went to the bathrooms at the end of the floor and showered. He shaved beneath the naked bulb that hung over the tiny sinks in the men's bathroom, then changed into a clean shirt and trousers from his locker.

He walked back to the team's incident room at the far end of the floor. The place was in darkness, and he flicked on the lights as he entered.

The room was large with two desks on either side. Across the back wall were three whiteboards which Packer had had brought up from storage in the station's cellars. A row of filing cabinets covered one wall beside them, and the other side held the door opening on to the only private office, which was Packer's.

Packer walked into his office and turned on the light as he went. He sat down and switched on his computer, then waited for it to power up.

There were about a dozen e-mails waiting for him, but he ignored them. One was a message from the officer taking photos in the alleyway. Packer opened it.

Attached was an image file and he double-clicked on it.

A separate window opened on the screen with the clear image of the dead woman from the alleyway. Her face was bathed in the bright, artificial glare of a camera flash, only her face and neck visible in the image.

For the first time, Packer got a clear view of her face.

Her cheekbones were high and round, the nose wide above thick lips that were open over a row of uneven teeth that contrasted sharply with her skin. Her eyes stared sightlessly upwards, red flares of broken vessels around the pupils from the strangulation. The woman's chocolate-brown skin was smooth, but marked on one cheek with a tiny patch of blemishes that may have been acne scars.

Her hair was tied into tight braids that were gathered together in a bundle above her head, the ends now splayed across her forehead and out on the plastic sheet beneath her head.

They were strong features, but she would clearly have been very attractive in life.

Packer stared at the image for long minutes, trying to gauge something about the woman, trying to get some feel for who she had been and how she had met her end.

Eventually, he sent the image to the shared printer outside his office, then got up and walked to the coffee machine on top of the filing cabinets.

He had only just poured a cup when there was movement behind him. Detective Constable Seoyoon Kim entered the incident room.

"Morning, boss," said Seoyoon.

"Hello, Seoyoon," Packer said.

Seoyoon was in her late-twenties. She was thin and petite, her glossy, black hair was pulled into a neat ponytail that hung down over the collar of her skirt suit.

Seoyoon put her handbag beneath her desk and switched on the computer.

"George said they found a body in Northbridge?" she asked.

Packer nodded. "Yeah. Wait for the others and I'll tell you what we know."

Seoyoon nodded and began dealing with other work on her computer, efficient as ever.

George Thompson arrived next, his heavy bulk squeezed into a fresh shirt. He was using one hand to run an electric shaver over his chins, while eating a service-station sandwich with the other.

He greeted them both and sat down at his desk to finish eating.

Before he had finished the sandwich, Detective Senior Constable Claire Perry arrived. She was in her mid-thirties and neatly dressed in a suit. Her blonde hair was cut short, and she was wearing minimal make-up.

Packer looked at his watch.

"Alright," he said, "We're not waiting for Mickey. Let's make a start."

The whiteboards across the back wall were mounted on metal stands with a pivot in the centre, so that they could be rotated horizontally. Packer pulled one forward and swiveled it over, so that the surface covered with another job was at the back and a clean surface faced outwards.

He collected the photo of the dead woman that he had printed earlier and placed it on the whiteboard, using a magnet to hold it in place.

"At about 2:00am last night, a street patrol in Northbridge was alerted to a dead body found in an alleyway off Lake Street. The deceased is female, approximately twenty years of age and of African descent.

"She was bound and strangled with some kind of garrote."

He recapped what they had learned at the scene last night and jotted the details down on the board as he spoke.

The others watched him. Tracking an investigation on the whiteboards was not something the team had done before Packer's arrival, but it was a method he intended to use on all their jobs moving forward.

"There was a handbag with her, but no ID in it. There was a purse, but the pockets were empty, so assume it was removed deliberately. Unless we get something else, we're stuck with checking fingerprints and DNA, which aren't going to help unless she's been in trouble with police before."

"Are we sure the couple who found her are not involved?" Claire asked.

"Fairly sure," Packer said, "but we don't have anything else to work with, so let's check. George, you confirm their whereabouts for the twenty-four hours before the body was found.

"Seoyoon, I want you to check all missing persons reports for anything that matches the physical description. If she's got family and didn't come last night, someone may have reported it. Check interstate, too. It's possible she was missing before she was killed, although it's a long shot. Put an alert on the system for any new reports that come in, too."

Seoyoon nodded.

"Claire, you organise with uniform to start knocking on doors in Lake Street. Someone dumped a body there yesterday evening. It's possible someone saw something without realising what it was."

"Do you need to run that past the inspector?"

"Get it organised, and I'll clear it with him when I speak to him."

"Is there any CCTV in the area?" Claire asked.

"I couldn't see anything near where she was found," Packer said, "but the nightclubs on the street will have it."

"Something might show up in the background," she suggested, "It's worth a look."

Packer nodded. "Yeah. See what you can get."

As he finished, the door to the incident room opened.

Detective Constable Mickey Simmons entered, grinning. Designer stubble covered his chin, and his blonde hair was fashionably tangled.

He saw Packer's stare as he entered.

"Sorry, I'm late, boss," he said, the grin disappearing, "I got stuck on the-"

"I don't care," Packer said, "Don't do it again. We're dealing with a murder now. Get a lift with Claire into Northbridge and help uniform doing doorknocks."

"I'm sure uniform can..." Simmons began. He tailed off, as he saw Packer's look. "Okay. I'm on it."

"Anyone got any other thoughts?"

"What was the woman doing in Northbridge?" Claire asked, "Street walker?"

"I wondered that, too," Packer said, "but if she is, she must be new to the game. She's healthy and in good shape. No evidence of drug use. No condoms or lube in her handbag. We'll keep an open mind about it for now, though."

"How do you get into the alleyway?" Seoyoon asked, "Are there other entrances?"

"I saw a gate at one end," Packer said, "but it was chained up. The narrow walkway we went through seems to be the only way in."

"Wouldn't it have been obvious if someone was carrying a body in there?" she asked.

"All the shops up that end are closed. There's minimal lighting and it was after dark. I'm assuming that's why the location was chosen."

"So the killer must know the area, then."

"Maybe. Or maybe he just knew it was some quiet."

Packer tapped the bottom of the photo near the dead woman's neck.

"The garrote's unusual. Murders are usually stabbings or beatings. It's difficult to kill someone by strangling them. I've never seen a garrote used before."

"Nor me," Thompson agreed.

"And the garrote's at the front, which means the killer was looking at the girl when he killed her. That doesn't help us find the killer, but it tells us we're dealing with someone dangerous. Most murders are done in the heat of the moment. Someone loses their temper. Not this time."

He let that sink in for a moment.

"Okay. Anyone got anything else? Right. Let's get moving, then."

As he returned to his office, Packer reflected on just how little they had to work with.

No leads and no ID.

They would need a lot of luck.

***

Packer sat at his desk. He had been at the station less than a month, and it felt like wearing a dead man's clothing.

The team had been headed by Senior Sergeant Frank McCain before Packer had arrived. McCain had retired unexpectedly. One day, he had been there, and the next he was gone. The official explanation was that he had had some sort of health scare, but he was uncontactable, which seemed very odd.

McCain seemed to have been well-liked by the team, and his sudden and unexpected departure had clearly affected them. This had led to some resentment towards Packer, particularly from Claire Perry and George Thompson, who had both worked with McCain for several years and seemed to have been on very good terms with him. But it was fading quickly. The team had referred to McCain as, 'boss,' and had now begun calling Packer this, too, which was an encouraging sign.

The office had been cleared out entirely before Packer had arrived, every trace of its former occupant removed, which added to the strangeness of the situation. The walls had faded patches where paintings or photographs had once hung, and even the stationery had been removed, leaving drawers and cupboards that were completely bare. It was as though McCain had been completely erased from existence.

Packer had been sitting at his desk for no more than ten minutes when there was a single tap on the door.

He looked up as Inspector Harold Base closed the door behind him and sat down. As always, Base was wearing his full uniform, which was impeccably pressed and looked like it had just come fresh from the dry cleaners.

"I'm told a body was found in Northbridge," Base said, without preliminaries.

Packer nodded but said nothing.

"What are the details?" Base asked.

"Woman of about 20 years. African descent. The body was naked, wrapped in plastic and dumped in Northbridge. The FME thinks she was killed somewhere else. FME thinks she was bound and killed with some kind of garrote."

Base frowned. "A garrote? Like a ritual killing?

"I don't think so. It's weird, though."

"Have you identified her?"

"Not yet. No ID on her. My team are checking missing persons."

Base nodded. "Alright. If you don't have an ID by the end of the day, organise for a media alert. I don't want complaints from the family that we didn't do everything we could to let them know."

It vaguely irritated Packer that Base's first thought was adverse media attention, rather than the actual investigation, but it didn't surprise him. In the little time he had been at the station, he had found that Base's priorities leant more towards appearances than policing.

"Are you going to ask for more officers?" Base asked.

"I need some uniforms to do some doorknocks in the area."

"Okay. Tell Sergeant Prior I've approved it. No more than ten officers, though. Our budget's tight."

Packer nodded.

"The media have contacted us this morning already," Base went on, "Get an outline of what you have to my secretary so we can send a press release. We need to be seen to be moving quickly on this, so don't piss about."

"Sir."

"I want a result quickly, Tony. Clear?"

Packer nodded.

"Right," Base said, "Get to it."

He got up and left.

The incident room fell silent as Base walked through the middle to the door. Everybody's attention was steadfastly fixed on their computers. Packer could almost feel the relief run through the incident room after Base closed the door behind him and left. Conversations resumed.

Thompson swivelled in his chair and leaned back to look through the doorway at Packer.

"Nice of the inspector to drop in," Thompson said.

"Just offering some encouragement," Packer said.

Chapter 5

Northbridge was transformed into a different place by day. The dealers who stood in closed doorways selling their wares without any attempt at subtlety were gone, and so too were the prostitutes who stood beneath streetlights along Fitzgerald Street watching for crawling cars to come to a stop by the gutter. The sunlight seemed to wash away the worst of the night's traffic.

But the underbelly of the city was still covered in dirt, even in the day.

Rubbish lay against street fronts, the occasional uncapped syringe or used condom amongst the broken bottles. Near the main intersection behind the Horseshoe Bridge, a man without shoes screamed at the cars as they passed, and another was passed out in the car park nearby.

Most of the homeless moved across the train track into the city to beg during the day, but there were still a couple of them sitting on the footpath with cardboard signs, hoping to pick up something from the commuters or the tiny number of tourists who walked from the train station towards the museum and the art gallery.

Uniformed police officers were a regular sight in Northbridge. Foot patrols had been replaced by bicycle patrols, who moved along the edge of the footpaths, dealing with the routine robberies and shoplifting offences, or moving on the drunks who had found their way down from the park at the far end of town.

Today, the uniforms were out in force.

Despite Base's firm command that only ten officers could be spared, Sergeant Prior managed to shift over twenty officers from routine duties elsewhere to Northbridge's streets. In twenty years of active service, Prior had learned the importance of gathering information in the immediate aftermath of a major incident and had mobilised as many officers as he could find.

They fanned out along Aberdeen Street and the streets leading off from it. Every shop and hotel that was open for business received a visit from a police officer seeking information about the day before.

At each street corner, officers stopped those passing by, asking whether they had been in the area the night before or if they lived nearby and had seen or heard anything.

The narrow alleyways leading off the sidestreets and the park at the end of Mountain Terrace were home to a shifting population of addicts and drunks. They were all combed by officers seeking any information that could be obtained.

The high number of break-ins and incidents of violence in the area meant that many of the local businesses carried CCTV cameras in the interiors of their shops or mounted above doors leading in from the street. Where it existed, CCTV was collected by the officers and sent back to the incident room in East Perth for Packer's team to sift through.

Many of the cameras were of poor quality or inoperative and used only for show. Dozens of recordings were obtained, but little of them were likely to be of any assistance.

Close to four thousand people were questioned during the first half of the day. Fewer than forty potential leads were found, and most of those were included only out of thoroughness.

The media began to comb the area, too.

Tipped off to the fact that police had located a body overnight, each of the nearby news groups sent people to Northbridge. The local news stations had sent camera vans and reporters to film reports from the outside of the alleyway on Aberdeen Street which remained cordoned off with uniformed officers guarding the area.

Reporters knew that the officers working the streets in the area would have no information to give, but questioned them anyway, hoping to gain something more than the scant details in the media release provided by Inspector Base's media officer.

One station managed a coup by finding a man who claimed he had been in the area and had seen what had taken place the night before. With two cameras trained on him and a microphone held in front of his face, he began to recount hearing screams and seeing the victim being dragged into the alleyway by three masked men. It was only when he mentioned in passing that the victim was male, a detail that the reporter was aware was incorrect, that it became apparent that he was nothing more than an attention seeker and he was sent on his way.

By lunchtime, the police numbers began to thin out. All the shops and businesses in the area had been canvassed and all the apartments had been checked or cards had been left under doors to contact police. Knowing there was nothing more to be seen here, the media began to drift away, too.

By afternoon, the streets of Northbridge had returned to their usual routine.

***

The first details of potential witnesses began to be sent back to the incident room soon after the doorknock began at 7:30am. Lists were collated and distributed amongst the team to follow up.

Mickey Simmons returned to the station with three USB drives containing CCTV from the local council's Safe City cameras and from a couple of local businesses. He began sifting through these, while more footage was ferried in by patrol cars as it was obtained.

The second and third whiteboards were used to record the details of potential leads, with lists growing as further information was received and shrinking as possible leads were eliminated.

The phone in Packer's officer rang and he walked in to answer it.

"I think you owe me a drink, laddie," said a thick Scots brogue on the other end.

"Have you got something?" Packer asked.

"Oh, yes, I have," Goodge said, "Yes, I have indeed. I'm e-mailing it over to you now."

In the background, Packer could hear the faint tapping of a computer keyboard.

"I opened up the bag of clothes your young lass had with her," Goodge said, "Pair of K-Mart trainers. Jeans and a T-shirt that looked like they come from the bloody Sally Army. Tucked away in the back pocket of the jeans was an appointment card for the dentists on Wellington Street."

As Goodge spoke, Packer clicked the refresh button on his e-mail system. A message from Goodge appeared on his screen and he opened it.

The message was blank apart from Goodge's signature block at the bottom, but it had an image file attached. Packer double-clicked on the file to open it.

A photograph of an A4 sheet appeared. It was crinkled and contained a series of creases where it had been folded to fit in the pocket of the jeans. The top bore the logo and address of a dentist in the city, while the rest of the sheet contained standard information about a dentist's appointment. Dotted lines had been left for a name, and the date and time of an appointment. Curly, feminine handwriting had filled in the name, 'Emily Mtuba,' and an appointment time of 9:30am on Friday.

Packer stared at the screen.

Emily Mtuba.

Now they had a name.

"There's a bottle of scotch on the way," Packer said.

"Better make that two, you tight bastard."

"You got something else?"

"There was a pair of knickers in the bag, too. She'd emptied her bowels and her bladder when she died, poor lass. But there's a smear at the top near the waistband at the back. You'll have to wait for the lab to test it, but I'd reckon it might be semen. Good chance it's been contaminated with her fluids, but you might get lucky.

"There was a bra in the bag, as well. Right big thing it was, too. Your lass must have been an impressive specimen. They have a wee, plastic buckle thing on the front to adjust the length of the straps, you know what I mean? Anyway, there was a hair caught under it. And not one of the lassie's."

"You're sure?"

"Aye, I'm sure. It was brown and straight. Hers are black and curly."

"You're a prince among men, Jock," Packer said.

"Aye, save your flattery, tight-arse. When am I getting the scotch?"

"It's in the mail."

"See that it is."

This was a familiar game. Goodge's chemotherapy forbade alcohol, but he still insisted that he wanted payment by the litre.

"Can you send me photos of the clothing?" Packer asked.

"Aye. Will do. Let me know if ye need anything else."

He rang off and Packer put the phone down.

This was an incredible find. At this stage, they had nothing to compare the semen or the hair with, but if they found a suspect, the DNA could be tested. If it could be matched to the suspect, it would go a long way towards securing a conviction.

If they could find a suspect.

Packer looked at the image on the screen of the dental appointment card, reading over it again.

He clicked 'print' on the image, then left his office.

He walked over to the printer and collected the image.

"I think we have a name," Packer said, walking over to Seoyoon's desk. Thompson stood up and walked over to join him.

"Alistair Goodge found a dentist's appointment in the pocket of her jeans," Packer said, placing the sheet down on the desk beside Seoyoon's keyboard, "Emily Mtuba."

Seoyoon opened up a search screen on her computer and entered the name.

A spinning hour-glass icon appeared on the screen and rotated for several moments, before being replaced by a box reading, 'No match'.

"She's not showing up in our database," Seoyoon said, "That's very odd. It pulls in details from driver's licence records, electoral rolls, the fines and penalties register, and a couple of others."

Moving the mouse, she opened another database. Packer and Thompson waited while she entered her username and password, then performed another search.

"I tried the electoral rolls directly. She doesn't appear there, either."

"Some variation on the name?" Packer suggested, "Maybe it's misspelt?"

They waited while Seoyoon tried various permutations of the surname.

Nothing.

"Interstate records?" Packer suggested.

"I don't have access to those," Seoyoon said, "I'll have to get someone at Intel to do it."

Packer nodded. "Alright. See what you can find."

"Could it be a fake name on the form?" Seoyoon suggested.

"Why use a fake name for a dentist's visit?" Thompson asked, "Doesn't make any sense."

Packer shook his head.

"What's going on here, boss? A girl who's been strangled using a fake name."

"I don't know. We'll see what the dentist says."

Chapter 6

"Yes, I remember her," said one of the receptionists behind the counter at the dentist's surgery.

There were two women behind the counter. One looked like she was pushing fifty and was clearly very organised. The other one looked like she was barely out of high school. She had green-tinged hair, a nostril piercing, and two arms covered in tattoos.

It was the younger one who remembered Emily Mtuba.

"What did she look like?" Thompson asked.

"African. She had her hair done in, like, braids. Must have taken ages to get them done."

"When did she come in?"

"Um. Wednesday last week."

The girl turned to look at the older woman. "It was your day off."

The older woman nodded.

"What did she come in for?" Thompson asked.

"She was in a lot of pain with a really bad toothache. She didn't have an appointment or anything. Just came in and wanted to see one of the dentists."

"And did she?"

The girl nodded. "Yeah. She was weird, actually."

"In what way?"

"She was, like, kind of, yeah, I don't know."

Thompson did his best to remain patient.

"Okay. So, there was something unusual about her?"

"Yeah. That's right. She was weird."

"What was it exactly that made you think she was weird? Something about the way she looked? The way she acted?"

"I don't know," said the girl, "She was just, like, um. Like, not friendly. Kind of, you know, trying to hide or something."

"Hide?" Thompson asked.

"Yeah, like, when I asked for her details, she didn't want to give them. She didn't have a Medicare card, or private health insurance. But I told her we had to have contact details. We always ask for credit card details, and she didn't have one. Not even, like, bank details or anything. She wanted to pay in cash. Like, not many people do that any more."

"Did she leave an address?" he asked, "or a phone number?"

The girl nodded. "Yeah, that was weird, too. Usually, we get an e-mail address, but she didn't have one. I mean, who doesn't have an e-mail address, heh?"

"Can you find the address and phone number for me?" Thompson asked.

The girl nodded.

She turned to the computer behind the counter and tapped briefly at the keyboard. After a moment, she read out the details and George wrote them down in his notebook.

He sent a text message with the details to Seoyoon so she could use them to search through records.

"Okay, thanks," Thompson said, "That's a big help. Who treated her when she came in?"

"Stuart did."

"Is Stuart here?"

The girl nodded.

"He's with a patient at the moment," the older woman said, "Doing a fairly lengthy procedure. Best if you make an appointment and come back."

"No, we'll wait," Packer said, from behind Thompson.

The older woman looked at him, a frown of annoyance appearing on her face.

"As I said, it's quite a lengthy procedure. I'm sure he could fit you in later in the week."

Packer turned to look at the younger girl.

"Why don't you go and ask Stuart how much longer he'll be?" Packer said, "Tell him the police want to see him and it's urgent."

The younger girl looked at the older woman for help. The older woman stared daggers at Packer for a while, then stood up.

"This is very inconvenient," she said, "but I'll ask him."

She moved out from behind the front counter and disappeared up a hallway towards the inner part of the office.

"What's happened to the lady?" the young receptionist asked, "Is she in trouble?"

"Something like that," Thompson said, vaguely.

The girl was about to ask more, when there was movement from beside them.

The older receptionist had returned with Stuart. He was a Chinese man in his thirties wearing black trousers and a white, collarless shirt with a name tag on the lapel pocket.

"I'm Stuart Chan," he said, "Can I help?"

His voice carried surprise, but no animosity.

Packer and Thompson both produced their identification and held them out.

"Detectives Thompson and Packer," Thompson said, "Is there somewhere private we can talk?"

Chan nodded. "Of course. Please come through."

He turned back the way he had come, and Packer and Thompson followed him along a corridor. Two small rooms with dentist chairs opened from one side of the corridor, and there were two closed doors on the other side.

Chan led them to a room at the back which had a table with four seats, a fridge and a kitchen bench.

"I'm afraid we don't have a visitors' room," Chan said, gesturing to one of the seats, "so we'll have make do with the lunchroom."

"That's fine," Thompson said.

He and Packer sat down on one side of the table. Chan sat on the other.

Thompson produced the photo of the dead woman he had been sent by the forensics officer in the alley.

"We believe you may have treated this woman recently," he said, placing the photo on the table.

Chan looked at the photo and nodded.

"Yes," he said, "I did. Has something happened to her?"

"I'm afraid she's been found dead," Thompson said.

"Oh, my."

Chan was staring down at the photo, clearly shocked by this.

"What happened to her?" he asked.

"We're still investigating," Thompson said, "so anything you can tell us will be helpful."

"Yes, of course," Chan said, looking up. He looked nervously between them. "What would you like to know?"

"I understand she came here last Wednesday?"

Chan nodded. "That's right. She was complaining of toothache. She was in a lot of pain and wanted to see someone straight away. It was very unusual."

"And you saw her?"

"Yes. I had other appointments, of course, but I pushed one back so that I could see her. She was in a lot of pain, as I said."

"And what was the problem?"

"One of the back molars was fractured. Almost completely split, and it had cut into the side of the gums. Frankly, I don't know how she was putting up with it. It must have been acutely painful."

"You treated it?"

"I did. I gave her a local and removed the tooth completely. It's not ideal to remove them, of course, but it was beyond repair. The tooth next to it was loose, and so was one on the other side. There was a lot of swelling to the gums on both sides, too. We made an appointment for her to return at the end of this week, so that I could examine those more thoroughly and work through a treatment plan with her to avoid losing the loose teeth altogether."

"What would cause damage like that?" Thompson asked.

Chan gave a low sigh.

"Someone punching her would be my guess," he said, "She kept saying it was an accident, but wouldn't give any details when I asked. I'm sure it was from someone punching her. There was bruising to her face, although that was not obvious because of her skin colour. But the damage to the teeth was from trauma, and it was on both sides of her face"

Chan shook his head, frowning.

"It was quite an uncomfortable experience, to be honest," he said, "She wasn't willing to provide any details about next-of-kin or anything else, so I wasn't comfortable about performing a procedure on her, even something as relatively uncomplicated as an extraction. But she signed the consent forms, and I could hardly send her away in so much pain."

"And she came alone?"

"Yes. I tried to engage her in conversation. We always do, it helps to relax the patient. But I couldn't get much of a response out of her. She was clearly evasive about what had happened."

Thompson nodded. "Is there anything else about her you recall?"

Chan looked down at the photo for a long moment.

"No," he said, eventually, "Nothing else."

"Thanks for your time," Packer said, "You've been very helpful."

He retrieved the photo and they returned to the reception area.

The two receptionists were watching them.

"Is everything okay?" asked the younger one, fishing for information.

"Fine, thanks," Thompson said, as they passed, "You've been a big help."

As they walked back to the car, Thompson's phone chimed with a new message. He took it out and read it.

"The girl's phone number is a prepaid," Thompson said, "The address is the same as one we just got from the dentist."

"She came to the dentist last Wednesday morning," Packer said, "So someone punched her in the face before then. Five days before she was killed."

"It's strange, boss."

"Yes, it is."

Chapter 7

The address for Emily Mtuba they were given by the receptionist at the dentist was in Richards Road in Girrawheen, one of Perth's poorest suburbs.

Packer and Thompson drove north. Closer to the city centre, the streets were filled with highrise apartment buildings and newer townhouses. These soon gave way to a mix of new developments and older properties that had been renovated and restored.

As they drove further out into Perth's older and less reputable suburbs, the change was stark.

Older houses nestled amongst overgrown yards and tumbled down fences. Rows of the plain brick flats that had been built as social housing in the eighties began to fill the streets. Playgrounds with broken equipment and vandalised public toilets nestled amongst them.

The police car they drove was unmarked, but the fact that it was a late model and in well-maintained condition clearly marked them for who they were. They passed a group of heavily-tattooed men standing around a letterbox at the front of one house, who looked up and watched them as they passed.

A few turns down back streets led them to Richards Street and Thompson slowed down as they looked for house numbers.

"Over there," Packer said, pointing across the street at the far side.

A squat brick building sat at the end, faded metal numbers reading, '14'. The yard was filled with dying grass and the chain-link wire fence had collapsed at one end. A row of six letterboxes sat on a poorly-repaired wooden beam near the driveway.

Thompson pulled in across the road and stopped the car.

He and Packer got out and crossed the road.

As they walked, Packer looked around.

They were in a cul-de-sac which was lined with similar blocks of cheap flats, with a couple of run-down houses amongst them. The yards were all neglected, littered with rubbish in places and a couple of broken windows had been repaired with plywood sheets here and there.

On the far side of the street, a dark-skinned man wearing a singlet sat on the concrete porch drinking from a beer bottle. He watched the two police officers cross the street with a dull expression on his face.

"Welcome to paradise," Thompson muttered.

They walked along the cracked driveway into the front yard of the block of flats. The building was fronted with two garage doors that were both closed. Peeling paint covered the surface of both and one had clearly not been opened in a very long time, rubbish and weeds covering its base.

A concrete staircase beside the garage doors led up to a balcony along one wall of the building, and a low concrete step ran along the side.

Thompson stepped around the corner and looked along the rows of doors at the bottom.

"This way, boss," he said.

Packer followed him along the side of the building.

Two grimy windows lined the wall followed by a door, then the same pattern again.

The last door had a number '3' hand-painted at its centre.

Thompson stepped up onto the low concrete porch and knocked on the door.

There was a long silence, and he was about to knock again, when they heard the sound of the lock being undone on the other side.

A man stared out at them, his features Indonesian or south-east Asian, his face covered with a straggly goatee and his long, wavy hair hanging down over his shoulders.

"Police," Thompson said, holding up his identification, "What's your name, mate?"

The man looked between them for a long moment in silence, then he said something in a foreign language.

"Sorry," Thompson said, "Didn't catch that. Do you speak English?"

The man repeated the same string of foreign words, then added something else. He began to close the door, but Thompson put his hand on it to hold it open.

"Hang on, mate," he said, firmly, "We need to talk to someone. Is there anyone else in there we can talk to?"

The man remained in the doorway for a moment. He was clearly unwilling to let them in, but made no further attempt to push the door closed either. He stood there, staring at them in silence.

"Hello," said a female voice from behind the man.

The man turned his head and hissed something unintelligible.

There was a reply from the female, and then he stepped back. An Indonesian woman who looked to be in her twenties stepped into the doorway. She was wearing a short skirt and a singlet, and was painfully thin, her arms little more than sticks below her narrow shoulders. Her brown hair was pulled back into a loose knot behind her head, a long fringe hanging down across her face.

Although her hair had been arranged to cover her face, it failed to mask the fact that the left side was heavily disfigured by scar tissue. From her forehead, down past her mouth, and extending almost to the bottom of her chin, the woman's skin was heavily wrinkled and puckered, pulling the corner of her eye and the edge of her mouth out of place.

"Police," Thompson said, holding up his identification once more, "Do you speak English?"

The woman looked at the identification card for a moment, then up at Thompson.

"Yes," she said, "I speak. What do you want?"

Her voice was heavily-accented, but understandable.

"Is this where Emily Mtuba lives?" Thompson asked.

The woman looked at him for a moment, then her eyes began to fill with tears.

"Is she hurt?" she asked, her voice rising in pitch.

"Best if we come in," Thompson said, gently, "Is that okay?"

The woman looked down at the ground and nodded. She stepped back, pulling the door open.

Thompson and Packer stepped inside.

They were in a kitchen. The wall was covered with ancient linoleum that was littered with burn marks and holes. The cabinets were decrepit and falling apart, held together with brown packing tape in places. In the centre of the room was a vinyl-topped table with a couple of packets of cigarettes and tin cans used as ash trays sitting on top.

Despite the poor condition of the place, there had been some attempt to keep it clean, although it stank of stale smoke and damp.

The man at the door had retreated to the far side of the table and stood there staring at them.

The woman stood near the sink inside the door, rubbing at her eyes.

"I'm Detective Thompson and this is Detective Packer," Thompson said, "What's your name?"

"Siti," the woman said after a moment.

"What about him?"

"Herman."

"He's your boyfriend or husband?"

"No. Herman lives here."

Packer looked over at the man, who stared back at him with undisguised hostility.

"Why don't we sit down?" Thompson suggested.

Siti sniffed heavily, rubbing at her eyes again, then walked over to the table. She pulled out one of the mismatched chairs and sat down in it.

She did not invite them to sit, but Thompson sat in a chair at the end.

Packer looked at Herman, then pointed at the chair in front of him.

Herman stared back at him for a moment, then begrudgingly sat down. He sat staring at Packer, who stared blankly back at him.

"So, Emily Mtuba lives here, too?" Thompson asked.

Siti nodded.

"Just the three of you?"

Siti shook her head. "Raghav and Tanvi as well. Sometimes others."

The flat was tiny. One or two bedrooms. Five or more of them here would clearly be a squeeze.

"Have you known Emily long?" Thompson asked.

Siti shrugged. "Less than one year. What did happen to her?"

"I'm afraid we have found a body we believe to be Emily," Thompson said gently.

"Is she injured?" Siti said, looking down at her lap.

"I'm sorry to say she's dead."

Siti's face crumpled and she gave a low moan of distress.

Herman hissed a guttural string of words at her, and she replied in the same language.

He spat further words at her, clearly in anger, and she shouted back at him.

He got up, pushing the chair back angrily and went into the bedroom behind them, closing the door.

Packer watched him go but said nothing.

"When we came to the door," Thompson said, "You asked if something had happened to Emily. You were expecting this?"

Siti continued looking at her lap. "She did not come home last night. I thought something bad."

"Does she have a phone or some way you could have contacted her?"

Siti nodded. "I tried to ring to her. But no answer."

"Any idea at all where she might have been?"

Siti said nothing, simply staring down at her lap.

Thompson glanced back at Packer. He said nothing for a moment.

"Listen, Siti," Thompson said, "You're not in trouble. We're trying to find out what happened to Emily. Anything you can tell us might help."

Siti stared at her lap, saying nothing. She had stopped crying but rubbed at her eyes.

She made no move to answer, but Thompson and Packer sat there, letting the silence do its work.

Eventually, Siti looked up.

"We do not have money," she said, "It is hard. We work when we can, but it can only be without papers."

"You're not here legally?" Thompson said.

Siti shook her head, her eyes clearly showing her fear.

"It's okay," Thompson said, "We don't care about that. We just want to find out what happened to Emily."

Siti looked doubtful about this but continued after a moment.

"Sometimes Emily can do the cleaning. Billy can make this jobs for us. But it is not all times."

"Who's Billy?" Thompson asked.

"He collect rent money."

"Do you know his last name?"

"Just Billy."

"Okay. And Emily was doing cleaning work?"

"Yes. For last year, every night if she can. But maybe for last two months, some nights she does not work."

Siti paused a moment. "But Emily has money. More money than before. I ask her how she get money, and she does not want to tell to me. But I think it is something *mesum*. Something bad. She cannot look to my eyes when I ask, you understand?"

Thompson nodded.

"Sometimes when Emily go out, she seem she does not want to go. And when she come home, she goes to shower. She stays there a long time. After, she is quiet, do not want to see others. But always when she does this, she has money."

"You said you haven't seen her since yesterday," Thompson said, "Was she quiet like this when she went out?"

"Yes, she is quiet. I worry. When she does not return, I worry. I know something bad has happen. Then you come."

Siti's eyes filled with tears once more, and she looked down at her lap.

Thompson and Packer waited in silence for her to regain some composure again.

"Did you ask Emily where she was getting this money?" Thompson asked after a moment.

Siti nodded. "One night, Emily say to go for drink, just for girls' night. We go to pub near here and drink alcohol. When she has some drunk, I try to ask her. She will not say. But she has plans. When she has made money, she will pay men to bring her brother here to Australia on boat. Then they can both work and make money to pay to bring other family."

"But to pay men to come here is cost very much. *How can you get so much money?* I ask to her. She looks to me with strong look, you understand? And she say, it will take much, and will be hard, but she will do this. She is very strong and she will do this."

"Did she mention any names? Anyone she was going with? Where she was going?"

Siti looked down at her lap again. Her tiny shoulders quivered slightly beneath the thin cotton of her singlet.

It was clear that there was something else she was having trouble telling them, something she was unwilling to talk about.

"You asked if she could help you make money, too," Packer said, quietly, "You wanted to make money to bring your own family here as well."

Siti took in a sharp breath, and let out a low wail. Her eyes squeezed shut, and her lips clenched shut. She nodded.

"What did Emily tell you?" Packer asked.

Siti rocked back and forth in the chair for a moment, her tiny body shaking, as she made a low keening sound.

Thompson and Packer waited, saying nothing.

After long minutes, Siti looked up, her eyes staring.

"Emily hold to my hands," Siti said, "and she say to me, 'You must promise you never do this. Even if somebody ask to you, you must promise never to do.'"

Siti's voice dropped to little more than a whisper.

"Emily say to me that the man she does this for, the man is *iblis*."

She looked at them.

"The man is Satan."

Chapter 8

The flat had two tiny bedrooms.

One was currently being used by Raghav and Tanvi. It had a double bed that had seen better days, and there were two suitcases and a backpack leaning against the end. There was a cabinet against the wall that was being held together with packing tape. On the other side of the room was a rolled-up sleeping bag and another backpack.

The other bedroom was used by Emily and Siti. It contained another double bed, and a single, together with another mattress leaning against the wall.

Herman, it seemed, slept on one of the lounge chairs, and the other two were sometimes used by others from time to time.

Siti was reluctant to let them see Emily's things, but Thompson again told her that they just wanted to find out what had happened to her. After some hesitation, she lifted back the fraying edge of the quilt that covered the single bed in the second bedroom.

Thompson leaned under and found a plastic-shelled suitcase that was scuffed and marked. He pulled it out and lifted it on to the bed.

He and Packer both pulled on blue examination gloves, before going through the contents.

The suitcase had a combination lock fastener, but luckily, this was not locked. One side of the case contained a small collection of clothing and underwear. Thompson pushed through them in case something was hidden under it, but there was nothing else there.

The lining of the lid of the suitcase had a zipper running its length, converting it into a large pocket. Thompson undid it and folded back the flap.

There were two more photographs of the same African family that had appeared in Emily's handbag in the alleyway, together with a single shot of the parents and a few photographs of the younger brother.

Nestled under these was a maroon-coloured passport.

"Look at this, boss," Thompson said, reading over the identification page, then handing it to Packer.

Packer looked at the cover of the passport, which had been issued in the Democratic Republic of the Congo, then turned over to the identification page. Emily Mtuba's face stared up at him, looking uncannily like the still image the forensic officer had e-mailed to him.

The details on the side were for 'Imani Mbanda'.

"Explains why she didn't show up in any of the records," Thompson said.

Packer nodded. He looked at the date of birth and calculated that Emily / Imani was nineteen and would have turned twenty in a few months' time.

Thompson was shuffling through a collection of folded papers in the pocket.

"There're letters and enrolment papers here for Edith Cowan University," Thompson said, "She was enrolled in an English language course under Imani Mbanda."

He handed them to Packer who skimmed over them.

"Anything else?" Packer asked.

"Nothing of importance," Thompson said, shuffling through a handful of brochures and bus timetables to the side, "Not much to show for a life, is it?"

"At least we've got a name now," Packer said, "Call Seoyoon and tell her not to waste any more time searching. Tell her to try ECU. See if they've got attendance records and contact details for student counsellors or lecturers."

"Righto."

Packer looked over the passport again. There was a single stamp on its pages, showing entry to Perth eleven months ago. The passport had been issued about six weeks before that.

Packer returned to the kitchen, where Siti was sitting at the table. Herman was sitting on the lounge chair. He glared at Packer as he emerged from the bedroom, then looked away.

"You told us Billy collects the rent," Packer said.

Siti nodded.

"What's the arrangement to pay the rent?"

"Billy come to collect money every Friday night."

"Is there some way to contact him? If you need repairs or something?"

"He has phone but say not to call unless very important. Wait until he come here for money."

"Can I have the number?"

Siti nodded again. She walked over to the kitchen bench and opened a handbag that was sitting there. She took out a grey mobile phone and began looking through the address book, then turned the screen towards Packer.

He read over the number and recorded it in his police notebook.

"You said he found cleaning work for you. How was that arranged?"

"Billy ask if we need to make some money. He make phone call, then tell us to go to this address at six o'clock. We go on train to there. A red bus is waiting in car parking to collect us and take us to office and factory to do cleaning. We do this in one place, then go in bus to somewhere else to clean. Then somewhere else. The man pay us at end of night. Sometimes no work for a few days, but always more if we wait."

"Emily did this cleaning work, too?"

"Yes."

"But you said sometimes in the last two months, she didn't do it?"

Siti looked down. She shook her head.

"Sometimes, Emily is hurt. She does not walk well. Sometimes, her back or arm is hurt."

"She told you this?"

"No," Siti said, still looking down, "But I see this. I see she is hurt."

Packer was silent for a moment, wondering what to make of this.

"Did Emily have another job? Not the cleaning, and not working for the bad man. Something else?"

Siti shrugged. "I cannot know. I do not think so."

Packer nodded.

"Does Emily have any other friends here? Anyone else she talked about or you saw her with?"

Siti shook her head. "Emily is very quiet. Maybe I am only friend."

"You said she went out two days ago. Did she say anything at all about where she was going?"

Siti shook her head.

"How did she seem before she went out?"

"She is quiet. Always when she goes to this other place, she is quiet."

"What other place?"

"To do bad thing. I cannot know where."

"And she was like this when she went out yesterday?"

"Yes."

"What time did she go out?"

"Maybe it was ten o'clock," Siti said.

"In the evening?"

"No. Before lunch."

"Ten in the morning?"

Siti nodded.

"Who was here when she went out?"

"I. No one else."

Thompson came out of the bedroom, carrying Emily's suitcase in one hand.

Siti looked at the suitcase.

"That is Emily things," she said.

"She won't be needing them any more," Thompson said, gently, "and it's evidence now."

Siti looked to Herman for help.

Frowning, he threw his hands dismissively in the air, then turned away, saying nothing.

Thompson found a business card in his pocket and gave it to Siti.

"That's my direct line," he told her, "If you think of anything else, or you want to ask something, you give me a call."

He took down Siti's number in his notebook.

Neither Siti, nor Herman had last names. Most Indonesians did not.

Packer looked over at Herman, who was staring daggers at him once more. When Packer looked at him, Herman looked away.

Thompson and Packer walked out to the car and Thompson put the suitcase in the boot. He started the car and turned around, heading out of the *cul-de-sac*.

"That Herman was a prick," Thompson said, "You reckon he knows something?"

"There's definitely something off about him," Packer said, "Bit obvious about it, if he does know something, though. Doesn't fit with what Siti said about Emily working as a prostitute, either."

"What about this Satan that she was working for? Her pimp?"

"Sounds like it. Who do we know running girls in Northbridge at the moment?"

Thompson scoffed. "How long have you got?"

"Anyone who does black girls as a specialty?"

"Nobody I can think of. You think the pimp killed her?"

"I don't know. Would be unusual if he did. You don't kill the cash cow, just kick them about a bit to keep them in line."

"Could have been an argument over money or something."

Packer nodded.

"Punter then?" Thompson suggested.

"Seems more likely."

"Shit. How are we ever gonna find him if he was a punter?"

Packer said nothing. Thompson was right. If Emily was working as a prostitute and had been killed by a customer, it would be impossible to track him down without something further.

But there was something about this that still didn't feel right. Pieces didn't fit. He couldn't put a finger on why, but Packer wasn't buying the idea of a customer turning violent and strangling Emily. The bindings and the garote suggested something much more organised, much more specific than that.

There was something else here, but Packer couldn't see what it was yet.

Thompson recognised the younger man's mood. He drove in silence, letting Packer brood over the information they had.

Chapter 9

It was mid-afternoon when they drew nearer to the city. Thompson insisted on stopping at a service station on the way back to buy lunch and returned to the car with a bag of microwaved meat pies and plastic-wrapped packets of sandwiches.

"Got yours, too," he told Packer, dropping the bag on Packer's lap.

Packer looked at the contents unenthusiastically. "Whatever I've done to piss you off, George, I apologise."

Thompson grinned. "It's good stuff, boss. It'll keep you going."

He patted his large stomach, before pulling out of the service station and heading back towards East Perth.

When they returned to the incident room, they found Clare and Mickey pouring over CCTV footage at their desks. A couple of empty takeaway packets sat on the desk beside them.

Seoyoon was eating stir-fried noodles from a Tupperware container.

She waved to Packer as they entered, chewing through a mouthful of food before speaking.

"I spoke to ECU, boss," she said, "They told me they did have an enrolment for Imani Mbanda at the start of the year. She was accepted last year as an overseas student from the Congo to study English, but never actually showed up at the beginning of the year."

Packer frowned.

"Did they contact her to find out why?"

Seoyoon shook her head. "I asked that. They said they didn't have contact details for her in Australia. The procedure is that they accept students while they're still overseas, so that the student can get a student visa issued to come to Australia. Then when they get here, the students arrange a phone and a place to stay, then contact the uni to let them know their details. Imani Mbanda was accepted, but they never heard from her again.

"They said it's not actually that unusual. They accept over two thousand international students every year, and a few hundred of them cancel before the start of the term, or just never turn up."

"We know she did come to Perth, though," Thompson said, peeling back the wrapping on one of the sandwiches, "so why not turn up at the uni?"

Seoyoon shrugged. "That's all I've got."

Packer turned that over for a moment.

He turned to Thompson. "Try the immigration department. See if they can tell us anything else."

"What about my lunch?" Thompson asked, through a mouthful of ham and salad sandwich.

"Alright. After lunch," Packer said. "Assuming you survive the food poisoning," he added, darkly.

He turned to Clare and Mickey.

"What have you got?"

"We got the city council's footage from Newcastle Street," Clare said, "It's rubbish. It always is. Out of focus and jerky."

"Got some stuff from a couple of nightclubs, though," Mickey added, "None of them are pointing in the right direction, but you can sort of see the street if you squint."

He rolled to the side in his chair to show Packer the screen.

"That's the alleyway there," Mickey said, tapping the screen with his finger, "See the graffiti at the edge?"

Packer peered at the tiny black slot at the far edge of the screen. It must have been fifty metres away from the camera and was barely visible at all. If he hadn't already seen the street himself, he would never have been able to work out what it was by looking at it.

"Is that the best you found?" he asked.

"Afraid so," Mickey said, disappointed that Packer wasn't more impressed, "I'm waiting for a call back from a guy who owns a Chinese takeaway place closer, though. Shop was closed, but there was a camera outside. We might get lucky."

Packer nodded and straightened up. He turned to Claire.

"We spoke to the flatmate. She seemed to think you might have been right about Emily working as a prostitute. Emily was scared of someone violent. Could be a pimp."

"Do you think he killed her?"

"I don't know. It's worth following up, though. Get the details from George and then start talking to anyone we know working the streets."

"Okay," she said, nodding.

"George, can you update the whiteboard?"

He headed in to his office without saying anything else.

"Don't forget your pie, boss," Thompson called after him. The others stifled a laugh.

Packer sat down at his desk. He took out his notebook to find the phone number he had been given by Siti.

He picked up the phone on his desk and dialled the number for Billy.

The phone did not even ring but went straight to the standard message from Telstra. The announcement told him that the person he was trying to call was unavailable and invited him to leave his name and number after the beep, which would then be sent as a text message.

"Police," Packer said and left his mobile number.

He put his phone down and nudged the mouse on his computer to activate the screen.

There were a handful of e-mail messages, which he ignored.

One message was from Alistair Goodge with the subject line, 'Photos'.

Packer clicked to open it. Four photos were attached.

He opened the first. It showed a view of a pink-coloured lace bra lying on a sheet of white paper on top of an examination table.

The second showed a closer image of the strap on the righthand side of the bra, with the adjustment buckle in the centre of the picture.

The third and fourth images showed extreme close-ups of the buckle from two different angles. With the harsh glare of a bright light shining on the buckle, the tiny hair could clearly be seen against the stark white paper beneath it. The hair was short, maybe a centimetre in length and a pale brown colour.

Packer stared at the final image on the screen for a while.

How would a hair have got there? The placement was odd. If the hair was on top of the assailant's head, it would not have come into contact with the buckle in order to become caught by it. Had the assailant had his face against the front of Emily's breast? Something about that seemed odd to Packer.

There was a tap at the door. Packer looked up.

Seoyoon was standing in the doorway.

"Visitor for you, boss," she said.

There was a woman standing behind Seoyoon, who took a step forward. She was wearing a grey suit, the jacket buttoned over a plain white blouse. Her long, dark hair hung loose behind her shoulders, a pair of oval glasses on her nose.

Packer didn't recognise her at first.

"Hello," Doctor Chandra said.

"Doctor Chandra," Packer said, "Come in."

He pointed at the seat on the other side of his desk.

Chandra sat down, crossing one long leg over the other. Packer could smell her perfume. It was something floral.

Chandra lifted one hand to her ear and pushed a lock of long, glossy hair back behind it.

"I wanted to apologise again," Chandra said, "This morning at the scene, I was very short with you. I'm sorry."

"I told you. It's fine."

"Death is never pleasant, especially violent death. I've only been working as a pathologist for a short time, and I'm still adjusting."

Packer nodded.

"I replaced Doctor Dupasquier when he retired," Chandra continued, "Did you work with him?"

Packer shook his head. "I've only been here a few weeks myself."

"You're new, too?"

Packer nodded.

"Good," Chandra said, "It's so nice to know I'm not alone."

She grinned at him.

"He's very highly regarded at the hospital," she went on "Nobody seems to miss the opportunity to let me know that I have very large shoes to fill."

Packer nodded.

"I'm forever hearing what a loss he is to the hospital," Chandra went on, "He wrote most of the course used to train the first-year surgeons. His textbooks are still the standard texts used in Western Australia.

"He was practicing longer than I've been alive. There doesn't seem to be a single person in the hospital who isn't aware of it."

Packer nodded again.

Chandra looked at his blank expression.

"I'm sorry," she said, "You're a busy man and I'm waffling."

"Not at all," Packer said.

Giving him a slight smile, Chandra reached down to her handbag beside her chair.

She straightened up, holding a buff-coloured folder which she placed on the desk in front of her. Her glasses had slid down her nose slightly, and Packer found he was looking into her eyes. She held his gaze for a moment, then leaned back.

She touched the frames of her glasses with her hand, repositioning them.

"My examination report," she said.

She reached across the table and placed one hand on the folder. Her fingers were long and slim, the maroon-coloured nail polish freshly applied.

"Very quick work, doctor," Packer said.

"Nish," she said.

"Sorry?" Packer said, frowning.

"My name. It's Nish."

Chandra smiled, her teeth startlingly white between her lips.

"Right," Packer said, "Tony."

"I assumed you'd want my report as soon as possible. I know you need to work quickly."

Packer nodded.

He put his hand on the report and pulled it towards him. He folded back the cover and skipped over the first few pages of preliminaries.

There was a full-length photograph of Emily Mtuba lying naked on an examination table. The metal surface of the table below her made her body seem cold, highlighting the fact that she was dead.

The next photograph showed a close-up of the woman's face from the side, giving a clear view of her profile. A series of close-ups followed, showing the marks around her neck and wrists.

"You can see the ligature marks clearly," Chandra said, "The tissue has swollen in places around the marks on the neck. The blood stops flowing after death, which means the tissue doesn't swell. All of this was pre-mortem."

"Meaning what?"

"I would say the garote around her neck was tightened, hence the swelling, then released. At some point, it must have been tightened and left there, causing death, but it was released before then."

"He was toying with her before he killed her?"

Chandra nodded, swallowing. She said nothing.

Packer turned over some more photographs, showing close-up views of the nose and face.

"You can see bruising around the nose and cheeks," Chandra said, "Because the blood stopped flowing, the bruising has not fully developed, but the tissue was quite badly traumatised. It would have resulted in significant bruising and swelling. If she had lived."

"Was a weapon used?"

"I don't think so. The skin is unbroken. I can't say for sure, but I would say a fist or a knee."

She tapped the photograph with her forefinger.

"You see the marks there?" she asked, "Two ridges close together, and the same pattern here, as well. I'd say it's the first two knuckles of a fist."

She demonstrated this by touching her knuckles with the index finger of the other hand, tapping her fingertip against each for a brief moment.

Packer returned to the report, turning over intimate photographs. A gleaming metal speculum had been placed inside the woman's vagina and used to spread it apart.

"I took vaginal and anal swabs," Chandra said, "There's some kind of substance on both. AP tests came up negative, so it's not semen. I'm guessing some kind of lubricant, but you'll have to wait for lab results to confirm it."

"Was she penetrated?"

"Yes. Both vaginally and anally."

"Raped?"

"Well, she was bound."

"Doesn't mean it wasn't consensual."

Chandra looked at him for a moment. "No, I suppose not.

"There's bruising around both her vagina and anus," she continued, "but not as much as I had expected, to be honest with you. She was bound, though, so could have done little to resist. If it was consensual, it would not have been enjoyable."

Packer turned over to the next photographs.

"There's bruising to her upper arms on both sides and to one of her buttocks," Chandra said, "It's difficult to date these accurately, but they're not recent. Based on the changes in colouration, I would estimate them to be two to three weeks old."

Chandra leaned forward and turned over the photo to the next one. It showed a close-up view of dark skin. It took Packer a moment to realise it this was upper part of the woman's back, between her shoulder blades.

"You see these marks here?" Chandra said, "They're faint, but it is still possible to make them out."

"Scratches?"

"Mmm. Perhaps. You can see that they trail down her back and there's bruising around them. It's possible they've been inflicted with some kind of weapon."

"What kind of weapon?"

"I don't know. The marks are too old to make out clearly."

"Not part of the attack that killed her, though?"

"No," Chandra said, "They're much older. They're almost healed now. Weeks older than the injuries that killed her."

She turned over the last photograph. Below it was an x-ray image of the woman's face from the side.

"When I was examining her mouth with my finger, I could feel a missing tooth," Chandra said, "so I arranged for x-rays. You can see here there's a molar on the top, right-hand side that's missing. The gum's not completely healed, so the tooth was knocked out recently."

Packer nodded. This matched up with what the dentist had told them.

"There's trauma to some of the others, too," Chandra said, "and the bruising to the cheek above them. That's consistent with her having been assaulted, but at an earlier time."

"Are you able to say when?"

"Difficult. The bruises were older than a few days. I can't be much more accurate than that."

Packer stared at the image for a moment longer, before closing the folder. "Okay," he said, "Thanks."

Doctor Chandra nodded and stood up. She held the bottom of her jacket and tugged it down to straighten it, which had the effect of pulling it tight over her breasts. Despite himself, Packer felt his eyes drawn there for split second before looking back at her face. Chandra gave a faint smile, letting him know she had seen this.

"Let me know if I can help further," she said.

"Thanks," Packer said, "You could have just e-mailed the report."

Chandra nodded, a smile playing at the corners of her mouth.

"I could have," she agreed.

They looked at each other across Packer's office for a moment.

"Call me if you need anything else," Chandra said, the smile growing slightly.

Then she turned and left.

Packer watched her walking across the office. Seoyoon stood up and mumbled something, then led Chandra towards the exit.

The door to the office had barely closed behind them before Thompson stepped into Packer's office.

"Phew," Thompson said, appreciatively, "She scrubs up alright out of the forensic suit, doesn't she?"

Packer handed him Chandra's report.

"She have anything interesting to say?" Thomson asked.

"The girl had been assaulted before. Lot of bruising to the back and face, but not from the attack that killed her."

"Fits with what Siti told us," Thompson said.

Packer nodded. "It does. Have a read of the report, then update the whiteboard."

"Okay, boss," Thompson said.

He turned to leave Packer's office, then turned back.

"Oh, boss," Thompson called.

Packer looked up.

"Did that Doctor Chandra say why she dropped the report in to you, instead of just e-mailing it? Surely, she must be very busy."

Packer said nothing but turned back to his computer screen.

Thompson grinned, as he left.

Chapter 10

Thompson rang the Department of Immigration. After waiting on hold for the better part of an hour, as his patience grew increasingly thin, he managed to speak to a switchboard operator, who offered to take a message and have someone call him back. She became agitated when he insisted on remaining on hold while she found someone for him to speak to immediately.

After a further lengthy wait, he was told that everyone in the compliance section had left for the day, but someone would return his call in the morning. Despite further protests, Thompson made an appointment to visit the office when it opened at 9:00am the next morning.

Packer emerged from his office half an hour later and walked out to the main part of the office.

"Did you talk to someone at immigration?" he asked.

Thompson shook his head. "Anyone who could help had gone home for the day. At four o'clock in the afternoon, mind you! Bloody public service. They're all useless bastards."

"We're part of the public service," Packer pointed out.

"Well, there are you, then," Thompson said, "Mickey works here. Proves my point."

"Oi," Simmons called turning around, "Who are you calling useless?"

"Have you found anything in the CCTV?" Packer asked him.

Simmons gave a resigned shake of his head.

Packer pointed at his computer screen.

Simmons knew better than to say anything. He turned back to his computer and resumed his search through the CCTV footage.

Thompson made no attempt to hide his grin.

The team spent the rest of the day working over the scant number of leads they had. The doorknock conducted by the uniformed officers in Northbridge had turned up a handful of possible witnesses, but none of these were panning out, and the list was growing steadily shorter as they eliminated each of them.

By six o'clock, the team had been on duty for twelve hours straight. Packer did the rounds to work through with each of them any progress that had made. There was little to report.

He told them to finish what they were on and resume in the morning.

Simmons turned off the CCTV on his computer with a small whoop of delight.

As the team began to drift out of the incident room, Packer returned to his office.

Packer looked at his mobile phone. It had been three hours since he left a message for Billy, and he had not received a return call.

He dialled the number again and got the same recorded message as last time.

"Police again," he said, leaving his number once more.

He wasn't optimistic about receiving a return call.

Packer got up and pushed his phone into the pocket of his trousers. He left the building and walked along Hay Street to an Asian takeaway shop. The shop was the closest to the police station, so he was a regular visitor after hours. He sat by the window and waited impatiently while his order was stir-fried.

He returned to the police station and put the takeaway food container on his desk. He stood by the coffee machine, waiting impatiently for it to fill his cup, then carried this through to his office and placed it on the edge of his desk.

He read over the forensic report from Alistair Goodge as he ate the takeaway food, tasting none of it.

Goodge's report contained a photographic record of his examination.

Each item of Emily's clothing had been laid out on a sterile sheet of white paper and photographed. Each item had then been checked under a blue light for stains. Wherever something had been located, it had been circled in white chalk and photographed, then swabs taken.

There were very few white chalk marks. Very little had been located.

Blue denim jeans were laid out on a sheet, with a tiny mark near the waistband. Nothing had been located on the K-Mart brand T-shirt.

The pale pink underpants were heavily stained where Emily had lost control of her bladder and bowels as she died. A tiny patch close to the waistband at the top had been marked with white chalk, and there was a series of images showing a swab being taken, then placed in a sterile tube for later testing.

There was a series of images of the bra, containing those Goodge had sent earlier, together with others. The first showed it laid out on a sheet. The second showed a close-up image of the plastic adjuster on the front above the right cup. Trapped between the plastic square and the strap was the tiny hair, clearly visible under the harsh lighting of Goodge's examination table.

The next image showed an even closer view, followed by an image of the hair being removed by a pair of metal tweezers and laid on a fresh sheet of paper, next to a ruler.

The hair was slightly shorter than the tweezers themselves, measuring a little over a centimetre in length. Against the stark background, the colour could be made out as medium brown or even dark blonde, and it was straight. It was clearly not one of Emily's hairs.

Packer skimmed over the rest of the images which showed the hair being packaged in sterile packaging, to establish the chain of continuity before the hair was sent for DNA-testing.

The final images showed a pair of heavily-scuffed sneakers. The brand marking had been rubbed away by heavy use, but they were clearly a generic brand of some sort.

Packer clicked on the screen to close the report.

As he did so, his hand caught the side of the coffee cup. It toppled off the desk and hit the floor, luke-warm coffee splashing across the carpet.

"Shit," Packer hissed.

He reached down for the cup and placed it back on the desk. A brown pool was seeping into the carpet.

He looked around the room for something to clean up the mess but saw nothing.

He hurried out to the incident room. There was a box of tissues on Perry's desk, and he grabbed this, then returned to his office.

Kneeling down on the floor, he began to mop up the coffee with the tissues, pushing them against the carpet until they had been soaked full of brown liquid, then dropping them into the wastepaper basket.

The cup had been almost full, and the coffee had splashed all the way across the floor to the cupboard behind Packer's desk. Methodically, he worked his way across the carpet, soaking up the mess as he went.

There were a few splashes on the bottom of the cupboard door and Packer cleaned these off. The cupboard was sitting on legs holding it a couple of inches off the ground, and the splash continued underneath.

Balling up a couple of tissues in his hand, Packer reached under the bottom of the cupboard and pushed them against the carpet.

As he lifted his hand, it brushed against something underneath the cupboard, and he felt it move against his knuckles.

Frowning, he dropped the wet tissues into the bin, then reached up under the cupboard.

His fingers came into contact with something hard and square, about the size of his thumb.

He scrabbled around for a bit and discovered it was held in place with tape. Gripping the edge, he pulled it out.

It was a plain black USB drive.

What was it doing up under the cupboard? Clearly, it had been taped there to hide it? But why?

Packer reached back under the cupboard and felt around. He moved his fingers along the length of the cupboard but felt nothing else.

He took out his mobile phone and turned on the light. Careful to stay out of the wet patch from the coffee, he lay on his stomach and slid as close to the cupboard as he could. Using the phone's torch, he looked under the cupboard, but saw nothing else.

It appeared the USB drive was the only thing hidden under there.

Packer returned to his desk.

He pulled the cap off the drive and inserted it into one of the computer's USB sockets at the front.

After a moment, a window popped up on the screen, reading, 'Password,' with a blinking cursor. Packer stared at it for a moment, then closed it.

He tried opening the file explorer on the computer to see the contents of the drive but got the same password prompt. Whatever was on the drive, he wasn't going to get access to it with the password.

Packer sat there for a moment longer, staring at the screen.

Who had hidden this under the cupboard? Frank McCain had had the office before him, so logically, it must have been his. Why had he hidden it there? He hadn't taken this with him, but he had left without warning. Had it been missed when the office was cleaned out?

The proper course of action was to report this to Base and leave him to sort it out.

But there was something about this that rang alarm bells for Packer.

What was McCain hiding? Did it have anything to do with his sudden departure?

Packer pulled the drive out of the computer and put the cap back on it.

He stared at the drive for a moment longer, then pushed it into the pocket of his trousers.

Whatever this was about, it would have to wait. Emily's murder was his priority for now.

He stood up and stretched his shoulders.

He had had only a couple of hours sleep the night before, and was feeling tiredness fill him, but it was pointless returning home now; he knew he would not be able to sleep and would spend the night thinking over the case anyway.

He made another coffee to replace the one he had spilled, then returned to his desk chair, and opened Doctor Chandra's medical report.

He turned to the first image of Emily's face. He ran the tip of his finger along the edge of lifeless features.

"When she has made money, she will pay men to bring her brother here to Australia on boat," Siti had told them, *"But to pay men to come here is cost very much. How can you get so much money? I ask to her."*

Packer tried to put himself in Emily's place, desperate to earn enough money to pay people-smugglers to bring her brother to Australia. The sums paid to the traffickers were astronomical by the standards of those living in third-world poverty. How far would Emily go to earn enough?

He looked at her cold, lifeless face in the photograph, the marking from the garote clearly visible around her neck.

How far would she go?

"Emily say to me that the man she does this for, the man is iblis... The man is Satan."

Packer's eyes closed and his head fell back against the headrest on the chair.

An image entered his mind.

Emily was on her knees, naked, her head facing up, braids falling across her back. Thick lips drawn back over clenched teeth stark white against her dark skin.

The attacker was in front of her. He was dark, bathed in shadows, his features completely hidden. Shoulders and arms tensed as he pulled the garote tight, but oddly calm; a coldness as he watched her die.

Emily struggled, sucking desperately for air that would not come.

The killer relaxed his hands, loosening the garote.

Desperately, Emily sucked in a lungful of air, eyes wide with terror, as she looked up at the man in front of her.

She opened her mouth to speak, to plead, to beg.

And he pulled the garote tighter again, cutting off her air once more.

She struggled, chest straining for breath.

He watched her, still, cold. Silent.

Packer jerked upright in the chair, eyes snapping open.

For a moment, he was lost, unable to work out where he was.

He took a deep breath, looking down at the photo of Emily in the report.

This wasn't a killer who took a life in rage or a moment of losing control. This was a killer disconnected from human emotion.

But there was something that didn't fit here, something that was moving at the edges, just out of sight.

Then he closed the report and stood up.

He walked around the desk, stretching his shoulders and back.

Christ, he wished he hadn't quit smoking.

<u>Tuesday</u>

Chapter 11

The Department of Immigration had its headquarters on Wellington Street, on the edge of the CBD. The massive building site of the university lay beside it, with the constant noise of construction and the occasional truck bringing building material into the barricaded off alley beside the building.

Packer and Thompson arrived on time for their appointment but were asked to wait in the front foyer.

Packer looked over the long lines waiting to speak to someone at the front counter. A number system was in use, with a digital display above the line of desks slowly moving upwards from '5' to '6', while they waited. Packer estimated there were over a hundred people waiting.

Nearly forty minutes after their appointment time, a man walked along the corridor. He was overweight with thick glasses and hair greased back over a receding hairline. A lanyard hung around his neck with a security pass on it.

"Are you the police?" he asked, looking at Thompson and Packer.

"Yeah," Thompson said, producing his identification, "Detectives Thompson and Packer."

"Chris," the man said, not offering them a surname or a handshake.

Without saying anything further, he turned and walked away, waving at them to follow him.

Thompson and Packer followed his back, as he waddled along a corridor to a bank of elevators.

In the narrow confines of the elevator, Chris's deodorant was powerfully strong.

"Looks busy downstairs," Thompson said.

"It hasn't even started yet," Chris replied, idly, "It'll be five times as busy in an hour or two."

The elevator opened onto an open-plan office space that was filled with endless cubicles of desks. Packer looked along the lines and estimated twenty or thirty cubicles.

Chris led them between a couple of narrow rows of partitions and into a tiny workstation with a computer and filing cabinet. The desk was piled high with papers, weighted down by a dirty coffee cup with, 'I FUCK ON FIRST DATES!', printed on the side.

Without offering to find them a seat, Chris sat down on the chair at the computer that creaked under his bulk.

The computer screen had a password entry box and Chris tapped in his password.

"You said on the phone you had a passport?" he said, looking at the screen.

"Yeah," Thompson said, producing an exhibits bag containing Imani Mbanda's passport. He pulled out the passport and held it out to Chris.

Chris took the passport and opened it to the identification page.

He placed it down on the desk, holding it open with one hand, while he tapped the passport number into a database on the computer.

After a moment, the same photo of Emily / Imani from the passport appeared on the screen, together with a display of all her details. Together with her date of birth and name, the computer screen showed details of her family, city and country of origin, and other details.

"She was granted entry to Australia last year on a student visa," Chris told them, "Standard conditions. She can remain here for three years, beginning in January, on the condition that she remains enrolled as a student at Edith Cowen."

"We spoke to them," Thompson told him, "They told us she never showed up at the start of the year, so they cancelled her enrolment."

Chris nodded. "Hardly surprising."

"Isn't it?"

Chris half-turned in the chair to face them. He looked bored.

"It's a pretty standard way to get entry. It's fairly easy to get a student visa, which gives you entry to the country. Once you're here, you can do whatever you want."

"Wouldn't the uni report it to you if she failed to show up?" Thompson asked.

"Why would they? They just accept the students. Visas aren't their problems. If the student doesn't show up, they just cancel the enrolment and that's the end of the problem for them."

"So why would she apply for a student visa?"

"Like I said, it's an easy way to get into the country. The alternative is to apply for a prospective partner visa or a family reunion visa, but you have to know someone already here who already has resident status."

"What about asylum seekers?" Thompson asked.

Chris smiled and gave a slight snort. "The numbers of asylum seekers are small by comparison. There's still a handful of people who come on boats through Indonesia, but then they have to wait in a detention centre on Nauru for a year. Who wants to do that? Much easier to come in with a legitimate visa. We do hundreds of thousands of those."

"But if they come in on a student visa or whatever and then disappear, don't they get caught?" Thompson asked.

Chris shrugged. "Some of them. But they work cash-in-hand so they don't appear on tax records, and they drive without licences. Unless they break the law and get arrested or something like that, they never get found. A lot of them are here for years before they come to our attention, and by then they've been living in the country long enough to qualify for citizenship that way."

"If they're here illegally, don't they get sent home?"

Chris shook his head. "Doesn't happen. We get a lot who've been identified as unauthorised because they've been arrested for raping or stabbing someone, or something like that. But if we begin deportation proceedings, they get Legal Aid to fight the proceedings. That takes years, and the outcome is always that they get granted citizenship anyway. We go through the motions, but it's always the same result. Once you're here, you're here for good."

"So why not just apply for citizenship?"

"You've got to pass good character tests, and a lot of them can't, because of criminal offences in their home country. Then you've got to pass language proficiency tests, which again, they can't, and citizenship exams. There're fees for all of this, too, and the numbers are limited each year. Getting a visa's much cheaper and much easier."

"How many people get a visa and then disappear?" Thompson asked.

Chris shrugged, bored of the conversation. "Who knows? We don't find out about most of them. One in three maybe."

"On in three out of how many?"

"Seven or eight hundred thousand a year? Something like that."

"So, two hundred and fifty thousand people disappear every year?" Thompson said, incredulously.

Chris held his hands up. "Look, I don't make the system, buddy. I just work here."

Thompson retrieved the passport and put it back in the exhibit bag.

"Well, you can cross her off your list," he said, "She was found murdered on Sunday night."

"Right," Chris said, without any sign of interest, "I'll make a note on the system."

He made no move to do so.

"Anything else you want to know?"

Thompson shook his head. "No, that'll cover it. Thanks for your help."

Chris nodded and stood up.

He walked them back to the elevator and pressed the button.

"Just turn right at the bottom, back the way you came," he said, when the elevator arrived.

"Thanks," Thompson said.

As the elevator doors closed, Chris turned back towards his desk, idly scratching his arm as he went.

"There's clearly a lot of job satisfaction working here," Thompson said, as they descended in the lift.

"Maybe the hours are good," Packer said.

***

"Alright," Packer said to the team, updating the whiteboard in the incident room when he and Thompson returned, "Immigration confirms that the victim came in on a student visa. Seems like it's a common scam to get entry into the country and remain here without authority. Working cash-in-hand to avoid detection seems to be common, which explains why the victim started working as a cleaner, along with her flatmates."

"We're working on the theory that she moved into prostitution?" Mickey asked.

Packer nodded. "Yeah."

"Why?" Mickey asked, "I mean if she was making money cleaning, why become a sex worker? The money's not great, but still."

"The flatmate, Siti, said she was planning to bring her brother, then the rest of her family here on a boat from Indonesia. It would take a long time to pay for that cleaning offices."

"Why couldn't they get student visas, too?"

"Judging by the photos, the brother was too young. The parents would be too old."

Mickey nodded.

"How are we looking with the CCTV?" Packer asked.

"We've finished the footage from the council and the nightclubs nearby," Mickey said, "There's nothing there so far."

"What about the Chinese takeaway you were waiting on?"

"Started on it this morning," Mickey said, "It's shitty quality but it shows the street, at least."

Packer nodded.

He turned to Claire.

"How are you getting on with the local girls?"

"Nothing so far. I'm waiting for a few calls back, but I'll go out later to visit a few of the girls I've dealt with in the past. Even if they don't know the victim, they might have been in the area Sunday evening."

"It's a bit of a long shot," Thompson said, making a face.

Packer nodded. "Agreed. But we don't have much else. Seoyoon, I want you to get a name and address for this phone number. It's the victim's landlord. Goes by the name of Billy. I've left a couple of messages, but I'm not getting a call back."

"Do you think he's involved?" Seoyoon asked.

"I didn't. But I get suspicious when people don't return my phone calls."

"Maybe he's just busy," Thompson suggested, with one raised eyebrow.

"Then he'll be very disappointed when I interrupt his busy schedule," Packer said.

He returned to his office to wade through e-mail.

He barely had twenty minutes to work.

"Boss," Simmons called from his desk.

There was something about his tone that made Packer look up sharply.

He left his office and headed for Simmon's desk.

Simmons was sitting facing his computer, leaning forward in his chair, so that his face was only a couple of inches from the screen.

Thompson walked over to stand behind him. Claire and Seoyoon moved across, too.

Simmons' screen was filled with grainy CCTV imagery, the colour so washed out that it appeared almost gray. The image was paused, flickering very slightly.

In the bottom left-hand corner was the date and time code. Last Sunday afternoon, 18:24.

The view showed the seating area of a takeaway shop, a long bench against a window running the length of the shopfront. Two people sat at either end of the bench, waiting to collect their orders, one idly playing with his mobile phone.

Through the window could be seen the footpath outside, bathed in twilight as early evening fell. One man walked casually along the street towards the shop entrance. A single car was driving past. A couple of people walked on the other side.

Simmons tapped the top, right corner of the screen with his finger.

"Look up here," he said.

The others peered closely at the screen. There was a tiny patch of the image, no more than two centimetres square. A darkened rectangle, with scrawl on one side.

"That's the alley?" Thompson asked.

"Yeah," Simmons said, "and watch this."

He tapped the keyboard on the computer.

For a moment, nothing happened.

Then a blurry, white rectangle crawled slowly onto the screen from the right, in slow motion. It drove past the darkened rectangle of the alleyway and stopped on the other side.

As the white rectangle stopped moving, the image focused very slightly. It became apparent that the image showed a large van. A windscreen and headlights could be made out. The image was far too distorted to make out a number plate or even the make of the van.

The driver's side opened, and a dark shape got out and walked around to the side of the van. The door slid open, and he leaned inside.

After a moment, he stepped back, hefting a long, dark shape in both arms.

He moved quickly around the back of the van and disappeared from view.

For long moments, nothing happened.

Then the dark shape of the man reappeared. He was now empty-handed.

He pushed the side door shut, then walked back to the front of the van.

The van drove down off the footpath, then turned back the way it had come and disappeared from sight.

"He's dumping the body," Simmons said, turning back to look over his shoulder at Packer.

Thompson placed a hand on Simmons's shoulder.

"That's good work, son," he said, "Well done."

"Play it again," Packer said, "at half speed."

Turning back to the screen, Simmons moved the mouse around and replayed the same section of footage but slowed right down.

"Pause it there," Packer said, as the van stopped, "What kind of van is that?"

"One of those big ones tradies use," Simmons said.

"Are they a Merc or a Renault or something?" Thompson added, "The bonnet sticks out slightly at the front, and it's got a really high top on it. Not like the Japanese ones."

"No markings and it's too fuzzy to see the number plate," Simmons said.

"Go forward a bit," Packer said.

Simmons continued playing the footage, until the driver was standing on the passenger side next to the sliding door.

"Pause there," Packer said, "Look at his height next to the window."

"He's not real tall," Thompson said, "Five nine? Five ten? Something like that."

Packer nodded. "Maybe. Could just be where he's standing, too. The image is too fuzzy."

"Doesn't look like he's struggling too much to lift the body when he gets it out," Simmons said, "Must be pretty strong."

"She wasn't a big lass," Thompson, "Wouldn't have taken too much effort to pick her up."

The blurry shadow was far too dark and out of focus to determine any further details.

"I can see if IT can enhance this," Simmons suggested, "They might be able to clean it up a bit, add lighting and stuff."

Packer nodded.

"He drives back along Aberdeen Street towards the park," he said, "See if you can get any CCTV from further along. The freeway might have speed cameras or something. We know we're looking for a white van now, and we know the time. Should narrow it down if you can find footage from anywhere."

Simmons looked unenthusiastic about the idea of spending more hours sifting through endless hours of CCTV footage but was smart enough not to say anything.

"Right, boss," he said.

"That was a good find, Mickey," Packer said.

It was as close to a compliment as he was likely to give.

Simmons smiled. "Thanks, boss."

***

Simmons managed to locate CCTV footage from the Mitchell Freeway through the Department of Transport. Traffic cameras had been placed at strategic locations around the main part of the city, where congestion was at its heaviest and the most traffic accidents occurred.

Simmons and Claire split the job between them and spent several hours sifting through the footage that had been provided.

There were four possible entrance ramps leading from Northbridge on to the freeway, so they began with those.

The white van did not appear in any of them.

At first, they sifted through the footage from all four entrances in the hour after the body had been dumped. They found nothing.

Working on the idea that the white van might have stopped for some reason, they went through the footage for the next hour. Still nothing.

Eventually, they were forced to accept that the van had not entered the freeway.

At some point between dumping the body and driving towards the freeway entrance, the van must have turned off and driven in another direction, somewhere out of the range of CCTV.

They had lost it completely.

Chapter 12

"I traced the phone number you gave me for the rent-collector, boss," Seoyoon said, "It's registered to a company named, 'Richards Road Holdings Ltd.'"

"A company phone? Makes sense, I suppose, if it's a work phone. Is the company local?"

"Well, that's where it gets interesting."

"Does it?" Packer asked, "Interesting how?"

"'Richards Road Holdings Ltd' is a shelf company. There's no physical address, just a PO Box. I did a company search on Richard Road Holdings. They own the block of units where the victim lived, plus another three properties in the same area."

"So, who owns Richards Road Holdings?"

"Another company, which is called 'P&R Holdings'. That company owns about another twenty shelf companies with similar names, 'Hewitt Street Holdings', 'Green Street Holdings'. I did an asset search on some of them. They all own rental properties, too."

"What about 'P&R Holdings'? Who owns that."

"The company director is Jeffrey Frazier. There's an address in Peppermint Grove near the river."

"Jeffrey Frazier?" Packer said, "That sounds familiar. Who is he?"

Seoyoon shook her head.

"He's in real estate, I think," Thompson said, "Some millionaire property developer. Friends with the mayor or someone. I'm sure I've seen him in the Sunday papers. The social pages and that."

Packer frowned as he thought this through.

"So, a millionaire in Peppermint Grove who owns half the slums in Perth. Our victim is living in one of his properties and paying the rent to this Billy, who also organises work for her and doesn't want to talk to the police."

"Even if the flat she lives in is dodgy," Thompson said, "Doesn't mean there's a connection to the murder."

"No," Packer conceded, "but something about it smells wrong. I think you and I are going to go and talk to Jeffrey Frazier."

***

Peppermint Grove was millionaire's row in Perth. Six small blocks of housing overlooking the north bank of the Swan River, heading out of the city towards the ocean. It had the highest income of any suburb in Perth by a very large margin, and its property prices were more than ten times Perth's average.

Even by the elevated standards of Peppermint Grove, Jeffrey Frazier's house was impressive. It sat on a raised section of Bindaring Parade, overlooking the river. High fencing of sculptured lattice concealed the front yard and revealed only the top of the three-story home inside.

There was no street parking anywhere along the road, and Thompson was forced to park the car some distance away. He and Packer walked back along the coast road towards the house.

"Christ on a bike," Thompson said, as they walked past the ornate houses that lined the street, "How much do you think these places are worth? One of these would cost more than I could make in a lifetime on a police wage."

"You need to start developing property in your spare time, George," Packer said acidly.

They climbed the hill and stopped outside the property. Steel gates two metres high and the width of two cars covered the driveway. An intercom was embedded in one of the white stone pillars beside the gate.

Thompson leaned on the call button.

There was a lengthy pause, and he was about the press it again, when there was a slight hiss from the speaker.

"Hello," said a woman's voice.

"Police," Thompson said, "We're looking for a Jeffrey Frazier."

There was another long pause. Thompson looked at Packer, who said nothing.

The pause went on for so long that Thompson was about to press the intercom button again.

"Do you have any identification?" asked the woman's voice from the speaker.

"Aye," Thompson said.

"Hold it out in front of you, please."

Packer looked up and saw that there was a tiny camera behind a dark glass bubble sitting on top of the stone pillar.

He and Thompson both got out their police identification and held them up towards the camera.

After a few moments, the gates began to slide back with a low hum of motors.

Thompson headed along the driveway, Packer a couple of steps behind.

The driveway ran towards the house and curved around a wide pond with a white marble statue of a naked woman pouring a jug. Water trickled steadily from the marble jug into the fountain below.

A black Lamborghini was parked on the far side of the pond outside a garage with three doors that were all closed.

The house was a huge mock colonial building, and fronted in white marble, with darkened bay windows across the bottom. It looked more like the Governor's official residence than a private home.

As Thompson and Packer drew closer to the house, the front door opened.

A woman in a skirt suit and glasses was standing in the doorway, waiting for them.

"Please come in," she said, her voice the one they had heard over the intercom. Her expression was blank, her manner business-like.

She stepped back to allow Thompson and Packer entrance to the house.

The inside was a huge foyer, tiled in grey marble with artwork placed tastefully around the walls. A white staircase curved up towards the second level, and closed doors led off from below. The entranceway was clearly designed to impress.

One of the doors at the far end was open. A man was waiting there and stepped forward.

He was tall, close to six feet, and heavily-built. A patterned shirt strained to cover a large belly, the top couple of buttons undone. He was wearing grey slacks over socks with no shoes. His thinning hair was slicked back.

He smiled slightly as he walked forwards into the room.

"G'day, officers," he said, "Jeff Frazier."

Despite the clear wealth of the place and his expensive-looking clothes, Frazier sounded like a builder. His accent was thick and nasal.

He reached out to shake hands, a thick golden bracelet hanging from his wrist.

Both detectives introduced themselves and shook hands.

Frazier's grip was surprisingly strong.

"Do I need my solicitor here?" Frazier asked, a faint smile on his face.

"I don't know," Thompson said, "Do you?"

The smile disappeared. "Two police officers turn up unannounced. Doesn't sound like its good news. You gonna tell me what this is about?"

"Is there somewhere we can talk in private?"

Frazier looked over Thompson's shoulder at the woman who was standing behind the two police officers.

"Nat's my PA," he said, "I got nothin' to hide from her, but come into the office if you want."

He turned and walked back towards the door he had emerged from. The detectives followed, with Nat trailing behind them.

The office was again large. A huge desk sculpted from some kind of dark wood with a computer on top of it sat in front of rows of bookcases lined with expensive-looking books. Two oil paintings hung on the walls. Incongruously, a glass-fronted display case containing a signed West Coast Eagles football jersey was hung beside them.

A row of lounge chairs circled a coffee table that matched the desk.

Frazier went and sat on one side. Thompson and Packer sat on the other side of the coffee table. Nat remained standing discreetly behind them.

Frazier leaned back in the seat, his thick legs apart, and one arm draped over the back of the couch.

"So?" he said, looking between Thompson and Packer, "You gonna tell me what's goin' on?"

Thompson retrieved his notebook from the pocket of his suit jacket.

"You own a company named P&R Holdings?" Thompson asked.

Frazier nodded. "Yep."

"Which owns another company called Richards Road Holdings?"

"Yep. I got a dozen or so companies that own a bunch of rental properties."

"One of those is a block of units at 14 Richards Road, Girrawheen."

Packer was half-expecting Frazier to say he didn't know all the ins-and-outs of the business or something similar. But Frazier nodded again.

"Yeah, it's a block of six. You obviously know all of this, though, 'cause you got it written down in your notebook."

"Do you know the tenants in the units?" Thompson asked.

Frazier shook his head. "I can tell you some of the addresses, but I got no idea at all about the tenants. I don't look after all that stuff myself."

"Who does?" Thompson asked.

"Nat pays the bills and looks after the accounts. I got another bloke who looks after the rent and the repairs and all that."

"What's his name?"

"Billy Harrison."

"What's the arrangement with the tenants? Are there leases in place for each of them?"

Frazier shrugged. "Some of them do, some of them don't. You'd have to ask Billy about all of that."

"One of the tenants at 14 Richards Road was found dead on Sunday night," Thompson said.

A slight frown appeared on Frazier's face. Packer was watching him closely for a reaction. If it was an act, it was a good one.

"Shit," Frazier said, "What happened to her?"

"Murdered," Thompson said, "Bound and strangled."

"Fuckin' hell," Frazier said, "Really? Wasn't in the flat, was it?"

"The lass was found in Northbridge," Thompson said, "in an alleyway."

"Northbridge, eh? You blokes must see a lot of suspicious deaths over there. Rough place, Northbridge. Wouldn't go near it after dark, myself."

Frazier shook his head slightly.

"Do any of your businesses own a white van?" Packer asked.

Frazier's eyes flicked over to him.

There was no change in his expression at all.

"White van?" Frazier asked, "Don't know, to be honest. Like I said, I don't have anything to do with the day-to-days of the businesses. Why? Is there a white van involved?"

"How long have you known Billy Harrison?" Packer asked, ignoring the question.

Frazier shrugged. "A long time. Twenty years probably. We used to work on site together."

"On site?"

"Yeah, that's where I made me money. Developing property. Started off as a fitter when I was fifteen and worked me way up. Last time I was working on sites was about ten years ago. I was foreman and Billy was me chief runner."

"And now he looks after your rental properties?"

Frazier nodded. "Yeah, he's a good fixer. Sorts out problems, you know? I don't have to worry about none of that, 'cause I know he'll just sort out whatever comes up. Just like he done on site."

"I've been trying to get in touch with him," Packer said, "He never answers the phone."

Frazier gave a snort.

"Too bloody right he doesn't, if he doesn't know the number."

"Why not?"

"Bloody tenants ringing up non-stop." Frazier raised his hand and imitated a mouth speaking, then broke into a high-pitched whine, imitating difficult tenants. "*'The water's not hot enough.' 'The front door sticks when I open it.' 'A dog shit on the front lawn.'* Never gets a moment's peace from the whinging pricks."

"That doesn't sound like the most sympathetic landlord."

"Look, officer," Frazier said, "Most of these properties are in Balga and Ghirrawheen, not fuckin' Peppermint Grove. They're cheap housing at cheap prices. If people are paying three hundred bucks a week, they know they're not gettin' a room in the fuckin' Ritz Carlton, right?"

"So how do I get in touch with Billy Harrison?"

"I'll get him to call ya."

"You got another phone number for him?"

Frazier let out a breath in frustration.

He lifted his bulk up off the lounge chair and walked over to the desk. He picked up a mobile phone that was lying there and began prodding it with his finger.

Packer was expecting Frazier to read out a phone number to him

Instead, Frazier lifted the phone to his ear.

"Yeah," Frazier said, after only a couple of seconds, "I've got a couple of police officers here at my place. They tell me one of the tenants from the Richards Road flats was found murdered in Northbridge on Sunday night. Apparently, they want to talk to you, but can't get in touch with ya.

"I want you to drop whatever you're doing and go see 'em."

Frazier looked over at Packer. "What station are youse blokes from?"

"East Perth. Near the Causeway," Packer said flatly.

"The East Perth police station," Frazier said into the phone, "Down near the Causeway. Can you get there at three o'clock? Fine. Thanks."

Frazier hung up the phone and put it back down on the desk.

He walked back over towards the lounge chairs but remained standing.

"Billy'll be down at your station at three o'clock to talk to youse," Frazier said, "Now, if there's nothing else, I've got a lot of stuff that needs doing. Next time, ring first and make an appointment, eh?"

Packer stared at him for a moment in silence.

Frazier looked back at him, clearly unwilling to be intimidated.

After a moment, Packer stood up.

Still looking at Frazier, he took out his wallet and retrieved a business card.

"This is my business card," he said, "It's got my contact details on it."

Frazier reached out a hand.

Packer turned and handed the card to Nat.

"I'd like you to check through your records. Let me know if any of Mr Frazier's companies own a white van."

She took the card from him, then looked over at Frazier.

Packer turned back to Frazier, who was now glaring at him with very obvious annoyance.

"Nat'll show youse out," he said.

He walked back to the desk and sat down, the chair creaking beneath him. He twitched the mouse and began looking at the computer screen, ignoring the two detectives completely.

In silence, Nat showed them out to the front door, and closed it behind them.

They walked back down the driveway. As they neared the gate, it opened for them with a low hum.

"It's not even one o'clock yet," Thompson said, as they began the walk back to the car. "Why do you reckon Billy Harrison needs two hours to get to the station?"

"Probably gives Frazier long enough to have a good, hard talk with him first," Packer said.

Chapter 13

When Packer and Thompson returned to the incident room, Seoyoon was standing behind Mickey, and they were both looking at the screen.

They looked up when Packer and Thompson walked in.

Mickey was almost bouncing with excitement.

"Look at this boss," he said, "I've found the van."

Packer and Thompson walked over to the desk.

A CCTV image was paused on the screen of Mickey's computer. It showed a view from high up, looking down over a freeway. Cars and trucks were driving along the lanes.

"We found the footage of the van dumping the body, right?" Mickey said, his words tumbling out rapidly, "but couldn't find the footage of it driving back on to the freeway afterwards. We figured it must have gone a different way instead of onto the freeway. Headed through streets where there was no CCTV."

Thompson nodded.

"It looked like we lost it, right?" Mickey said, "But then it occurred to me this morning."

He paused for dramatic effect.

"We didn't know where it went after dumping the body. But maybe we could find where it came from *before* dumping the body."

Thompson grinned. "Bloody brilliant," he said

"And?" Packer asked.

Mickey turned proudly back to the screen.

"And there's the van," he said, "Comes along the freeway and takes the exit to Northbridge six minutes before the body is dumped."

"Can you follow it backwards?" Packer asked.

"Already have," Mickey said, "Got all the footage from the Transport department along the freeway. I just spent the last hour going through it."

Mickey put his hand on the mouse and moved it around the screen, pulling up other windows showing paused images of CCTV footage.

"The van's moving south to get to Northbridge, so I followed it north along the freeway. There's a couple of black spots where there's no cameras, but you can see it on the cameras that are there."

Mickey moved to another window and clicked on play. The image showed a view of the freeway with one of the entrance ramps curving into view from the side. A couple of cars entered the freeway from the entrance ramp.

The white van was in the middle.

Mickey paused the image again.

"Which entrance is this?" Packer asked.

"Osbourne Park," Mickey said, "so we know the van came from there."

"Unless he was just driving through there to get to the freeway," Thompson pointed out, "He could have come from anywhere in the Northern suburbs."

"No, I don't think so," Mickey said, "Look, you can see the van coming from one of the side streets before it gets to the ramp leading on to the freeway. See there? Right at the edge of the screen. He's come out of Osbourne Park. He's not just driving through there."

"Okay," Thompson said, "That narrows it down. But that area's huge. There's about thirty blocks of workshops and commercial units in there."

Mickey's face fell. "Well, yeah," he conceded, "but there's tons of commercial properties in Osbourne Park, repair shops and shit. There'll be heaps of CCTV in there. It'll take us a while to go through it all, but we can work backwards from the freeway entrance. We should be able to trace it."

"Well, it's a start," Thompson said.

He looked at Mickey, seeing his look of disappointment.

He put his hand on Mickey's shoulder. "Nice bit of work, son."

Mickey nodded, and managed a half smile, but was clearly disappointed nobody was more excited about this.

Packer was looking at the screen, staring at the frozen image of the van.

"Seoyoon," he said, "You told me P&R Holdings has a long list of shelf companies that own properties throughout the suburbs."

"Yes," she agreed.

"Can you see if there any in Osbourne Park? Or near there?"

"I can do a company search and see what's listed on the assets registers for each one."

Packer nodded.

He looked back at Mickey, who was listening to the conversation.

"What are you waiting for?" Packer asked, "You've got CCTV footage to find."

***

Claire knocked on the door again, harder this time.

There was still no answer.

Working in Northbridge, it was inevitable that she got to know many of the local prostitutes. Many of them lived in the area, so that it was not far to take the clients, and Claire had spent the last few hours visiting those she knew who lived locally.

Despite this, she had so far learned absolutely nothing.

Claire knocked again and got no response again.

She half-turned, ready to give up, when she heard the latch on the other side of the turn scraping.

The door opened with a slight creak.

"What do you want?" croaked the woman on the other side.

"Hello, Gloria," Claire said, cheerfully, "How's things?"

"Claire?" the woman said, squinting at her through sleepy eyes, "What bloody time is it?"

"It's after lunchtime," Claire said, "Time you were up and about."

"I've been up half the bloody night."

But Gloria took a step back, holding the door open.

Claire stepped forward into the kitchen. The curtains were drawn, bathing the room in a dull twilight, and there was an unpleasant odour of unwashed dishes from the sink.

Gloria closed the door behind them and gave a low sigh of tiredness.

At night, under the dim lighting of Northbridge's streetlights and with heavy make-up, Gloria could have passed for fortyish. Here and now, tired and with the remnants of make-up hastily cleaned off the night before still on her face, Gloria looked even older than her fifty years. She had been working the streets a long time and it had clearly taken its toll.

She pulled the toweling dressing gown tighter over her breasts.

"Put the kettle on, love," Gloria said, "I need a pee."

She headed out of the room while Claire headed towards the bench.

There was an electric kettle on the bench next to a power point, but it was completely empty. Claire picked it up to refill it, but the sink was completely blocked with unwashed dishes smeared with the remainders of microwaved meals.

Awkwardly, Claire lifted out the dishes and placed them on the edge of the sink, so that she could fill the kettle with water and turn it on.

There was a sponge next to the tap that was nearly as dirty as the dishes. While she waited for the kettle to boil, Claire squeezed a couple of drops of detergent from the bottle on the bench onto the sponge and began to clean the dishes.

There was the sound of the toilet flushing and Gloria returned a few minutes later. She was now wearing track-suit pants and a Nike T-shirt, and her scraggly hair was pulled back into a loose ponytail.

"Thanks, love," she said, watching Claire washing the dishes.

"That's alright," Claire said.

Gloria took two mismatched mugs out of the cupboard and spooned instant coffee into them. She placed three teaspoons into her own mug.

"I haven't got any milk," she said, "Sorry."

"That's fine."

Claire rinsed off the last of the dishes as Gloria carried the mugs over to the tiny table, then she sat down with her.

"This is about the black girl?" Gloria asked.

"You know about that, then?"

"Of course I do, love. Word spreads pretty fast. Specially if it's a girl getting killed near where we work."

Claire nodded. "I should have realised. Did you know the girl?"

Gloria shook her head. "Was she a working girl?"

Claire gave a slight shrug. "We don't know for sure. Her flatmate thought she was."

"If she was, then she must have been new. None of us knew her, and we all know each other."

"Is it possible she could have been just starting out?"

"Yeah. Happens all the time, love." Gloria gave a wry smile. "A lot of these silly, little girls think it's easy money. They think you do a couple of blowies or a few roots and go home with a handbag full of money. They find out pretty soon that it's not that easy."

"If what we're hearing is right, then she might have started a couple of months ago."

Gloria shrugged. "I didn't know her if she did. I would have seen her in Northbridge if she was working there, but she might have been working in Highgate or doing home calls or something."

"She was African. Probably would have stood out."

Gloria nodded. "Yeah. I haven't heard about any African girls. There was one a few years ago, but not lately. A lot of blokes want the Asian girls, and there's a few of them. Don't know about Africans, though."

"She was found over on Aberdeen Street. Do you work down there?"

Gloria shook her head. "It's too isolated down there. Too risky. None of us take clients down there, even if we know them. Better to stick closer to the main drag in case of trouble."

"Well, we actually don't think she was killed there. We think she was killed somewhere else, then dumped there. I was really asking if you would have seen something over that way."

Gloria shook her head. "No. I work further up past the TAFE. The blokes know where to stop if they're looking for a girl."

"Did anything unusual happen that night? Anyone driving past who was acting weird, or anyone hanging around that stuck out? Anything like that?"

Gloria thought about it for a moment. "No, love, I don't think so. Like I said, though, I don't work down that way, so I probably wouldn't have seen anything anyway."

Claire nodded.

"What about anyone violent hanging around? Any of the girls been beaten up in the last few months."

Gloria gave a snort. "Last few months? We've all been knocked about the last few months, love. A bloke can't get it up or decides he doesn't want to pay. Getting knocked about is part of the job."

"This is really violent, though. This bloke would have really stood out. Something about him would have felt wrong."

Gloria shook her head. "Can't think of nobody."

She took a mouthful of black coffee and swallowed it.

"What they're saying is that this girl was beaten up and choked. Is that how it happened?"

"Pretty much," Clair said.

"And she was only a teenager, too?"

"Nineteen. Twenty years old in a few months."

"Fuckin' hell," Gloria said, "That's rough."

Claire sipped her own coffee. It tasted terrible, but she kept her face blank.

"She had marks on her," Claire went on, "Her wrists and ankles had been tied, and she'd been strangled with something around her throat."

"Fuck," Gloria hissed, her eyes widening slightly, "I never heard that part."

She shook her head slightly, as she absorbed this. She lifted the coffee cup, then lowered it again without drinking from it.

For a moment, she chewed her bottom lip, a slight frown on her face.

"What is it?" Claire asked.

Gloria shook her head. "Nothing."

"Come on," Claire said, "Out with it. What?"

Gloria wrinkled her nose. "Oh, look. It's probably nothing. Something about what you said, though. There was a girl here a couple of years ago. What was her name? I can picture her. Skinny bitch with long, curly hair. She was using speed pretty hard. There were a couple of dealers chasing her for money. Shit. What was her fuckin' name?"

She sat there for a moment longer.

"I can't remember," she said eventually, "but you know who might know is Suzy Sue. I think she's down in Canningvale somewhere now."

"This other girl with the curly hair. What about her?" Claire prompted.

"Oh, I don't know. Like I said, it's probably nothing."

"No, what was it?"

Gloria shrugged. "I don't know. I'm probably not even remembering this right. There was some story about her. She reckoned she went with some bloke, and he tied her up and whipped her or some shit."

"Is she still working now, this girl?"

Gloria shook her head. "No, she pissed off. This was about two years ago. She owed money to a lot of blokes."

"But she said she was tied up and whipped? You're sure about that?"

"That's definitely what I heard, yeah. Made me think of it when you said this dead girl had her wrists and ankles tied. That's what this other girl said, too. It's probably all bullshit, though. Like I said, she was using a lot of speed."

Gloria frowned again. "Thing is, though, I'm pretty sure she said something about being choked, too. Reckons she was lucky to get out alive. She said the bloke put a belt around her neck and choked her with it 'til she passed out."

Chapter 14

Billy Harrison was standing in the reception area at the station when Thompson and Packer went down to get him.

Harrison was short, maybe five foot six or seven. He was heavily-built, with solid shoulders and thick arms, like a boxer run to fat. Packer would have put his age at mid-forties.

He was wearing jeans and a plain-coloured shirt with the sleeves rolled up over large forearms marked with green ink. They looked like prison tattoos to Packer.

Harrison looked warily at Thompson and Packer.

"Billy Harrison?" Thompson asked.

Harrison nodded. "Yeah. You Sergeant Packer?"

Frazier hadn't mentioned Packer's name when he had rung Harrison from his office. Clearly, Frazier and Harrison had spoken about the visit after Packer and Thompson left.

"I'm Detective Thompson," Thompson said, "This is Detective Packer."

Harrison shook hands with Thompson, then Packer.

His grip was firm, but there was something odd in his eyes. He looked evasive to Packer.

Thompson led Harrison through to an interview room that led off the reception area.

"So, Jeff said you wanted to talk to me?" Harrison said.

"I left a couple of messages on your phone," Packer said, "You didn't return them."

"Yeah, sorry about that," Harrison said, grimacing slightly, "It's the phone I use for work. I have to give a number to the tenants in case of emergencies, but a lot of them ring up at all hours of the day and night with the most trivial shit. I ignore most of it."

"I said I was police."

"Well, you said, 'police,'" Harrison replied, "I didn't think it meant you were police. I thought it meant police had come to one of the flats."

"Is that common?" Packer asked.

Harrison nodded. "It's not unusual. They're not the best quality tenants in these places, right? A few of them have been arrested. A lot of them don't speak much English and don't know anyone here. I tell them they can ring me if it's an emergency, so if they get arrested, they say it's an emergency and ring me."

Packer looked at Harrison but said nothing.

"Where do these tenants come from?" Thompson asked.

"Word of mouth, mostly," Harrison said.

"And it's all legit, is it? Leases and everything?"

Harrison gave a shrug. "Okay, a lot of them shouldn't be here. I know this, right? I don't care about any of that shit. I hear One Nation on TV spouting all this, 'Fuck off, we're full' crap that they go on with. I don't buy into any of that White Australia shit. If people want somewhere to live and they pay the rent each week, I don't care who they are. Doesn't make any difference to me, one way or the other."

"Do you know the tenants in these places?"

Harrison shrugged again. "Some of them. But they move around a lot. They're there one week when I come for the rent, and they're gone the next week."

"Bit risky if you don't know who they are."

"Not really. There's always a lot of them staying there, so if someone leaves, there's someone else there to cover the rent. I've had a few times where they've all taken off, but it's pretty unusual."

"You're not worried about these places getting damaged?"

"Not much to damage in most of them," Harrison said, "They're cheap flats. Worst that can happen is a window gets smashed or a door kicked in or something like that, and I can fix that myself."

"Is there ever trouble getting the rent?"

"Yeah, happens a lot," Harrison said, "but they know they don't get much leeway. Fuck me about twice in a row and they're out. Simple as that. Cuts both ways, though. They know if they do the right thing by me, I'll look after them."

"How's that?" Thompson asked.

"Most of them need work. Jeff's got this mate, Tom. They go to the races every Saturday night. Tom runs an industrial cleaning business. He used to clean up properties after Jeff's company had finished building them, but now he does office and factory cleaning. I put the people from Jeff's flats in touch with Tom and he gives them cleaning work."

"That's very good of you."

Harrison gave him a look. "Yeah, well, I don't do it for free. I get a kickback from Tom for everyone I put in touch with him."

"Ah," Thompson said, feigning sudden understanding, "and it's all above board, this work, is it?"

Harrison gave a small sigh. "Look, I told you I don't buy into that white power shit. If people come here and want to work, why not give it to them? Otherwise, they're on the fucking dole, and all the racists are complaining about that. They get cash-in-hand work from Tom, and Tom gets some cheap labour. Everyone wins except the tax man, but who gives a fuck?"

"What's Tom's last name?"

"Kirby."

"Did you know Emily Mtuba?" Packer said, throwing the name in from nowhere and watching for Harrison's reaction.

Harrison turned to look at him, his face blank.

"Who?" he asked.

"Emily Mtuba."

Harrison shook his head. "Is she the one that got killed?"

Packer nodded.

"Jeff said that's why you were asking questions," Harrison said, "I don't know her."

"She was a tenant at 14 Richards Road," Packer said.

"Okay. I didn't know her. They're mainly Indonesians in those flats. Some Pakis and Indians in a couple of them. Didn't see any black girl in there."

"She lived at unit 3."

Harrison gave a slight snort. "That prick, Herman, lives there."

"Herman?" Thompson asked, feigning ignorance.

"Yeah. Real bad fucking attitude on that bloke. You should be asking him about the murder."

"Why's that?"

"Go and meet him and you'll see what I mean."

"Why don't you tell me what you mean?"

Harrison shrugged. "He's just a nasty prick. Always has an attitude about him if he's there when I go around. They didn't have the money one week when I went around, and I nearly got into a blue with him. He was fucking gibbering away at me in Indonesian and waving his arms around. He tried to take a swing at me. The girlfriend had to calm him down."

"Who's the girlfriend?"

"Siti." He waved his hand down the side of his face. "She's all fucking burned to one side of her face, poor girl. She's easy to deal with. Keeps him under control, too, when he gets a bit wild."

"When did this happen with Herman?"

"Oh, months ago," Harrison said, "June or July? Something like that."

"When was the last time you were at those flats?"

"Would have been last Friday night. I do the rents at different places on different nights. I do the rents in Ghirraween on Friday nights."

"Anything unusual happen last Friday?" Thompson asked.

Harrison shook his head. "Nuh. I just turned up and collected the rent. Siti answered the door with the money ready. I counted it and left. Everything was fine."

"Anyone else home that night?"

"Yeah, I think so. I didn't go in, just stayed at the door, but the TV was on. I think there was someone on the lounge, watching it."

"Was Herman there?" Thompson asked.

"Didn't see him if he was."

"Do you drive a white van?" Packer asked.

Harrison turned to look at him. There was no reaction.

"No," he said, "Why?"

"What do you drive?" Packer asked.

"A Ford Falcon."

"You said you fix windows and doors sometimes. How do you transport them to the flats?"

"It's a wagon. Plenty of room in the back when the back seat's folded down."

"Where were you last Sunday afternoon?"

Harrison shrugged. "Home probably."

"Were you home or not?"

Harrison nodded. "Yeah, I was. Had a couple of beers and watched something on Netflix."

"What was it?"

"Dunno. Something about fucking zombies."

"Anyone with you?"

Harrison shook his head. "No. I live on my own. Wife pissed off a few years ago. Took the kids with her to Queensland."

Harrison's hands were resting on the table, palms down. They were large hands, with heavy calluses on the fingertips and dirty nails. There were a few scrapes and marks on the fingers. Two of the knuckles on his right hand were scraped.

"How'd you get those marks on the backs of your right hand?" Packer asked.

"What?"

"The marks on your hands. How did you get those?"

Harrison looked down at his hands for a moment, then shrugged.

"I mow the grass at these places and clean up the yards. I was cutting back trees at one of them last week. Probably from that."

"What about that?" Packer asked, pointing at his palm. Harrison had a long scrape along the palm on the right-hand that was half-healed over.

"Same trees," Harrison said, "I was up on a ladder, holding on with one hand and cutting with the other. The branch fell and I reached out to grab it with the saw still in my hand. Stupid thing to do, but you don't think, do you?"

Packer looked at him for a long moment, saying nothing.

Harrison offered nothing further.

Packer leaned back in his chair, as a signal to Thompson that he had finished.

"Well, I don't think we need to keep you any further," Thompson said, standing up, "Thanks for your time."

Harrison gave a slight frown and looked at him as he stood up.

"Okay. No worries."

He followed Thompson towards the door.

"If you get another message from the police," Packer said, from behind him, "Return the call this time."

"Yeah, alright," Harrison said, turning back to him, "Will do."

Packer walked a few steps behind as Thompson led Harrison back to the reception area, then opened the front door for him. He stood by the door and watched Harrison walk across the car park to a white Ford Falcon wagon.

As he got to the car, Harrison looked back at the police station.

He gave no reaction to seeing Packer standing there.

Harrison got in the car and started the engine.

"What do you reckon about Herman getting agro with Harrison?" Thompson asked.

"What about it?"

"It matches up with what I saw at the flat. Herman's living with the victim and he's aggressive. My money's on him."

"Alright," Packer said, "Let's have a closer look at Herman."

Packer said nothing, as he watched Harrison driving out of the car park.

"You're thinking about Harrison?" Thompson asked.

"I think we should have a closer look at him, too," Packer said.

"He was happy enough to admit to knowing a lot of the tenants were illegals and he was getting them under the counter work cleaning from this Tom Kirby bloke. Matches up with what Siti told us, and he wasn't trying to hide it."

"No," Packer agreed.

"No reaction to any of the important questions, either" Thompson pointed out.

"No," Packer agreed, "but he spoke to Frazier first, so he knew what we were going to ask."

"Seemed pretty genuine to me. Maybe he just didn't know anything."

"Maybe."

"You don't sound convinced, boss," Thompson pointed out.

"Did you see the tatts?"

"Prison ink?"

"Looked like it. Do some background on him. See what you can find out."

"Alright," Thompson said, "but I didn't get the vibe from him."

Packer watched Harrison's car leave the car park and turn on to the main road.

"Emily's been living at the flat since the start of the year," Packer said, "and Harrison comes to collect the rent from the flat every week. But he never sees a black girl at the flat. Not even once. Does that seem a bit odd to you?"

Chapter 15

When they returned to the incident room, Simmons was leaning back in his chair, watching CCTV on fast-forward, Seoyoon was working at her computer, and Claire was out.

"Where's Claire gone?" Packer asked.

"Still talking to the working girls, I think," Simmons said.

Packer nodded. "Alright."

"The inspector came down before looking for you," Simmons said, "I told him you were downstairs. He said he'd be back."

Packer nodded. He had been expecting it.

He returned to his office and waited.

He didn't have long to wait.

There was a single tap at the door and Base walked in. Once again, his uniform was freshly pressed. He gripped the front of his trousers and pulled them to preserve the creases as he sat down.

"What progress have you made?" he asked.

"We've identified the girl," Packer said, "She was here illegally and using a false name. Living in a cheap flat in Ghirraween. One of her flatmates thinks she was on the game, so Claire's doing the rounds, talking to the girls she knows. Mickey's tracked down CCTV of a white van that appears to be dumping the body and followed it back to Osbourne Park."

"Have you traced the owner?"

Packer shook his head. "The quality of the footage is too poor."

"Then get it enhanced. I shouldn't have to tell you that."

Packer nodded, not bothering to engage with this.

"Have you got a suspect?" Base asked.

"One of the flatmates is an Indonesian national," Packer continued, "He's a possible. George and I will speak to him again."

"The flatmate's another illegal?"

Packer nodded.

"So here illegally," Base said, "and living with the girl. Sounds like a winner to me."

"There's a rent-collector, too, who I don't like the look of."

"Why not?"

"Something about him feels off."

Base gave a sigh of frustration. "Can we connect him with the deceased?"

Packer shook his head. "He denies knowing her. I'm not convinced about that."

"Yes, well, I'm not really interested in your 'feelings about things being off', Tony. I want a result. Focus on the flatmate. Pull him in for a formal interview. You can hold him for up to 48 hours, which give you enough time to connect him with this white van. Let me know as soon as you've made an arrest."

Packer nodded.

"I told you yesterday, Tony. I don't want any pissing about with this. Get a result and get it fast."

Base got up and left.

Packer waited until the incident room door closed behind Base, then got up and left his office.

"Follow up on Harrison," he told George, "I want to check up on something else."

Thompson nodded and sat at his desk.

"Right, boss."

Packer went down to the car park to his car. He drove west along Adelaide Terrace towards the city centre. He turned along Victoria Avenue and drove past the church into the car park for the Royal Perth Hospital.

The hospital had been regularly expanded over the years as the city had grown, and now consisted of a dozen buildings in mismatched styles that spread over three blocks with a major road in the middle.

Packer walked in through the main entrance and spoke to the receptionist, showing her his identification.

An orderly was summoned to the counter and appeared fifteen minutes later, wearing dark blue scrubs.

He asked Packer to follow him and led him down through the rat's warren of corridors leading to the lowest level of the building.

The morgue consisted of a row of examination rooms with offices at the far end.

The orderly tapped discreetly at one of the office doors, then gently opened it.

"Senior Sergeant Packer to see you, doctor," he announced, before retreating back along the corridor.

"Hello, officer," Doctor Chandra said, standing up from behind her desk, a slightly playful smile on her face, "It's been less than a day. Can't stay away from me, can you?"

"I was in the area," Packer said, keeping his face neutral.

"Were you? Well, please sit down, then. Can I offer you tea?"

"I'm fine. Thanks."

Packer sat down in front of the desk and looked around the room. The office was scrupulously tidy, with a row of filing cabinets on one side next to a computer printer. The other side contained two higher cabinets that were closed.

The desk had a computer terminal and a neatly organised collection of papers that Chandra was working on.

The shelf behind her desk contained two rows of medical textbooks and a small wooden-framed photograph that showed Chandra holding a girl of about ten. Her skin was paler, but her features clearly matched Chandra's.

Chandra saw Packer looking at the photograph and turned to look at it, too.

"My daughter, Mina," she said, "She's twelve now. They grow up so fast."

"She's very pretty," Packer said, "Looks just like you."

Chandra gave a closed-mouth smile at the compliment.

"She lives with her father half the time. When she's away, I can't wait for her to come back. Have you any children?" Chandra asked.

Packer shook his head.

"You should," Chandra said, "Children are the greatest thing in the world. The only thing that gives life any real meaning, if you ask me.

"Anyway," she said, "How can I help?"

"I've been thinking about the garote. Would it take a lot of strength to strangle someone with that?"

Chandra considered.

"It really depends on what was used. Strangulation would take several minutes, so the device would have to be held tight enough to cut off the air supply for quite some time. If the device was something with a fastener that could be secured and ratcheted tight, the same way that cable ties work, then it would simply be a matter of pulling it tight and letting it do the rest. If, on the other hand, it was simply a belt or something along those lines, it would have to be pulled tight and held for several minutes until the victim passed out. That would require considerable strength to do."

"Do the marks on the neck give you any indication one way or the other?"

"Unfortunately, not. Either way would have left the same kind of marks."

"What about the man holding the garote. Would it leave marks on his hands?"

Chandra thought. "Possibly. If he had to pull the garote tight and hold it in place until the woman died, it might cause something like rope-burn to his hands."

"But not if it was a device with a ratchet?"

"No."

"You found older bruising on the body, from an earlier assault."

"Yes."

"Were the bruises bad enough that they would have left marks on the hands of whoever did it?"

Chandra gave him a slight smile. "I expect so. But you hardly need me to tell you that. You must have seen more than a few assaults in your time."

"I have, yeah," he said, "You said she'd been sexually penetrated."

"Yes."

"Are you able to say if that was before she died or after?"

Chandra raised her eyebrows slightly in surprise. "You think she may have been killed first, and then raped?"

Packer shrugged. "Are you able to tell?"

Chandra thought this over.

"No, I'm not. There was some trauma to both the anus and the vagina, but nothing substantial. If there had been lacerations to the skin or significant bruising, I might be able to tell from the blood flow whether it was post- or pre-mortem, but it's not substantial enough.

"Forgive me, officer," she said, "but that's a very morbid question. Have you some reason to think the sexual assault may have been after she died?"

"No," Packer said, "I'm just asking questions."

Chandra nodded, but she clearly had some doubts about that.

"Is there anything to suggest drug use?" Packer asked.

"No needle marks or damage to the nasal cavities. I sent a blood sample off to toxicology, but I haven't seen the results yet."

"Okay. Let me know if anything shows up."

"Of course."

Packer stood up to leave.

"You've been very helpful," he said, "Thanks."

Chandra walked around the desk to join him. She walked over until she was standing beside him.

Once again, Packer could smell the faint jasmine scent of her perfume.

"You know, you could have just phoned to ask me these things," Chandra said.

"Yes," Packer agreed, "I could have."

He stood there for a moment. A faint smile curved at the edges of Chandra's lips as she looked at him.

"Thanks again," Packer said, after a moment.

"Any time, officer," Chandra said, "I'm always available."

Packer left her office.

***

When he returned to the incident room, Thompson was on the phone.

Seeing Packer walk in, Thompson beckoned him over.

Packer waited, while Thompson listened on the phone.

"Aye, well, thanks for that, love," he said, "I'll be in touch if we need anything else. Cheers."

He hung up the phone and turned over his notes.

"I got that background on Billy Harrison while you were out," Thompson said, "Did six months for assault when he was nineteen. Probably where the prison tattoos came from."

"What was the assault?"

"A pub fight. It was twenty-five years ago, so the records don't have much detail, but that seems to be about it."

"Anything else?"

"Several drink-driving offences. One nine years ago that got him a caution, and another seven years ago that resulted in a licence suspension, and another one barely a year after that. Nothing else on his record."

"What about the ex-wife?"

"That was her on the phone."

"And?"

"She was married to Harrison for sixteen years, then left him four years ago. Two kids, a girl of fifteen and a boy of nine. She took them both with her and moved to Queensland, just like Harrison said."

"Did she say why she left?"

"She did, indeed," Thompson said, "She tells me Harrison's a drinker. This had been a problem for a long time but got worse and worse in the last two years before she left. Says he used to get a bit busy with his fists when he'd had a few brews.

"He used to give her a good pasting every now and then," Thompson went on, "which she put up for the sake of the kids. But when he started giving the daughter a hiding, too, she decided enough was enough and took off. She's got a couple of restraining orders on him to prevent him contacting them."

Packer absorbed that. "Was it just her and the girl he used to hit?" he asked, "Did he ever hit the son?"

"She says not," Thompson said, "Sound like Harrison only likes hitting women."

"Maybe. Although the boy is a lot younger, and Harrison's got a record for a pub fight. Did you ask her if he ever tried strangling or tying her up?"

"I did," Thompson said, "and it's hard to slip that into a conversation subtly, let me tell you. She was quite surprised when I asked that, though. She says it never happened. He just hit her when he was off his tits."

Packer nodded thoughtfully.

"That might fit with Emily being beaten up at earlier times," Packer said, "She has some kind of relationship with Harrison, who gets drunk and knocks her about."

"He told us he never met Emily, boss. Siti seemed to think that was correct."

"She wasn't sure, though. It's possible he met Emily some other time. Harrison used to do repairs at the units, so he might have been there another time when Siti was out. And there were times in the last two months when Siti was out cleaning and Emily was not. Harrison could have seen her then without Siti knowing about it."

Thompson nodded. "Okay. That's possible."

"The marks on his hands bother me, too."

"He said he was cutting trees."

"I spoke to Doctor Chandra again," Packer said, "She says the garote might leave marks on the killer's hands, depending on what sort of garote was used."

"Did she?" Thompson said, eyebrows raised slightly, "Just phoned you up out of the blue, did she, or..?"

Packer ignored the question.

"Let's keep Harrison in mind. Goodge found a hair and a semen stain. If we get enough on Harrison to get a warrant for a DNA sample, we can get a comparison done."

"Right, boss."

Packer looked at his watch.

"Let's go and speak to Tom Kirby."

Chapter 16

It was close to four o'clock when Packer and Thompson headed into Leederville and traffic was heavy with the afternoon rush.

Like many of the inner suburbs of Perth, Subiaco had expanded rapidly and was now home to multiple high-rise apartment developments, but unlike other parts of the city, there had been little space to expand the main thoroughfares. Hay Street ran past the older shops and pubs and its narrow street was now heavily congested with traffic.

After fighting through the traffic, Packer and Thompson found themselves outside a row of commercial offices on the border of Jolimont. Predictably, the handful of parking spaces were full, and they were forced to park in a side street a couple of blocks away and walk back.

Focus Commercial Cleaning had the office in the middle of the row.

Parked outside was a large, red mini bus marked with the company logo, with a small, enclosed trailer hitched to the back.

They walked inside to find a tiny office space with a circle of lounge chairs and a coffee table next to a water cooler.

A desk lay at the back beside a door leading to the back of the shop.

Sitting behind the desk and talking on the phone was a man in his forties, wearing work trousers paired with a business shirt.

Still talking on the phone, he gave them a smile and pointed towards the lounge chairs.

He carried out a few more minutes of conversation before telling the caller he had to go and hanging up.

"Sorry about that," he said, walking over to them, "Busy afternoon. Tom Kirby. How can I help?"

"Police," Thompson said, introducing them both as they showed Kirby their identification.

"Shit," Kirby said, giving them a look of mock fear, followed by a smile, "What's this about?"

"We're following some enquiries," Thompson said, vaguely, "Focus Commercial Cleaning. Do you own the business?"

"Yep, that's right. Had this one for about three or four years now."

"What about before that?"

"I had another business that did cleaning on building sites and demolition grounds, but it went belly up. Left me with a ton of debts to pay off. It was a lot of hassle, too, 'cause of all the WHS rules on construction sites. Some of it was classed as cleaning up hazardous waste, too, which meant special licenses and insurance. This is much less hassle."

"What do you clean now?" Thompson asked.

"Offices mainly. Some factories and warehouses, too."

"What sort of areas do you do?"

"Anywhere. Mostly around the city, but we go out as far as Joondalup. A couple of places down south, too. Bull Creek, Curtin."

"How many people do you employ?"

"I've got a girl that does the books twice a week. Otherwise, it's just me. All the actual work's done by contractors."

"How many of those do you employ?"

"Well, I don't employ them. Like I said, they're contractors. I pay them casual rates by the hour. If I employ them directly, I have to get insurance and pay superannuation and all that stuff. Paying them as casual staff means I don't have to worry about all that."

"And that's all above board, is it?" Thompson asked.

"Yes, it is," Kirby said, firmly, "Part of the reason the site cleaning business went under was because of all the extra stuff I had to pay. The accountant suggested I could avoid all of that this time by just paying casual staff instead. You're gonna tell me you're here because he's wrong about that?"

Thompson shook his head. "No, that's not why we're here."

"So, why are here?" Kirby said, looking between them, "What's this all about?"

"How do you actually do the jobs?" Thompson asked, ignoring the question, "What's a typical night look like?"

"I have a list of jobs for the night. There are a few places that get me to clean every night. Some are twice a week, and some are weekly. I have a meeting place near the train station for the contractors who are doing the cleaning. I pick them up in the bus and drive them from site to site. At the end of the night, I drop them back near the station, pay them and they go home. That's it."

"That's the bus outside, is it?"
"Yeah."
"Do you own any other vehicles?"
"Well, I don't use the bus at home," Kirby said, "I've got a 3-series BMW when I'm not at work."
"Any others?"
"No."
"Do you have a white van?"
"Not any more," Kirby said.
"You used to have one?"
"Yeah, got rid of it a couple of years ago."
"Why's that?"
"It wore out. Wasn't big enough any more, either. It was fine when I had about eight or ten contractors, but I need more like thirty now. There wasn't enough room in the van for them."
"What happened to it?"
"It broke down one day and wasn't worth fixing. There were only a couple of months left on the rego anyway. The bloke who towed it gave me a couple of hundred bucks for it to use for scrap. I got the bus the following week."
"Do you remember the rego of the van?"
"No, but I probably can find it for you if you want it," Kirby said.
"Yes, please."
"Look, what's going on?" Kirby said, "I keep asking you this, but you're not telling me. What's this about?"
"We're making some enquiries after a girl names Emily Mtuba," Thompson said, "We believe she may have been doing some cleaning work for you."
Kirby shrugged. "Alright."
"So, was she?"
"I wouldn't know, to be honest," Kirby said, "They come in and do the work. I pay them at the end of the night and that's it. I learn a couple of first names if they turn up regularly, but not that many."
"She's an African lass. About twenty, long hair in braids. Bit of a looker."
Kirby shrugged again. "Maybe. I've had a few Africans doing the work, but I don't know any of them specifically."

"Do you know a girl named Siti?"

Kirby shook his head.

"Indonesian. One side of her face is burned," Thompson said, touching the left side of his face.

"Oh, yeah, I know who you mean," Kirby said, "I didn't know her name, but I remember the scars."

"The African lass would have been with her."

Kirby thought for a moment. "Don't remember her. The girl with the scar used to bring her boyfriend along. I told him not to come back after a while, though."

"Why's that?"

"He was a troublemaker," Kirby said, "He used to yell at the girlfriend, and it made everyone a bit wary around him. Then one of the clients rang one day to say they were missing some tools from the warehouse we were cleaning the night before. I paid them for it, but they still took the work elsewhere. Never got to the bottom of that one, but I told the boyfriend to piss off the next night, and nothing ever went missing again. Can't have been a coincidence."

"Where do you find these people who do the work?" Thompson asked.

"I used to run ads in the paper, but I haven't done that for ages. Now it's mostly word-of-mouth. Everyone knows someone else who wants to make a few extra dollars by doing some night work."

"Anyone send people to you for extra work?"

Kirby nodded. "Yeah. A couple of people I know put the word out."

"Billy Harrison?"

"Yeah. Billy sends me people every now and again."

"What's the arrangement there?"

"He sends me people. If I need them, I use them, and send Billy a spotter's fee."

"How do you know Billy?"

"He works for one of my mates."

"Who's that?"

"Jeff Frazier," Kirby said, frowning again, "Look, what's all this about? You said you were looking for some African girl. What's she done?"

"She was murdered," Packer said, "and dumped in an alleyway in Northbridge."

"Shit," Kirby said, his eyes widening slightly, "I mean, Northbridge is a pretty rough place. You reckon this girl was doing work for me?"

"We have some information suggesting she was," Packer said.

Kirby shook his head. "Look, it's possible she was. Like I said, though, I don't know who they all are. If they turn up and I can use them, they do the work and I pay them. I don't know anything more about them than that."

"Where were you last Sunday?"

Kirby smiled nervously with surprise. "You think I killed this girl? I certainly wasn't in Northbridge on Sunday, that's for sure."

"Where were you?"

"I don't know, really. At home in the morning. I picked up some cleaning supplies from Bunnings after lunch. I usually do."

"Which Bunnings did you go to?"

"Belmont. It's the nearest one to my place. I've got an account there."

"Where do you live?

"Near the stables at Ascot."

"What about after that?'

"I was planning to go to a mate's place for a barbeque for dinner, but I didn't really feel like it in the end, so I stayed at home."

"Anybody else with you?"

"No, there wasn't," Kirby said, the smile becoming a frown, "Seriously, you reckon I did this?"

Packer shook his head. "No. Just asking standard questions."

"Fair enough."

"How long have you known Billy Harrison?"

"Billy? A long time. Ten years or more."

"How did you meet him?"

"He used to work for Jeff. He was his 2IC. Whenever I used to go out on site with the other business to clean up at the end of the build, Billy was there running the site."

"Is he a friend?"

Kirby shrugged, then nodded. "Yeah. We get along pretty well. I don't hang around with him outside of work or anything, but we've had a drink a few times."

"Married?"

"Not any more. Barbara left him a few years ago and took the kids. She said Billy was hitting her and the kids."

"And was he?"

"I doubt it, to be honest. He's got a bit of a temper, especially when he's had a few drinks. I don't know about him hitting Barbara and his kids, though. If I had to guess, I'd say she made that up to avoid any custody issues, but it's none of my business."

"Have you seen him lose his temper?"

Kirby shook his head. "Oh, not really. He used to yell at some of the blokes on site years ago, and I remember him getting into a knuckle at a Christmas party once, but it's not like he was a psycho or anything."

Packer nodded. "Okay. Thanks for your help."

Thompson gave him a business card. "That's my contact details there. If you can send me the rego and details of your van as soon as you get a chance, I'd appreciate it. If you can send me the receipt from Bunnings, that would be good, too."

"Sure. No dramas," Kirby said, looking at the card. He stood up to open the door for them. "Let me know if there's anything else."

Thompson and Packer headed back along the road towards where the car was parked.

"Check out the van and rego and the Bunnings account," Packer said.

"Is he in the frame?" Thompson asked, surprised.

"We don't have a lot of suspects, George. Not many people knew Emily."

"Kirby didn't know her."

"Kirby *said* he didn't know her."

"You think he did?"

"I don't know. Siti says Emily was doing cleaning work for months. Seems odd that Kirby wouldn't remember her at all."

"You said that about Harrison."

"Seems odd that he didn't know her, either."

"My money's still on Herman. We saw the way Herman was treating Siti back at the flat. Billy Harrison says he was violent, and now Kirby is telling us the same thing. Plus, he nicked stuff from one of the places they were cleaning."

"Doesn't make him a murderer," Packer said.

"No, but it makes him an aggressive little shit who mistreats women and breaks the law. And he was living with Emily. Like you said, not many people knew Emily, but Herman did."

"Alright. We'll go back to the flat and have a chat with Herman," Packer said, "We can check with Siti about some of the stuff Harrison and Kirby told us, too."

"Boss," George said.

They walked back to the car in silence.

Chapter 17

Thompson drove the car north, heading out from the city centre and through the suburbs, towards Ghirraween once again.

As they drove, Packer felt something inside his pocket press against his leg. It was the USB drive he had found hidden under the cupboard in his office.

Again, he wondered what it was doing there.

"You worked with Frank McCain for a long time?" Packer asked.

"Aye. Four years. Five maybe."

"What was he like to work for?"

"Grand," Thompson said, "He was a good copper. Had a great feel for people, understood what made them tick, and he was good at getting them to open up."

"What about the way he ran the team?"

"Aye, well. Maybe his people skills could have used some work. He had a temper on him. If you thought you'd made a mistake, he certainly let you know about it."

Thompson sighed slightly. "Actually, he'd had some bad breaks. He had a daughter who died a few years back. She was barely out of her teens. Leukemia, I think. It took her a few months to go. Frank had to watch it happen, knowing there was nothing that could be done about it."

"What about his wife?"

Thompson shook his head. "Jenny couldn't handle it. She left a few months after Genevieve got sick. Didn't even come back for the funeral. Frank changed after his lass died. He got more... withdrawn, I suppose. Started playing his cards close to his chest, you know? Always seemed like he knew more than he was letting on. He wasn't much of a talker."

Thompson looked at Packer from the corner of his eye.

A lot like you, he thought, but said nothing.

"What about when he left?"

"It was odd," Thompson said, "He was late to work one day and wasn't answering the phone. I was planning to go around to see if he was okay, and then the message came down from on high that he'd left and wasn't coming back. No hint of it from Frank, mind. It came out of nowhere."

"Someone said he had some health problem?"

"That was what he heard. Made sense, I suppose. He was a bit of a drinker, Frank. He'd had some heart issues a few months back, a minor heart attack. So, we all thought it was probably connected with that. Strange that he didn't come to say goodbye."

Thompson gave a slight snort. "Or maybe it wasn't. The spirit went out of him after the lass died, and he was getting more withdrawn, especially towards the end. I can't imagine him giving thank you speeches at a farewell do or anything like that."

Thompson turned to look at Packer.

"Why are you asking about Frank?" he asked.

Careful to keep his face blank, Packer shrugged.

"Something Base said the other day," he lied, "He thinks I'm failing to measure up to Frank McCain's performance."

"Does he now?" Thompson said, raising his eyebrows, "I think Base is playing mind games with you, boss. He never liked Frank much, and I think he was relieved when Frank left. Just like the bastard to pretend otherwise, though, if he thinks it'll help him push you around."

Packer nodded.

He wanted to ask more about McCain but knew doing so would make Thompson suspicious.

He let it go.

"What about Mickey?" he asked, changing the subject, "What do you make of him?"

"Bloody Mickey," Thompson said, shaking his head, "He's bright enough. Got the makings of a decent copper. Just so bloody disorganised, you know, and can't keep his mind on the job."

"He's been thorough enough with the CCTV."

"Aye, that he has. He just needs to focus. I can't help but wonder if there's something going on outside of work that's causing problems."

They chatted about Simmons for a while, and Packer felt little concern that Thompson was suspicious about his asking about Frank McCain.

After another twenty minutes, Thompson drove them through the same streets of run-down units and social housing, before turning into the *cul-de-sac* of Richards Road once again. He stopped at the end of the road.

"No spectator this time," he said, looking over at the house where the man with the beer bottle had been watching them last time.

"Probably gone to his evening class," Packer said.

They walked along the side of the block of flats to unit 3 and knocked on the door.

There was a long wait.

Thompson tapped again.

Eventually, the door was cautiously opened, the chain holding it open only a couple of inches.

The sun was falling, and it was growing dark, but the kitchen was in darkness. Siti stood back from the door. Thompson could barely see her face in the gloom.

"Hello, love," he said, cheerfully, "Remember us?"

Siti looked at him for a moment before answering.

"Yes," she said, her voice quiet.

"Can we come in?" Thompson asked, "Just want to ask a few more questions."

She peered at them from the darkness for a moment in silence.

"I tell you everything," she said, "I do not know more."

"That's okay, love. We just want to check a few extra things with you. Won't take too long."

She looked at them for a longer moment without speaking.

When it became clear that they were not going to leave, Siti closed the door again. They could hear the chain being removed, then she opened the door again and stepped back. She stood on the other side of the table as they entered.

The curtains across the kitchen windows and the lounge windows were closed. Only the light in the hallway was on, bathing the place in semi-darkness.

But even in the poor lighting, the damage to Siti's face was obvious. Her eye was swollen and bruised, tissue red and puffy. The skin around her mouth split and there were several raw cuts filled with blood.

"You've been in the wars," Thompson said gently, "Can I see it?"

Siti looked down. "No. It is not bad."

"Doesn't look too good to me," Thompson said.

He stepped slowly forward, raising his hands very carefully. Gently, he put his hand under Siti's chin and turned her towards the light. He lifted her head slightly, so that he could see the damage. Her fringe had fallen across the side of her face, and he moved it carefully to the side with his fingers.

The broken lip had begun to scab over, and the bruising around her eye had turned red. There was also bruising around her arm and shoulder. The damage was recent, but not completely fresh. It was a day old.

Probably just after they had been here last time.

"Have you seen a doctor?" Thompson asked.

Siti shook her head.

"I'm gonna feel around your eye. Make sure there's no fracture. It'll hurt a bit, I'm afraid."

Cautiously, he placed his thumb above Siti's eye socket and moved it along, feeling for a step beneath the swollen skin. Siti winced and gave a high-pitched grunt but let him examine her.

Thompson checked all the way around the eye but found nothing other than bruising.

"I can't find any sign of a fracture, love," Thompson said, lowering his hands, "but you should still go to the hospital to make sure."

Siti did not reply.

While Thompson was examining Siti's face, Packer had checked the other two bedrooms and the bathroom. Nobody else was home. He caught Thompson's eye and shook his head.

"Why don't we sit down?" Thompson said.

He pulled out one of the chairs and Siti sat down.

Thompson sat at the end of the table beside her, the chair back from the table.

"Who did this to you?" Thompson asked.

Siti looked down at the table but said nothing.

"Was it Herman?" he asked.

Siti shook her head.

"We can do something about this," Thompson said, "Make sure it doesn't happen again. But you need to tell us who it was."

Siti shook her head again.

"It was nothing."

Thompson looked at her for a moment longer. He had seen enough battered women in the last twenty-five years to know he was not going to get anything out of her.

"Alright," he said, "but you should still get it looked at. And if you change your mind, you know where I am. Okay?"

Siti gave a slight nod.

"We need to ask you a few more questions," Thompson said.

"I do not feel so good."

"It's important, love. To help us find out what happened to Emily."

"I do not feel so good," Siti said again.

"Herman doesn't want you to talk to us," Packer said, from the other side of the table, "That's why he hit you."

Siti kept looking down but held her breath.

She said nothing.

"Emily was killed," Packer said, "It could happen again if we don't catch the man who did it. You can help us do that."

Siti remained silent, but a tear ran down her cheek. Another followed.

She nodded.

"Brave girl," Thompson said, gently, "Thank you."

"Billy comes to collect the rent every Friday," Packer said, "Is it always him that comes?"

Siti nodded.

"And he's been doing it as long as you've lived here?"

Siti nodded again.

"Was Emily home sometimes when Billy came here?"

Another nod.

"Did Billy ever speak to her?"

Siti thought for a moment, then shook her head and gave a small shrug.

"Think about it for a moment," Packer said, "It's important."

There was another pause.

"I cannot know," Siti said, her voice very low, "Emily was scare of seeing people. She did not want to be sent home. If somebody come here, she stay in bedroom."

"Who gave the rent money to Billy when he came here?"

"I."

"But you all knew the rent was due on Friday nights? Emily knew that, too?"

Siti nodded.

"So, when there was a knock on the door on Friday nights, you all knew it was just Billy. Emily must have known that, too."

Another nod.

"But she stayed in her room?"

A nod.

"Did Herman ever pay the rent money to Billy?"

Siti shook her head.

"Did he speak to Herman sometimes?"

Siti was silent for a long moment.

"Sometimes there was trouble," she said eventually, her voice so low it was almost impossible to hear.

"What kind of trouble?"

"Sometimes we cannot pay. We know Billy angry. Shout at us. Say we must get out if we do not pay. Say we will tell police on us."

"What did Herman do?"

"He go to door to yell to Billy. One time, they fight."

"When you say, 'fight,' you mean shouting at each other?" Packer asked.

Siti shook her head. She lifted one tiny fist and gave a feeble imitation of a punch.

"There was a physical fight? With hitting?"

Siti nodded.

"Did Herman hit Billy? Or did Billy hit Herman? Packer asked.

"Both hit."

"Who hit first?"

Siti shrugged.

"This happened one time?"

"More than one time. Maybe three. Maybe four."

"Herman hit Billy?"

Siti nodded.

"Just like Herman hit you?"

Siti sat still.

"Because you spoke to us last time we were here?"

"I tell him we must help to Emily. He say Emily dead. Police do it. Police kill her."

"Did he say why he thinks police killed Emily?"

"Herman hate police. In our country, police make trouble to Herman. Try to kill him."

"Did you come here with Billy from Indonesia?"

Siti shook her head.

"Did you know him before you came here?"

"My uncle know to his father. When Herman come here, they say to help him. They tell him where to come I live."

"Where is Herman from? What part of Indonesia?"

"Deket."

"What is his father's name?"

"Bintang. He is a shop-keeper."

"Where is Herman now?"

"He go to work. He has some job taking furniture down south. Come back tomorrow, maybe dinner time."

Siti sat in the chair, her narrow shoulders shaking slightly as she breathed.

"Does Herman hit you often?" Thompson asked.

Siti gave a small shrug.

"The man who runs the cleaning work, Tom Kirby, told us Herman got upset with you when you were cleaning. Is that right?"

Siti took in a breath then let it out. "Yes," she said eventually.

"Why was that?"

"Herman does not like this man, Tom. He tell me to not be too friendly with this man."

"Why didn't Herman like him?"

"Herman say he too friendly with the women. Sometimes Tom touch them, like a man touch a wife."

"Did Tom touch you like that?"

Siti raised her eyes to Thompson and gave him a sad smile, the scar tissue pulling one side down. "What man want to touch me?"

"So what was Herman worried about, then?" Packer asked.

"He say this to all of us. To Tanvi and to Emily, too. He say we must be careful of this man. When I am friendly to Tom, Herman is angry that I do not obey what he say to do."

"Did you see Tom touch other women?"

Siti shrugged. "Sometimes. But it is not a big thing. Sometimes he touch bottom or rub shoulders. No more than this. Some men are like this."

"Did you ever see him touch Emily?"

Siti shrugged. "Maybe. Tom touch many women. It is just his way."

"Tom told us Herman stole something from one of the places you cleaned. Is that true?"

Siti shook her head. "No. Tom want reason to sack Herman because he does not like. He make up this stealing."

"How did Herman react when Tom sacked him?"

"He is very angry. Very angry. I think he will fight Tom. But he knows that we need to get money. So we continue to work for Tom without Herman, but Herman does not like this."

"Did Herman ever hit Emily?" Packer asked.

Siti shook her head. "Emily is very beautiful. Every man see this. Herman see this, too. He try to be friends with Emily, but he does not know how."

Siti swallowed, then sniffed. Tears appeared in the corners of her eyes. Talking about Emily was clearly still difficult.

Packer watched her for a moment in silence.

"Have you got friends you can stay with?" Thompson asked, "Just for tonight, maybe."

Rubbing at the eye that was not swollen, Siti shook her head.

"I am fine here," she said, her voice barely intelligible through her tears.

"You shouldn't be alone," Thompson said.

"I will not alone. Raghav and Tanvi will come back soon."

"They won't be home tomorrow, though, will they? What if Herman comes back earlier?"

Siti did not answer.

Thompson was unhappy about this, but they could not force Siti to leave.

"Alright," he said, eventually, "but keep the chain on the door and if there's any sign of Herman, you call '000' immediately. Promise?"

Siti nodded.

Thompson had some doubts that she would, but there was really no alternative.

They left Siti in the kitchen and began the walk back to the car.

"You reckon he'll come back here, boss?" Thompson asked.

"Not tonight, maybe. But tomorrow. Where else is he gonna go?"

***

It was nearing ten o'clock when they reached the city again. Thompson yawned a couple of times on the way.

"Drop me off at the station," Packer said, "You keep the car."

"Why don't you go home and get some sleep, boss?"

"Later," Packer said.

He hadn't slept for three days but felt fatigued rather than tired. It was always like this when he was working a case.

They drove the rest of the way in silence. Thompson dropped Packer at the corner of Hay Street near the police station and kept driving.

Packer used his security card to let himself into the building and made his way up to his office. He turned on the coffee machine and headed into his office.

While he waited for the computer to power up, he sat looking out the window behind him at the city. Streetlights cast cones of light over the darkness.

He closed his eyes.

Just for a moment.

Emily's hands were bound to the ground. She pulled backwards, straining to get free. Her braids flicked at her naked back, as she tugged hopelessly, the bonds cutting into the flesh of her wrists.

Suddenly, she stopped, her head flicking around.

A man was walking towards her, his footsteps echoing dully through the darkened room. The shadows obscured him, making him a black silhouette as he silently approached with measure steps.

A belt swung in his hands.

Emily whimpered as she saw it, terror leaving her unable to speak.

The man stood in front of her.

Emily pulled desperately as he wrapped the belt around her neck, threading the end through the buckle.

He pulled it tight, one hand wrapped around the end of the belt, pulling it hard while the other held Emily's throat in place. His shoulders shook with the effort.

Emily's gasped, her breath cut off.

Her eyes widened, staring, begging silently.

There was a loud buzz from the coffee machine, and Packer's eyes snapped open.

He sat in the chair for a moment, then blinked.

Rubbing a hand across his face, he got up and walked out to the coffee machine.

Wednesday

Chapter 18

Packer stood under the shower in the bathroom at the end of the corridor. He rested with his head against the tiles, letting the hot water run over the aching muscles in his neck and back.

After a long moment, he turned off the shower and dried off.

Wrapping a towel around his waist, he headed for the sinks and began to shave.

The door to the bathroom opened and a woman in a green uniform walked in carrying a mop and bucket.

She saw Packer at the sink and gave a slight start.

"Sorry," she said, "Didn't know anyone was here yet."

"It's okay," Packer said, looking at her the mirror, "Don't mind me."

Awkwardly, the cleaner mopped the floor, while Packer shaved.

He only had two clean shirts left in his locker. He was going to have to organise some laundry.

Thompson was sitting at his desk when Packer returned to the incident room.

"Morning, boss," Thompson said, looking up.

He gave a slight frown as he saw Packer's hair was damp.

"Jesus. Did you sleep here?"

Packer shrugged as he walked over to the coffee machine.

"Tom Kirby sent me a text message with his van details while we were at Ghirraween yesterday," Thompson said, turning to his computer screen, "I've just checked it out now. All supports what he said. He had a white VW Transporter, but the rego lapsed sixteen months ago.

"He sent me a picture of his Bunnings receipt, too. He was at the Bunnings at Belmont on Sunday at 1:42pm. Bought a load of cleaning chemicals, a new ladder, three mops and three buckets."

Thompson looked up. "No plastic drop sheet, though, boss. Put it all on account, just as he said."

"Has he got any history?"

"Couple of fines for possession of cannabis, but nearly twenty years ago. Nothing else."

Packer poured coffee from the machine and stood next to the filing cabinets drinking it.

He looked at the whiteboard. In the centre was the image of Emily's face, her eyes cold.

Radiating out from the photo were the handful of leads they had. Emily needing money to bring the rest of her family here. Working as a cleaner but finding something that paid better. Siti's belief that she was working as a prostitute for someone violent. The old injuries and evidence of earlier beatings.

What connected all of this?

Somewhere, there was a missing piece. Something would help them join the dots, but they needed to find it.

"Boss," Thompson said after a few moments, a note of resignation in his voice.

Packer turned towards him

"Why are we bothering with this?" Thompson went on, "I mean, it's Herman, isn't it? All the connections are there."

"Maybe."

"It has to be."

Packer shrugged. "I don't think it's that simple, George."

"Why not? You always have to bloody complicate things. He's a violent prick who beats up women and he killed her."

"What about the other job she had? And telling Siti about working for the devil?"

Thompson shrugged. "Who knows? Just a coincidence."

"There are no coincidences, George. There's something else happening here."

***

Seoyoon arrived not long afterwards. Her skirt and jacket were immaculately pressed, and her glossy black hair hung neatly in place behind her back.

"I want you to get on to AFP," Packer told her, "They'll have a contact with Indonesian police. See if they have any record of Herman, the flatmate."

"Okay," she said, "Why are we looking into him?"

"'Cause he did it," Thompson muttered from his desk, without turning around.

"We went to see Siti again yesterday," Packer said, "He beat her up. She thinks the police in Indonesia are looking for him. If that's right, I want to know why."

Seoyoon nodded. "It'll probably take a couple of days. Indonesian authorities aren't usually very forthcoming."

"Tell AFP to let them know it's a murder enquiry. See if that hurries them up."

"I'll tell them, but you shouldn't hold your breath."

Packer nodded. "Alright."

"Oh, Claire texted me, too," Seoyoon said, "She's gone to Canningvale to talk to someone. Be in later."

Simmons's computer screen was blank, his desk empty.

Packer didn't bother to ask.

***

The car park was busy, but Claire managed to find a space near the end next to the section fenced off for shopping trolleys to be collected.

The wooden fence on the other side was sprawled with graffiti and three boys in their late teens watched her as she locked the car and began walking back towards the shops. She wondered if the car would still be there when she came back.

As the city expanded outwards, a lot of these older shopping centres were being bought up and renovated, but clearly the urban renewal efforts had not reached here yet. The glass doors fronting the shopping centre were dirty and the industrial tiles on the other side were heavily marked.

A Wiggles coin car sat inside the doorway with a handwritten sign on it reading, 'Out of Order', and the shop behind it was empty. Claire walked past a two-dollar shop and a discount chemist, towards the grocery shop at the end.

There were three cashiers on duty at the narrow check-out counters, and Claire read their name badges as she walked past.

The woman at the end was pushing fifty, with black-dyed hair and a tattoo visible beneath the sleeve of her uniform. Her name badge read, 'Suzanne'.

The woman was moving groceries along the counter and scanning them, then dropping them into canvas shopping bags, with a bored expression on her face.

Claire took a Mars Bar off the impulse-buy rack at the end of the counter, then placed it on the conveyor belt and stood in line.

Suzanne slid the full canvas bags along the counter and charged the customer without bothering to look up.

"Just that?" she asked in a dull, nasal voice, as she scanned Claire's chocolate.

"I'd like a quick chat, too, please," Claire said, "Suzy."

Suzanne's eyes snapped up to look at her. There was a look of recognition in them. Though she had never met Claire before, she clearly knew a police officer when she saw one.

"I'm working," Suzanne said.

"That's fine," Claire said, giving her a slight smile, "I can wait until your break."

Suzanne glared at her for a moment, then looked around to see if any of the other cashiers or the supervisor was looking. Satisfied that they were not, she turned back to Claire.

"Twenty minutes," she hissed.

Claire nodded, as she touched her keycard against the scanner to pay for the chocolate.

"I'll wait down the end near the entrance," she said.

Claire walked back towards the entrance way. There were a couple of benches opposite the broken Wiggles car, and she sat down. She ate the chocolate bar while she waited.

After about half an hour, Suzanne walked along the floor towards her.

"Outside," Suzanne said, without stopping, and left the shopping centre.

Claire followed her along the outside of the shopping centre and down the side. A couple of industrial bins and some broken pallets lay next to a closed roller door.

Suzanne reached into her handbag and retrieved a packet of Marlboros.

She pushed one between her lips and lit up, glaring over the top of the cigarette at Claire as she inhaled.

"Well?" she said, breathing out a lungful of smoke from between her nostrils.

"My name's Claire Perry," Claire said, "You're not in trouble. I'm trying to find out about someone. Gloria Keefe said you might have known her."

"Gloria?" Suzanne said, clearly surprised, "I haven't spoken to her in ages."

Claire nodded. "She said it had been a while. Took me a bit of work to find you."

"Yeah, well, I'm not doing that any more. I'm working here now. I don't talk to none of those girls any more."

Claire nodded again. "Looks like you've done well. I don't want to cause any problems for you."

"So, what do you want to know?"

"I'm hoping you can remember another girl who was in Northbridge a while ago. Gloria thought it was about two years ago."

Suzanne frowned. "Two years ago? What's her name?"

"Gloria couldn't remember."

"So how the fuck am I gonna know her, then?"

Claire smiled. "Sorry. I know how vague that sounds."

She watched as Suzanne took another drag on the cigarette.

"I'm investigating a murder," Claire said, "A girl was found in an alley. Her wrists and ankles were tied, and she'd been strangled with some kind of garote or something around her neck."

Suzanne said nothing, but she gave a noticeable flinch. She raised the cigarette to her mouth again.

"We don't know for sure," Claire went on, "but there's a possibility she was a working girl. Gloria said she remembered another girl a couple of years ago who said she'd gone with a client who tied her up and whipped her. Might have tried to strangle her with a belt, too."

Suzanne was still silent, but she was staring hard at Claire. She lifted the cigarette to her mouth and sucked hard on it.

Her hand was shaking slightly.

"Gloria couldn't remember her name, but she said this girl disappeared not long after this."

Suzanne flicked the cigarette butt onto the ground.

"Do you know who I'm talking about?" Claire prompted.

Suzanne reached into her handbag and took out the cigarette packet. She pushed another cigarette into her mouth with a hand that was clearly shaking now. She fumbled with the lighter and almost dropped it. Holding it up to her mouth, she lit the end of the cigarette and puffed on it.

Claire watched but said nothing.

After a moment, Suzanne nodded.

"Yeah, I know her," she said quietly.

"Do you know her name?"

Suzanne nodded. "Georgia."

"Was she a friend of yours?"

"She's me ex. Haven't spoken to her in a year or more."

"Do you know where she is?"

Suzanne shook her head. "Nuh. I think she went down south somewhere, but I don't know."

"Did she tell you about a man who tied her up."

Suzanne lifted a shaking hand to her mouth and inhaled a lungful of smoke again.

She looked at Claire and shrugged.

"She didn't tell me much. Didn't want to talk about it. But she used to have nightmares about it. Woke up at night, yelling and that. One day, we were out shopping, and she reckoned she saw the bloke that done it. Started having a fuckin' meltdown and we had to go home. Couldn't even finish buying the food. She just had to get out of there."

"Did she tell you anything about him? His name or what he looked like?"

Suzanne shook her head.

"Nuh. But I was still working in Northbridge at the time. Every night when I went out, she used to tell me to be careful. And she used to tell me, 'Don't ever go with a bloke in a white van.'"

Chapter 19

It was nearly ten o'clock when Simmons turned up.

"Where have you been?" Thompson asked.

"Went out to Osbourne Park on the way in this morning," Mickey said, "Managed to track down a few places with camera out the front."

"Do you know," Thompson said, innocently, "I was starting to wonder if you might be getting sick of watching all the CCTV. It's really great to see that you're still so enthusiastic about it that you're going out before work to look for it."

Simmons gripped the edge of his chair and made a show of restraining himself from getting up to attack Thompson.

Thompson grinned at him, and he turned around, switching his computer on.

"Yeah, well," Simmons said, "The sooner I find something, the sooner I can get on to something more interesting than watching bloody CCTV."

He slotted a USB stick into the front of the computer. "Did you spend your early years in the job sifting through CCTV, George?"

"Oh, Christ, no."

"Probably before the days of CCTV, was it?"

"Oh, no, there was plenty of it around," Thompson said, "It's just that nobody thought I was a useless prick who was incapable of doing anything else."

Simmons picked up a CD from his desk and frisbeed it across the room at Thompson's head.

With surprisingly fast reflexes, Thompson caught it and sent it flying back again.

The phone rang, but neither of them took any notice. Rolling her eyes, Seoyoon answered it.

Simmons was trying to find something else to use as ammunition, when Seoyoon interrupted.

"George," she called out, "That was reception. Tom Kirby is downstairs to see you and the boss."

***

When Packer and Thompson went down to the reception, Kirby was standing up, looking nervous.

"Mr Kirby," Thompson said.

"Yeah, g'day again," Kirby said, giving him an awkward smile, "Can I, um, have a quick word?"

"Sure," Thompson said.

He led Kirby back through the door to the inside of the station. He found an empty interview room and waved Kirby inside.

Kirby sat in the chair, looking around the room.

"What can we do for you, Mr Kirby?" Thompson asked,

"Um, well, it's probably more what I can do for you," he said, "See, last night, I started thinking more about what you were asking yesterday. And I remembered a couple of extra things."

"Did you?"

"Yeah. Look, I was kind of surprised yesterday when you showed up out of the blue. I wasn't expecting the police to turn up and start asking me about a murder, right? But I thought about it more after you left. And I thought I'd better come down and tell you, 'cause if you find out some other way, you'll think I was lying to you or something."

"And what is it that you've remembered, Mr Kirby?"

"You were asking yesterday about an African girl? I told you I didn't know her, but thinking about it overnight, I think I know who you mean."

"Do you?"

"Yeah. You were talking about the Indonesian girl with the burnt face? There was a girl came in with her and the boyfriend a few times. I thought she was Indian, but after you left yesterday, I thought about it, and she probably was this African girl you were looking for. You said she had braids, which is what sort of threw me, 'cause this girl always had her tied up in a scarf kind of thing at the back."

"There's a difference between Indians and Africans, Mr Kirby," Thompson pointed out, "even when they're wearing scarves."

"Yeah, I know," Kirby said, "but they've both got dark skin and I don't really look at them that much, right? I get a lot of Indians and Pakis working for me. There're tons of them moving to Australia. Most of them only last a few weeks and I don't really take much notice of any of them, unless there's some reason why they stand out - like the girl with the burned face or the boyfriend who was thieving."

"Okay. So, this African girl. Is there anything else you can remember about her?"

"Not really. She would have only come in a few times, and it was months ago. Showed up, did the work without any hassles and that was it. I probably wouldn't have even realised that she was with the girl with the burns, except that you said that yesterday, and when I thought about it, I do remember them talking to each other.

"The only other thing about her, is that I remember one night the burned girl and her boyfriend were having a blue about something and this African girl got involved. Like, tried to break it up or something."

"A blue? Does that mean physical or verbal."

"Oh, just verbal. He was shouting at the other girl and the African one sort of jumped in, like telling him to calm down or something."

"Do you know what the argument was about?"

"No. No idea at all. It was over pretty fast, so I didn't get involved. I only really remember because you were asking about them."

"Right. Anything else about this girl?"

Kirby shook his head. "Nah, that's it. There is one other thing, though."

"What's that?"

"You asked whether I've got a white van."

Thompson raised an eyebrow. "And you've remembered that you do have one?"

"No," Kirby said, "I told you I don't have one, and I don't. I did borrow one back in July, though. The bus was off the road for a while. Blew a valve one night. Cost me a fucking fortune to get it fixed, and I had to cancel three nights' worth of work while it was at the mechanic's.

"Anyway, I had a ton of cleaning equipment I needed to shift from the suppliers back to my shop, and I wasn't going to use the BMW to shift it. So, I borrowed a van from a mate. Only had it for the day, though."

"When was this?"

"14 July."

Thompson raised his eyebrows. "That's a very specific date."

"Yeah, well, you were chasing the Bunnings receipt yesterday, so I thought you'd probably ask, so I dug out the receipt for the repairs on the bus engine. That was 13 July, and I borrowed the van the next day."

"And what's the name of this mate you borrowed it from?"

"You know him already. It was Billy Harrison's van. Ask him. He'll confirm it."

***

They stood in reception, watching as Kirby crossed the car park and got into a late model BMW. Its windows were so heavily-tinted that they were almost black, and it sat close to the ground on wide tyres.

Even from behind the glass, they could hear the loud, throaty sound of the engine as it started, and the car crawled across the carpark towards the entrance.

"Interesting," Thompson said, as they began the walk back to the elevator.

Packer said nothing.

"Looks like Mr Harrison's got a few questions to answer," Thompson said.

"I thought your money was on Herman."

"Still is. And now we've got Kirby witnessing Herman having a go at Emily, too. Maybe Herman killed her, and Harrison dumped the body."

"Why? They weren't exactly friends."

"Maybe Harrison didn't want the hassle of a murder investigation at one of the properties he was managing."

"So, he dumped the body himself? Covering up for the tenant he got into a fist fight with a couple of months earlier?"

"Well, I don't know, boss. Harrison wasn't straight with us about the van, was he? Why did he lie?"

"Didn't we check to see if he had a white van registered to him?"

"Yeah. Nothing came up under his name. But his phone's registered to a business. The van must be, too."

"Strange how Kirby suddenly remembered all this."

"Well, it's not unusual, is it, boss? How often do we take a witness statement and then the next day, they ring up and want to change it? And he was surprised when we turned up there yesterday, like he said."

"I suppose so."

"So, we talk to Harrison again?"

Packer considered for a moment. "Let's see what we can find out about the van first. See if we can find something concrete before we ask him."

***

Thompson and Seoyoon set to work on the van registration while Packer returned to his office.

"Yes!" Mickey yelled from the incident room, an hour later, "You bloody beauty!"

Packer left his office and walked over to Mickey's desk.

A blurry CCTV image was frozen on his screen.

"I've found the white van," Mickey said, triumphantly.

Thompson and Seoyoon gathered around to stand beside Packer.

"Okay," Mickey said, "In the footage from the traffic-cams on the freeway, we could see the white van leaving one of the sidestreets before getting to the freeway. We knew it came from Osbourne Park, but not where it had been before that."

"Spare us the re-cap, son," Thompson said, "Get on with it."

"I rang all the businesses along that street looking for CCTV footage that faced out on to the street. There were six of them with cameras, so I went and collected copies this morning. I spent the last three hours sifting through them. I could only see the van in two of them, but it goes along the street and then turns right at the end.

"There's a couple of businesses along there, but none with CCTV, so I thought I'd lost it."

Thompson let out a sigh of annoyance. Mickey was clearly milking his moment of triumph.

"But that street turns left into Cuthbert Street and there are a few more businesses along there. Right at the end is a ceramic tile importer. They had a break-in earlier in the year. Nothing stolen, but a lot of damage was done, so they got a security camera installed."

"Which part of, 'Get on with it,' wasn't clear to you?" Thompson asked.

"Alright, alright. Hang on," said Mickey, "I'm getting there."

He turned back to the screen and pointed with his finger.

"Further along Cuthbert Street from the tile importer is this place. It's a row of commercial units."

The image showed a street at dusk. There was a streetlight near to the camera and one further down, but the rest of the street was in grey gloom as night approached.

The time code at the bottom of the screen read 17:41.

At the edge of the screen could be seen another side road and next to it was a high chain-link fence with a car park behind it. There was no lighting in the carpark or nearby, but a row of low buildings could just be made out on either side of the carpark despite the approaching darkness.

"Now watch this," Mickey said.

He clicked the mouse, and the footage on the screen began to move.

There were ten or fifteen seconds of nothing happening.

Then a white shape moved from the side street and the van drove into view at the top of the screen. Despite the distance and the approaching night, the image was surprisingly clear, although the van itself was only about a centimetre high in the image.

The van drove past the chain-link fence, then turned off the road and moved into the car park. The brake lights flashed red as the van left the road, then it turned to the side, so that it was facing one of the commercial units, with the passenger side towards the camera.

The cabin of the van grew bright as the driver's door was opened and the interior light came on, then winked out. It was just possible to see a tiny figure move away from the front of the van towards one of the units.

Then the figure disappeared from view.

They watched in silence.

The van remained in place and nothing else seemed to be happening.

There was a strange feeling of anti-climax as they watched, but there was no further movement.

"Can you speed it up?" Packer asked.

"Yep," Mickey said.

He moved the mouse and the pointer on the screen moved down towards the bar at the bottom. He clicked and the image began to move at triple speed.

The time code in the corner of the screen ticked over rapidly as night fell at high speed over the image. Soon the car park was bathed in darkness and the van disappeared into the gloom.

After a few long minutes of this, there was a sudden flash of light.

"Stop," Thompson said, "Go back a bit."

Mickey used the mouse to rewind the footage slightly and began playing it at normal speed.

Two tiny, white glares appeared in the darkness, then shifted off to the side.

"That's the headlights," Thompson said, "He's leaving."

"18:13," Packer said, reading the time code aloud, "So he's there for about half an hour, then leaves. Say, twenty-five minutes to get to the city and another five to get from the freeway to Aberdeen Street."

"What's he doing inside for half an hour?" Mickey said.

"What do you think he's doing?" Thompson said, a note of frustration in his voice, "He's picking up a 'delivery' to take to Northbridge."

"No," said Mickey, turning around, "I mean why's it take him half an hour? If he's just sticking the body in the van and driving off, how come he's in there so long?"

Thompson looked at Mickey for a moment, then turned to look at Packer.

"Do you know, that's actually a very good question. This lad might even make a detective one day."

"I'm not putting money on it," Packer said, "Go back to where we first see the van arriving."

Mickey moved the mouse around and clicked on the screen while they waited.

After a few moments of playing around, the van drove along the side street once more.

"Stop there," Packer said, as the van began to enter the carpark, "Can you make out the number plate?"

They all stared at the screen.

"It's too hard to see 'cause the brake lights come on," Mickey said, "The first number's a 1. Then a B maybe. Could be a D after that. I can't make out the rest."

"No, it's not BD," Thompson said, "It's EO."

"It's a B, not an E," Mickey insisted.

"Could be anything," Packer said, settling the argument, "It's too hard to make out."

"See if you can get IT to enhance this," Thompson said, "They might have more luck."

"They tried that with the footage from the alleyway," Simmons pointed out, "It was no better. You still couldn't see anything."

Thompson nodded. "No. And this'll probably be useless, too, but let's give it a go."

Packer turned to Seoyoon.

"Seoyoon," Packer said, "Get an address for those units. Find out who owns them all."

"We don't know that the owner of the white van does."

"No," Packer agreed, "but he goes into one of them in the CCTV, so he's got access to it. Even if he doesn't own it, he's using it to store a dead body before he can dump it."

"Okay, boss. I'll get on to it."

"Have you found any businesses connected to Billy Harrison that have a white van registered to them."

"No, but I'm still looking. Do you really think that's Harrison's van?"

"Tom Kirby does. See what you can find."

"Boss."

She moved back towards her desk.

"What are we doing, boss?" Thompson asked.

Packer stared at the CCTV on the screen for a moment longer.

"We're going for a drive, George."

Chapter 20

Packer and Thompson drove north along the freeway, retracing the route taken by the white van in the CCTV footage.

"What are you expecting to find out here, boss?" Thompson asked.

"I don't know," Packer said, "I just want to have a look. Get a feel for the place."

They turned off the freeway exit and into Osbourne Park. The offramp led them a back street and endless blocks of commercial properties. While the main street was lined with car yards and furniture retailers, the back streets here were lined with car detailers and panel beaters, display rooms of tilers and carpet layers, and wholesale warehouses for plumbing supplies and roofing material.

Further back from the main road, the buildings became steadily more rundown and poorly maintained.

A large self-storage facility took up almost a whole block, its entrance gate now chained up after the company had gone into receivership. Rows of roller doors were covered in graffiti, broken windows left unrepaired after the business had gone broke.

An electrical cabling wholesaler was open beside them, but most of the others were closed.

Up ahead, at the end of Cuthbert Street, they could see the expanse of broken concrete car parking from the CCTV footage. The chain-link fencing was standing at an angle.

Thompson turned the car off the road and onto the concrete. He drove slowly between the rows of faceless commercial buildings. A few of them bore the names of businesses across the front, while a lot were simply blank. Some of the businesses might still have been in operation, although they were closed at this time of day if they were. It was clear that it had been a long time since most of them had seen any activity.

Thompson parked the car, and they got out.

They walked along the rows of shuttered workshops.

"This side?" Thompson asked, recalling the CCTV footage.

Packer nodded.

They walked along the row of units that lined one side of the broken concrete space, checking doors and windows as they went. They were locked, padlocks securing doors and some of the windows covered over.

They reached the unit third from the end.

The front of the building had once had a business's name painted across it, but it had been poorly painted over with off-white paint that was now dirty and peeling. The front door was securely locked and the windows beside it were curtained off with heavy, black drapes, giving no indication of what lay inside.

Thompson Leaned against the glass, trying to peer inside, but was unable to see anything.

He stepped back and looked around. The back of the car park was lined with the same chain-link fence that covered the front. Here, though, it was damaged. Two posts had collapsed, and the fencing had fallen over completely, giving access to a vacant lot and another row of warehouses behind the car park.

"This is a waste of time, boss," he said, "Maybe he just parked here and walked somewhere else. Nobody's been here in ages."

"There are tyre tracks in the mud over there," Packer said, "Someone's been here since it rained last."

"Could be anyone. Security guards doing a patrol. Someone selling drugs in the car park."

Packer didn't answer. He was standing outside the commercial unit, looking around the car park.

The noise of the freeway was faint in the distance, and he could barely hear anything from the main street. Despite the fact that they were in one of the suburbs closest to a major traffic zone, the area they were in was isolated and lay in the middle of warehouses and sheds that were mainly empty and disused.

"Want me to call Seoyoon? See if she's found an owner for any of these places?" Thompson asked, "Someone might be able to tell us if anyone has been here recently."

"Can you smell that?" Packer asked.

"What?"

"I don't know. Like paint stripper or something."

Thompson moved closer to Packer and stopped. He inhaled heavily.

"Yeah," he said, "but it smells more like bleach to me. No, not bleach. That shit the council uses to clean oil off roads."

He sniffed again. "Christ, it's strong. Do you think there's been a spill or something?"

Packer said nothing.

"Do you want me to have a look around the back?"

Packer shook his head.

"No. Get some uniforms down here. And a locksmith."

***

Thompson had grown impatient now. He shuffled from foot to foot impatiently, letting out loud breaths every now and again, while the locksmith crouched down in front of the door.

Packer watched in silence.

"Come on," Thompson muttered a couple of times.

The locksmith looked back over his shoulder, once or twice, frowning in irritation.

"Are we nearly there, mate?" Thompson asked him.

"I'm getting there," the locksmith protested, "It's not like just putting in a key, buddy. It takes a bit of work."

Thompson opened his mouth to respond, but Packer drew in a deep breath.

"Alright, George," he said, "Let him do his job."

With a frustrated sigh, Thompson stepped back and paced around behind the uniformed officers. He lifted one hand and rubbed the back of it across his bald head, the rubber glove squeaking slightly over the skin.

The locksmith turned back to the lock, maneuvering the metal prongs inside the lock once more.

After another fifteen minutes, the locksmith turned the lock to the side, using the prongs. It rotated slowly to the side, and he straightened up.

Putting one hand on the handle below the deadlock, he pushed it down. The door creaked slowly open.

"She's open," the locksmith said, trying to peer around the corner of the doorway.

"Okay," Packer said, "Step back."

The locksmith stepped to the side as Packer moved closer to the door.

Impatiently, Thompson shouldered his way past the uniformed officers to get onto the doorstep behind Packer.

Using the tip of his finger, Packer pushed the door open.

The reek of chemicals was so strong, it made him wince. Bleach or ammonia or something even stronger filled the air.

"Christ," Thompson grunted from behind him, holding his hand across his mouth.

Packer stood on the doorstep and pushed the door all the way back.

The room beyond was almost completely black. The only light was coming in from the open doorway that they stood in.

Packer took out his mobile phone and shone the torchlight through the entrance.

The inside of the building consisted of one very large room with two doors leading off on one side. One door was partially open, and Packer could see a toilet and sink on the other side. The second door was closed.

The floor of the main room was covered in industrial carpet that was dark grey with a dull pattern of oblique lines running across it. The centre was completely covered with a huge puddle of damp that must have been five metres across. Smaller patches of damp lay around its edges and there were large, dry patches of staining where chemicals had dried out and left a white residue behind.

Packer lifted his arm and left his shirt sleeve across his mouth and nose. It did almost nothing to reduce the overpowering chemical stench. His eyes began to water from the heavy fumes that filled the air.

Cautiously, Packer took one step forward into the room. The carpet squelched under the protective covers over his shoes.

Thompson pushed forward behind him.

"Christ," he said again, "What a fucking stink."

Packer said nothing. He looked around the room.

He pointed with his free arm.

"Look at the windows," he said.

They had been painted black.

The walls were lined with thick, rubber-backed material a couple of inches thick.

"What the fuck's that on the walls?" Thompson asked.

"Roofing insulation, I think," Packer said, "The room's been soundproofed."

They stood inside the doorway, looking at the space beyond.

Thompson turned back and lowered his hand to speak to the uniformed officers behind them.

"Get on to forensics," he said, "We need a full team down here as soon as they can get here. Tell them it's priority."

He turned back to Packer.

"Fucking bastard," Thompson spat, "He fucking set this all up. It's all been set up to kill her."

Packer stood there, looking around the room, but said nothing.

After a few moments longer, he stepped back out of the room and down the steps.

He breathed heavily, trying to clear the smell of chemicals from his lungs. The fresh air burned his throat slightly as he breathed in and out.

Thompson stood behind him. He was shuffling on his feet, pacing slightly.

"What the fuck is this, boss?" Thompson said, voice rising, "Who does this? He's a fucking serial killer or something."

Packer stood there, looking back at the doorway. The uniformed officers were clustered around, looking in.

"Fuck, boss," Thompson said, "He's a fucking psycho."

He ranted for a few minutes longer, while Packer said nothing.

Eventually, he calmed down enough to look at Packer and see the expression on his face.

"What?" Thompson asked, "Have you got some idea about this?"

Packer frowned and shook his head slightly.

"You do. What is it?" Thompson asked again.

"I don't know," Packer said, impatiently, "Something about this is off, George. Why set up a whole room like this and then dump her in an alley? This doesn't make any sense."

"He panicked."

"Maybe," Packer said, unconvinced.

"What else could it be?"

"I don't know."

Packer shook his head again.

They stood there in silence for a moment, Thompson staring at Packer while he tried to make some sense of this.

A thought suddenly occurred to Thompson.

"You think there's others?"

Packer looked at him

"He's killed other girls," Thompson asked, "Why set up a kill room for one victim?"

"It's not a fucking kill room," Packer said, impatiently.

"Well, what is it, then?" Thompson said, pointing angrily at the door.

"This is not a TV show, George. Nobody sets up a 'kill room' in real life."

"Well, what is it, then? Huh? Look at it, for fuck's sake. The windows are painted over, the walls are covered with sound proofing. And now it's been doused with fucking bleach to destroy the forensic evidence. What is it, if it's not a kill room?"

Some of the uniformed officers were looking over at them, alerted by Thompson's shouting and waving arms.

"That's enough," Packer said, "There are no serial killers in Perth. That's not what this is."

"Bradley Edwards," Thompson said, "Catherine Burnie."

"How many serial killers have you ever arrested, George?"

"They exist. It was bound to happen again sooner or later."

Packer closed his eyes and rubbed at his forehead.

There was something gnawing at the edge of his consciousness, something that explained this. But he couldn't quite see what it was. It was hovering in the dark, indistinct and out of sight.

He walked away from Thompson and the other officers, standing in the middle of the car park and trying to make sense of this.

***

Surprisingly, the forensics team appeared relatively quickly, taking little more than forty minutes to arrive.

There were four officers, two carrying large plastic toolboxes and the other two carrying a box filled with supplies. They made their way over to Packer and Thompson who were standing near the front doorstep.

The one at the front was an overweight man with a ginger beard. Packer recognised him but couldn't remember his name. He had a vague feeling that he disliked him

"What's going on?" asked ginger beard, grinning, "Is Ed Sheeran staying here?"

"We're investigating a murder, you fucking wanker," Thompson spat at him, "Don't making fucking jokes about it."

"Whoa, sorry," said ginger beard, raising both hands in front of him. His grin faded, but he didn't look particularly sorry.

Packer remembered why he disliked him.

"There was a murder victim found in an alley off Aberdeen Street two days ago," Packer said, "FME thought she'd been killed elsewhere, then dumped. It's possible she was murdered inside here."

Ginger beard nodded. "This is the African prostitute with the…"

He mimed having a noose around his neck, pulling it up into the air with one hand and making mock gasping noises as he rolled his eyes and stuck his tongue out, simulating being strangled.

Thompson stepped forward, jabbing out a finger.

"Look, you prick-" he started, but Packer interrupted.

"This is the girl who was strangled, yes," Packer said, "and it's possible it was done in here."

Ginger beard was staring warily at Thompson, the grin gone completely now. He swallowed, as he looked at Thompson.

"The place has been cleaned very thoroughly," Packer continued, "There's bleach or something similar all over the floors and the walls. There are two other rooms on one side. I haven't been in, so I don't know if they've been cleaned, too."

Still looking at Thompson, ginger beard nodded.

"We probably won't find much if it's been bleached," he said.

"Oh, no shit, Sherlock," Thompson said.

"But we might be able to recover hair fibres or something like that if they're in there," ginger beard finished lamely.

Packer nodded. "Alright. Thanks."

With a last look at Thompson, who was still glaring at him, ginger beard turned back to the rest of the forensics team. One of them opened one of the cardboard boxes and started handing out disposeable paper overalls.

Packer watched as the four officers pulled the hoods up over their heads and then pulled on blue gloves. Ginger beard and one of the others stood in the doorway, looking around inside.

Ginger beard then began issueing orders and the others opened the toolboxes ready to begin work.

"Fucking dickhead," Thompson muttered, loud enough for them hear.

"Why don't you go for a walk?" Packer said, "See if you can find a cafe or something near here. Get us some lunch."

"I'm not hungry."

"Well, just go for a walk, then," Packer said, "and phone the others. Tell them what we've found."

Thompson looked hard at him for a moment.

Then he nodded. He needed to calm down.

And there was something else, too. Packer wanted to be alone to think.

"Alright, boss," Thompson said, "I'll see you in a bit."

Packer nodded.

He looked back over at the open door to the room, suddenly feeling exhausted.

He closed his eyes for a moment.

Emily was on her knees, head back, braids jerking as she struggled. The man in front of her was clothed in darkness, his face hidden. His shoulders tensed as he pulled at the garote, tightening it around Emily's throat.

Emily croaked, struggling for breath.

Packer's eyes snapped open.

One of the uniformed officers was staring at him. He looked away when he realised Packer had seen him.

Packer stood for a long moment, looking at the open doorway.

He really wanted a cigarette.

Chapter 21

They drove back to the city in silence.

Still irritable over Packer's refusal to accept his theories about the unit, Thompson drove aggressively, muttering insults at drivers who were moving too slowly on the freeway or failed to indicate long enough when merging into traffic.

Packer ignored him, which made his mood worse.

It was a relief for both of them when they turned off Hay Street into the underground car park of the police station and Thompson parked the car.

They made their way up in the elevator in silence.

Simmons was still watching CCTV, trying to work out where the van had come from before getting to the commercial unit.

Seoyoon was at her desk.

They both looked up eagerly when Packer and Thompson walked in.

"It's definitely the place?" Simmons asked, "The place where she was killed?"

"Looks like it," Packer said, "I can't see any other reason for dousing the place in cleaning chemicals. Forensics are out there, but I doubt they'll get anything."

"Shit," Simmons said.

"Did you have any luck finding the owner of the unit?" Packer asked Seoyoon.

She nodded. "Yes, but there's a problem."

"Is there?"

"The unit is owned by an Allan Robb. He lives in Victoria. He owns four of the units in that block. He used to run a business from one of them, but it went broke during the pandemic, and he moved interstate two years ago. The unit was empty for ages. He couldn't sell it and he couldn't rent it out. He was surprised when someone got in touch about wanting to rent it from him."

Simmons had turned around at his desk to join in. Clearly, he had already heard this news from Seoyoon before Packer and Thompson arrived.

"The tenant is a Roger Scheffler," Seoyoon continued, "Robb's never met him. It was all arranged over the phone, because he's in Victoria and Roger Scheffler's in Perth. They both signed the lease in different states and sent them to each other by e-mail. The rent payment comes in every fortnight by bank deposit."

"So, who's Roger Scheffler?" Packer asked.

Seoyoon gave him a wry smile.

"There is no Roger Scheffler," she said, "There's no record of him and the contact details on the lease are bogus."

"The place is being held in a false name," Thompson said, a small note of triumph in his voice, "so it was rented with the intention of using it as a kill room."

Packer gave a sigh of annoyance. "It's not a kill room."

"Well, what is it then?"

"What do you mean 'kill room'?" Simmons asked.

"The windows are covered over, and the walls are soundproofed," Thompson said, "so that nobody knows there's a murder happening inside. Lot of trouble to go to if you're only killing one lass, eh?"

"Fuck," Simmons hissed, "So he's killed more of them?"

"We have no reason to think that," Packer said firmly, "and we will continue to work on the basis that Emily is the only one."

Thompson opened his mouth to argue, but Packer silenced him with a stare.

"Why don't you update the whiteboard, George?" he said, pointing at it.

He turned back to Seoyoon.

"Can you trace the bank account where the rent is transferred from?" he asked Seoyoon.

"I'm working on it. The owner is going to send me the bank details, but I'll have to get a search warrant for the bank. They won't give out confidential details without a warrant. Might not be today."

Packer nodded.

"Okay. Keep on it. Good work."

"Oi," Simmons said, listening from his desk, "How come you never tell me I'm doing good work?"

"Have you found where the van came from?" Packer asked, pointing at the CCTV footage on Mickey's computer screen.

"Not yet," Mickey said, his voice dropping.

"That's why."

Packer went into his office and turned his computer on.

There were a handful of e-mail messages, most of which were internal management messages. Packer deleted them without reading them.

There was also a message from Alistair Goodge with the subject line, 'Call me'.

Packer picked up the phone and dialled Goodge's number.

"Have ye found our man yet?" Goodge asked him when he answered the phone.

"I'm working on it," Packer said.

"Aye. Well. I'm afraid I'm not gonnae make ye job any easier. I told ye I found the hair under the lassie's bra?"

"Yeah."

"I sent it off to the lab. They've done some preliminaries on it."

"And?"

"Eh, it's not a hair after all," Goodge said, a note of apology in his voice, "Looked just like one, but when they examined it, it wasn't. They tell me it's a synthetic fibre."

"What, from a wig or something?" Packer asked.

"Probably not," Goodge said, "Filling from a pillow or something like that. Could be the bristle off a paintbrush or summat. Don't think you're gonnae get a DNA match from that any road."

"Alright," Packer said, "Thanks for letting me know."

"Nae problem. There's still the jizz on the panties, mind. That might still come up with the goods."

Packer hung up the phone, wondering what to make of that.

He could hear the others talking out in the incident room.

"But the others have never been found," Simmons said, "I mean he dumped the latest one in the alley, so what about the others? Did he bury them or something? Why not do the same with this one?"

"Something might have happened this time," Thompson said, "He had time to dispose of them in the past, but not this time."

Packer got up and closed the door with a bang.

***

There was a faint tap on Packer's door.

He had spent the last hour in his office, reading over Chandra's report and the photos from Goodge, trying to draw some kind of connection.

"Yes," he said loudly.

Seoyoon opened the door tentatively.

Thompson and Simmons were both sitting at their desks but looking towards his office.

Packer looked at her.

"Sorry to interrupt, boss," she said, "but I thought you'd want to hear this."

"What?"

"We assumed that Allan Robb was telling the truth when he said he was renting the unit to someone using the fake name, Roger Scheffler. It occurred to me that Allan Robb might be lying to us and have set up this fake lease to distance himself from the unit in case what was inside was ever discovered."

Packer raised his eyebrows.

"Good thinking."

Seoyoon gave a brief smile at the compliment. "So, I started checking what Robb had told me to make sure it was true. When I spoke to him, he said he'd bought the units about five years ago. I went back through the property register to make sure that was true."

"Is it?"

She nodded. "Yes, it is. There are property transfers registered for all four units at the same time."

"Okay. So, he's telling the truth about that."

"Yes. But here's the thing. The previous owner of the units is a deregistered company named, 'Aussie Park Developments No 3.'"

Packer felt his stomach twist.

He knew where this was going.

"And the owner of the company is Jeffrey Frazier?"

Seoyoon nodded. "That's right."

Packer leant back in his chair. He rubbed at his eyes while he tried to make sense of this.

"How does it fit, boss?" Thompson asked, moving over to stand behind Seoyoon, "Emily's living in a flat owned by Frazier and killed in a workshop he owned five years ago. What's the connection?"

"The connection's Frazier."

"Yeah, but there's five years in between. Frazier doesn't own the workshop any more."

Packer shook his head. "I don't know. There's something we're missing here."

"And who's this Roger Scheffler?"

"If we knew that, I think we'd have the killer."

Packer took in a breath and let it out slowly.

Something would make this fit together. He couldn't see what it was, but it was close.

"Any luck connecting the van to Harrison?" he asked.

Seoyoon shook her head. "Not yet."

Packer nodded.

"I think we should have another chat with Jeffrey Frazier," he said.

"He was pretty insistent that we phone first if we want to speak to him again," Thompson pointed out, "Do you want me to see if he's free this afternoon?"

Packer was silent as he toyed with the idea of simply turning up unannounced at Frazier's house once more. He didn't like being dictated to by anyone, especially someone like Jeff Frazier.

But at this stage, all they had on Frazier was a tenuous connection to the commercial unit in Osbourne Park, and still no actual evidence that this was where Emily had been killed.

"Phone him," Packer said, "and ask him to come here. Make it clear that we'll pay him a visit if he declines."

"Okay," Thompson said, unconvinced, "I'll give him a call."

Packer looked at his watch. "Better make it tomorrow. You and I have somewhere else to be this afternoon."

Thompson nodded. "Aye."

He went back to his desk.

To Thompson's surprise, Frazier agreed to come in to the station with little real resistance. He told Frazier he would be there the following morning at 9:00am.

Packer nodded when Thompson relayed the information to him but said nothing.

"Are we seriously looking at Frazier, boss?" Thompson asked.

"Emily lived in a flat he owned, and she was killed in a commercial unit he owned five years ago. I don't believe in coincidences."

"He's a millionaire property developer."

"He's a brickie with a lot of money. There's something off about him, George."

Chapter 22

"This place is starting to look familiar," Thompson said, as he turned the car into the back streets of Ghirraween, "It's almost like coming home."

"Talk to Billy Harrison," Packer said, "I bet he can do you a good price on a flat."

Thompson turned along the same street that they had driven down every day now. But instead of turning into Richards Road, he drove past the *cul-de-sac* towards the next.

The car was unmarked, but in an area like this, a white, late-model sedan screamed 'police car'. If Herman saw it parked in Richards Road when he returned home, he would keep right on going.

Thompson turned into the *cul-de-sac* and drove to the end. Then he turned around, so that the car was facing back towards the road and stopped. They were close enough to the end of the street to get back to the car quickly if they needed to, but far enough away that it would not be seen from the entrance to Richards Road.

They locked the car and walked back towards Richards Road. Thompson looked along the road, half-expecting to see Herman walking along the footpath towards them.

But the street was completely empty.

They reached the block of flats and knocked on the door once more.

After a moment, the door opened, and Siti peered out at them. The chain held the door in place.

"Hello, love," Thompson said.

Siti gave him a nervous smile, then closed the door again. She took the chain off and let them in.

The mass of bruising around her eye had begun to yellow and now looked even worse than it had the day before and her upper arm had a huge yellowing patch running along its length.

"You on your own?" Thompson asked.

"Yes," Siti said.

"You haven't heard from Herman?"

Siti shook her head. She seemed oddly calm.

"Did you get your eye looked at?"

Siti looked down and shook her head again.

"Aye, well. Never mind."

Thompson made them tea and they drank it with her. He attempted to make small talk, but she was unresponsive, and he got no help from Packer, so gave up. They finished the tea in silence.

Thompson looked at his watch and found it was after three o'clock.

"Why don't you wait in the bedroom?" he said to Siti, "Close the door."

Siti nodded. Silently, she got up and headed into the bedroom. Thompson closed the door behind her.

"We haven't got enough to pull him for murder, boss," Thompson asked, keeping his voice low, so Siti could not hear.

Packer shook his head. "We're pulling him for hitting her."

"She won't make a complaint," Thompson said, "We'll never get a statement from her saying it was him who hit her."

"Worry about that later."

Thompson nodded. "Okay."

He walked over to the kitchen benches and sat on the floor, leaning back against one of the cabinets.

Packer waited in the lounge, sitting below the window far enough away that he could not be seen in the shadows, but close enough that he could see movement behind the grimy curtain.

Then they waited.

***

By the time it had gone five o'clock, Thompson was beginning to wonder if they were wasting their time. Siti had said Herman was coming back, but there had been no sign of him. What if he stayed down south? What if he had come back from the other direction and seen the car parked at the end of the next street? He might never come back.

He looked over at Packer, who sat impassively by the window, unmoving.

And then there was a scrape outside the flat.

A shadow moved across the outside of the curtains, momentarily obscuring the light.

Packer stood up silently, looking across at Thompson, to make sure he'd seen it.

Thompson nodded.

His legs had gone numb, after sitting on the floor for so long, and he felt a few twinges, as he pushed himself up. But the adrenaline was flowing now.

There was a scratch of a key in the lock of the front door.

Herman pushed it open and stepped inside, a plastic carrier bag in one hand.

He turned to close the door, and as he did so, Packer stepped forward, reaching for his shoulder.

But Herman's head whipped around, catching the movement from the corner of his eye.

He stared at Packer, as Packer lunged forward.

Moving surprisingly fast, he swung the carrier bag at Packer.

The bag struck Packer in the side of the face, something hard inside it slamming into his cheek and sending a flare of pain up through his face.

Reflexively, Packer flinched back, moving his hand towards his face.

Herman pulled the door open again and stepped through.

Packer got his hand on Herman's upper arm, but Herman tugged his arm free and ran.

Shoving the door back, Packer ran out into the narrow passage outside.

Herman's back was disappearing along the fence line. He was wearing a singlet, leaving the corded muscles of his arms uncovered. His arms whipped up and down as he sprinted along the fence line.

Packer was sprinting after him, but Herman had a head start and was fast.

Herman's feet hit the driveway with a dull slap. He was about ten metres in front of Packer.

"Stop, police," Packer yelled after him, knowing Herman was already well aware of who he was, but going through the motions anyway.

As he got to the road, one of Herman's feet twisted on uneven ground, and he stumbled very slightly.

He barely slowed, but it was just enough for Packer to narrow the gap to five metres.

But then Herman was moving again.

As soon as he got to the road, Herman increased his pace. With nothing under his shoes but smooth surface, he was away. His arms whipped up and down with precision, moving with the frantic grace of a runner.

Packer thundered after him, sprinting along the bitumen with every ounce of speed he could find. He was fit and quick on his feet.

But Herman was much faster.

Try as he might, Packer could see Herman beginning to inch ahead of him.

As they tore along the bitumen towards the end of the road, Herman widened the gap between them.

Five metres.

Six metres.

Seven metres.

Eight metres.

They were drawing closer to the end of the *cul-de-sac*, and Herman was steadily moving away from Packer.

Packer put more effort into running, his chest heaving, but he knew it was a lost cause. Herman would escape.

And then the unthinkable happened.

As Herman raced from the end of the *cul-de-sac* and onto the road, there was a red flash from the side.

Tyres screeching, a car slewing across the road with a stink of scalding rubber.

Herman corrected course, shifting away from the car.

But the sudden shock had spooked him and thrown him off his step.

Reflexively, his head turned to look at the car sliding across the road towards him, and he slowed his pace.

He looked around, his eyes fastening on Packer, then he turned and sprinted away once more.

But Packer had not slowed at all.

As Herman began to run again, Packer slammed into the back of him.

His hands gripped the back of Herman's singlet, and he tugged him forward, forcing Herman to lunge to his left.

For a few metres, they ran together, Herman being pulled to the side as they moved.

Then Herman's feet slid out from under him, and he fell.

Packer went with him, hitting the bitumen hard and grunting with shock. He felt the ground tearing at his elbow and one knee but ignored it.

Pushing down on Herman's shoulders, he shoved him against the ground, trying to get his knee up to pin Herman in place.

Herman wriggled desperately, his whipcord-thin body squirming beneath Packer's arms.

He managed to move on to his side, frantic eyes staring up at Packer from inches away.

Herman's elbow slammed into Packer's jaw, snapping his head and making Packer grunt with pain. He felt his teeth hammer together, pain shooting up through the side of his face.

Resisting the urge to let go of Herman's singlet, Packer straightened his arms, pushing Herman down to the ground.

Herman was whipping around, desperation giving him strength, but Packer was bigger and had the advantage.

With a surge, Packer shoved Herman down, pushing his chest against the ground.

"Police," Packer shouted in his ear, "You're under arrest."

Herman squirmed some more, trying to break free. He managed to get his knees up under his stomach and pushed upwards, almost breaking free.

Packer moved one hand up to the back of Herman's head, fingers clutching at greasy hair. He pulled Herman's head up, then slammed it back down again, smashing it against the bitumen.

"Stop moving," Packer shouted, "Stop!"

Herman pushed with his legs again, but there was no real effort in it now. He was caught and he knew it. His energy was spent.

Packer lay there for a moment, pushing down on Herman in case it was a feint.

Herman lay still, chest heaving beneath Packer's arm.

"Fuck, mate," said a voice from behind him, "Are youse cunts alright?"

"Aye," he heard Thompson say, panting hard, "Fine. Police. Step back...sir, please."

Still panting hard, Thompson knelt down on the other side of Herman. He gripped Herman's hands, pulling them back behind his back. Herman offered no resistance, as Thompson cuffed his wrists together.

Packer pushed himself up off the ground and sat up.

Standing a few metres away was a man in a pair of dark glasses and a beanie, the driver's door of the red car open behind him.

Thompson was holding Herman down with one hand, trying hard to catch his breath.

"Well done, boss," Thompson panted.

Packer nodded, breathlessly.

"It's your turn next time," he said.

***

Having come in an unmarked car, they had no way to securely transport Herman back to the station. Thompson called for uniform from the local station, who arrived fairly quickly in a police van with a secure pod at the back.

Herman sat on the road and glared at them.

He had said nothing the whole time, although Packer was fairly confident, he understood what they were saying.

After Herman was loaded into the back of the van with little fuss, Packer and Thompson walked back to the flat.

Siti was back at the kitchen table, sitting silently, although it was clear that she had been crying.

"He's coming with us, love," Thompson said, "and he won't be back any time soon. You don't have anything to worry about. Is there anyone we can call to come over?"

Siti shook her head.

He thought about trying to get a statement from her about the beating but decided to let it go for the moment. There would be plenty of time for that later. Herman wasn't coming back.

They walked back along the *cul-de-sac* to where Packer had parked their car.

"What a nasty little shit," Thompson said.

Packer said nothing, thinking as they walked.

"You'll think he'll talk?" Thompson asked.

Packer shrugged. "I doubt it. But we'll see."

They drove back through the suburbs, the towers of Perth's city centre growing steadily closer along the way.

When they arrived back at the station, Herman was sitting outside the cells with the two uniformed officers from Ghirraween on either side of him. His head was down and he was staring at the floor.

"Have you not got a free cell?" Thompson asked the custody sergeant.

"I've got a cell," the sergeant told him, "but I can't process him until the translator gets here. Doesn't understand a word I'm saying to him."

Thompson looked around, to find Herman watching them. He put his head back down again.

"Oh, I think he understands just fine," Thompson said, "but wait for the translator. We need to cross the T's and dot the I's."

"For a DV?" asked the sergeant, surprised.

"It's a bit more than that," Thompson said, darkly.

Packer and Thompson headed upstairs to the incident room.

When they got there, Mickey was sitting at his desk, but the chair was facing away from it. A CCTV image was paused on his screen, ignored, as he looked over at Seoyoon.

Claire was standing behind him, watching Seoyoon, too.

Packer looked around at Seoyoon, who was moving the mouse around her screen. She had her head cocked to one side, long, black hair hanging down as she held the telephone receiver to her ear with her shoulder.

"Okay," she was saying, holding a conversation with someone who was talking far too much on the other end, "Yes. Yes, I think I have it. Okay. No, that's really okay. I will. Okay."

"What's going on?" Thompson asked.

"It's that bloke you've got downstairs from Indonesia," Mickey said, his eyes slightly wide, "Seoyoon's on the phone to AFP, who've been in touch with Indonesian police."

"And?"

"He's got-"

Mickey broke off, as Seoyoon said, 'thanks,' and hung up the phone.

They all turned to look at her.

She was staring at the screen, moving the mouse around.

"Come on," Thompson said, "Out with it."

Seoyoon looked up at them, almond-shaped eyes wide with excitement.

"I got AFP to check up with Indonesian authorities about him. They're sending someone over here."

She looked at them.

"He's been on the run in Indonesia for over a year. They had no idea he had made it to Australia. They've been searching for him over there."

"Why?"

"He murdered a police officer."

Chapter 23

It took them a lot of phoning around to find an Indonesian interpreter, who was available to come down to the station, and even then, he couldn't be there for another two hours.

The delay did not bother Packer. They couldn't charge Herman on the strength of what they had, so the delay gave them more time to chase down what they had.

Eventually, the custody sergeant phoned the incident room to tell them that the interpreter had arrived at the station, so that Herman could be processed.

To Packer's surprise, the custody sergeant rang back again half an hour to tell him that Herman had agreed to be interviewed, and he was sending the translator up.

When the translator arrived, he was white, rather than Indonesian.

"Patrick," said the interpreter, shaking hands with Packer and Thompson, "Before you ask, I'm NATI-certified. My wife's Indonesian, so I've been speaking the language fluently for over ten years. I had to learn how, so that I could go and visit the family. We go four times a year now. I'm planning to retire over there one day, too. Fantastic golf courses near Denpasar."

Patrick, the interpreter, kept up a steady monologue about his life history and future plans all the way up in the elevator and along the corridor to the interview room.

Packer was beginning to wonder if they would ever get the chance to interview Herman, or whether Patrick's spoken-word routine would last all afternoon.

Thankfully, as soon as they reached the interview room, Patrick was all business.

Herman had been brought up from the holding cell and placed inside the interview room. He remained handcuffed but had been given a meal and now sat with a cup of tea on the table in front of him.

Packer and Thompson watched through the two-way glass window looking into the interview room as Patrick sat down beside Herman and began talking to him in Indonesian.

Herman sat mutely for a while, listening, but nodding occasionally.

After a couple of moments, he replied, his voice calm and showing none of the tightly-held hostility that Packer and Thompson had seen at the flat.

There were a few more minutes of this before Patrick stood up and headed towards the door.

Thompson opened it, and he and Packer walked in.

Patrick sat down beside Herman once more.

Thompson walked around to sit on the other side, facing him.

Packer stood near the door for a moment, keeping his face blank.

Feeling eyes on him, Herman looked up at him.

Packer held the stare until Herman looked away.

Then he sat down beside Thompson.

He had a plain, brown folder with him, which he placed on the table in front of him. He watched Herman's eyes go to it.

"The date is 1 October, and the time is 7:47pm," Packer said, looking at his watch, "I'm Detective Senior Sergeant Tony Packer and this is Detective Senior Constable George Thompson. We are interviewing Herman, no last name, with the assistance of Patrick Johnson, a qualified interpreter."

As he spoke, Patrick mumbled away, interpreting Packer's words.

"Can you indicate that you understand what I have said, please?" Packer asked.

Before Patrick had finished, Herman nodded.

"Yes," he said, in heavily-accented, but clear English.

"Before we begin, I wish to inform you that you have a number of rights," Packer continued, "You have the right to an interpreter, which we have arranged for you. Are you satisfied with the interpreter that we have provided?"

"Yes."

"You have the right to remain silent. You do not have to have answer any questions that we ask you. You may choose to answer some, none or all of the questions I ask. That is your choice. Do you understand that?"

"Yes."

"If I ask you ten questions, how many so you have to answer."

There was an exchange in Indonesian between Herman and Patrick, then Patrick translated.

"I do not have to answer any of them if I do not want to."

"You have the right to speak to a lawyer. You indicated to the custody sergeant downstairs that you did not want to speak to one. Do you wish to speak to one now."

"No," Herman said, again answering directly in English.

"Are you certain?"

"Yes."

"If you change your mind at any time, please let me know immediately and we will stop this interview. You also have the right to medical treatment. I'm informed that you were examined by a doctor in the cells downstairs, but he found no injury other than minor bruising caused during your arrest. Is that correct?"

Herman looked at him without blinking, as this was translated. Then he nodded.

"Yes."

"Good. This interview is being recorded on the camera on the wall over there. You see that? And the microphones built into the table here record everything we say."

"Where do you live, Herman?" Thompson asked.

Herman's eyes flicked across to him.

Packer and Thompson had discussed this before the interview. To keep Herman off guard, they would switch topics between them.

"Richards Road, number 3," Herman told them, through the interpreter.

"How long have you lived there?"

"More than one year."

"Who do you live with?"

"Siti, Raghav, Tanvi. Emily until last weekend. Sometimes others, but not at the moment."

"Do you pay rent for the flat?"

Herman spoke to Patrick in a stream of Indonesian. The name, Billy, appeared in the middle of it, with a clear emphasis on the name.

"We pay the rent to Billy. He comes to get it every week."

"Describe Billy."

"White, fat, ugly. He tries to get women for sex."

"What women?" Thompson asked, keeping his voice flat.

"Tanvi. Another who used to live at the flat. Other women living in the building have complained about Billy, as well."

"What about Siti?" Thompson asked.

"No. Her face is marked."

Patrick said the word, 'marked,' hesitantly, showing some confusion. He spoke to Herman in Indonesian.

"Disfigured," Patrick clarified, "Burned when she was young."

Thompson nodded.

"What about Emily?"

"I did not hear Emily say this about Billy," Patrick translated.

"Did you ever see Billy talking to Emily?"

"No."

"What about when he came to collect the rent?"

"It was always Siti who went to the door to give him the money," Patrick translated, "He felt sorry for Siti because of the burns, so he was kind to her."

"Did you ever go to the door to speak to Billy?"

Herman's face darkened noticeably.

"Sometimes."

"Why did Siti not go?"

"Sometimes we did not have the rent money to give to Billy," Patrick translated, "Billy became angry and started shouting at Siti, so I went to the door. We argued."

"What does 'argued' mean?" Thompson asked.

"We shouted at each other?"

"Just shouted?"

"Sometimes we fought. Billy pushed me and I pushed him back."

"Did it go any further than pushing?"

"Billy hit me with his fists once. I did not hit him back, because I did not want him to make us leave the flat."

"Sure about that?"

"Yes," Herman answered in English, "Not hit Billy."

"Tell us about Emily," Packer said.

Herman looked at him, surprised by the sudden change in topic. For a moment, he looked at Packer, breathing for a moment.

He spoke a string of Indonesian, which Patrick translated.

"Emily is very beautiful. She is from Africa. She wants to bring her family here, where they can have a better life."

"Was she your friend?"

"I tried to be her friend," Patrick translated, "but she was very hard to be friends with. She was very shy, and she was scared of men."

"Scared of all men?"

Herman's eyes darkened.

His voice rose, as he spoke in Indonesian.

"I did not kill her," Patrick translated.

"I didn't ask if you did," Packer replied.

"You came to the flat and told us Emily had been murdered, then you returned and arrested me. You think I did it."

Packer fell silent. For a moment, he sat looked at Herman, trying to get a feel for the man.

Herman looked back at him, his brown eyes staring into Packer's. There was something predatory about those eyes. They were the eyes of a man who had lived a difficult life and was constantly on guard.

And the eyes of a man who had done bad things.

Packer leaned back in his seat, a signal for Thompson to take over.

"How did you come to Australia?" Thompson asked.

Herman looked at him, clear defiance in his eyes.

"I came on a boat."

"What sort of boat?"

"It was a fishing boat."

"Australia's a long way to go for a fishing trip," Thompson said.

Herman gave him a look of irritation.

"It was not a fishing trip," Patrick translated, "It was a fishing boat, but it was bringing people to Australia to live."

"Were you aware that that was illegal?"

"Of course," Patrick translated, "but life is easy in Australia. It is hard in Indonesia."

"How did the boat get here?"

"It travelled across the ocean. Many boats are stopped by the coast guard before they get to Australia, but some people know places the coast guard does not."

"Did you pay for the trip on the boat?"

"I paid some money. But the price was less because I helped to get the boat ready and helped to get the people to the boat."

"You helped the people smugglers?" Thompson asked.

"I do not like this word, 'smugglers,'" Patrick translated, "Everybody has the right to choose a better life."

"That's why you came here?" Thompson asked, "To choose a better life?"

"Yes."

"Did you know the people who owned the boat?"

"Other people in the village knew them."

"Do you know their names?"

"I will not tell you," Patrick translated, "because my family would be in danger if I did."

"Okay," Thompson said, letting it go, "Where did you arrive in Australia?"

"North. Near Port Hedland."

"How did you end up in Perth?"

"There are people there who take us to Perth for money. Truck drivers."

"Why come to Perth?"

"Siti was here."

"You knew Siti?"

"My family knew her. I was told how to find her."

"How do you make money here?"

"I work. Sometimes cleaning with Siti and Emily. Sometimes helping to move furniture with another man from Indonesia who speaks good English. There is a restaurant that lets me work in the kitchen on weekends because the owner is from Indonesia."

"Do you work there every weekend?"

"Yes."

"What sort of hours do you do there?"

"All day Saturday and Sunday. They are the most busy days for them."

"Were you there last Sunday?"

"Yes."

"What's the name of the restaurant?"

"If I tell you, the owner will be in trouble for giving me work."

"So, we only have your word that you were there last Sunday?" Thompson asked.

"I am not lying."

"Why did you leave Indonesia?" Packer asked.

Herman's eyes looked across at him.

He stared at Packer, his face impassive.

"There is no future in my village. In Australia, life is easy."

"Any other reason?"

Herman was silent for a moment, sensing a trap.

"No," he said in Indonesian, with Patrick translating.

"Where did you live in Indonesia?"

"I lived in several places."

"What were their names?"

"Turi, Lamongan, Sekaran."

"Deket?"

Again, Herman was silent for a moment. His face remained blank, but this had clearly unsettled him.

"I lived there for a time," he said eventually, with Patrick translating.

"Were you living there before you came to Australia?"

"Yes."

"How were things in Deket?"

"I do not understand what you mean?"

"Is it a peaceful place? Are people happy there?"

"There is no work. People are poor."

"Did you ever get into any trouble there?"

Herman fell silent again. He stared at Packer with unblinking eyes.

"Many people get into trouble."

"Did you?"

"Sometimes."

"Give us an example."

"Sometimes I drank too much alcohol. Sometimes I got into fights or had arguments."

"With your friends?"

"Yes."

"With other people?"

"Sometimes."

"With the police?"

Herman's face shifted noticeably, his eyes widening a fraction, and his jaw clenching.

He sat there silently.

"Did you ever get into trouble with the police?" Packer asked again.

Herman looked at him and gave one solitary nod.

"You nodded," Packer said, for the recording, "That means, 'yes'?"

"Yes."

"Tell us about that."

"About what?"

"How did you get in trouble with the police?" Packer pointed out.

Herman fell silent once again.

"Did you leave Indonesia because the police are looking for you?" Packer asked.

Herman stared hard at him across the table.

He muttered something in Indonesia.

"I want to see a lawyer," Patrick translated.

Packer and Herman looked at each other across the table.

"Interview suspended at 8:27pm," Packer said.

Chapter 24

"It's him," Thompson said, as they walked back towards the incident room, "He put the weights on Emily and she turned him down, so he killed her. Fucking prick."

"Get on to Legal Aid," Packer said, "See if they can send someone here to talk to him."

"They'll advise him not to continue the interview."

"Yeah," Packer agreed, "but we need to make sure all the boxes are ticked if it is him."

"What do you mean if?" Thompson asked, "Of course it's him. He's killed before and he knows the victim. He's got no alibi apart from this bullshit story about working in a restaurant that he won't tell us the name of."

"It's not enough, George. We can't build a case out of that."

"What about the forensics on the girl's underwear?"

"We don't know if it's his. If she was working as a prostitute, it could be anyone's."

Thompson gave a low sigh of frustration.

"So, what now then?"

"So now we get him a lawyer and we keep looking."

***

Thompson rang Legal Aid, who arranged to send a duty lawyer to speak to Herman.

She arrived an hour later and was placed in an interview room with Herman.

"Custody just rang, boss," Thompson said, tapping on Packer's office door, "Legal Aid have sent the Priest."

Packer said nothing but felt a sinking feeling.

Melissa Priestley was a senior lawyer at Legal Aid, who was difficult and obstructive. She was convinced that every police officer in the country was corrupt and made a regular habit of filing complaints against officers that had no foundation but wasted precious time to deal with. She had put in complaints against both Thompson and Packer previously, which had taken months of internal investigations before being dismissed.

She spent an hour with Herman before sending word that she 'required' Packer and Thompson.

They went down in the lift.

Priestley was sitting at the table in an interview room. She was wearing a grey suit, her hair pulled back into a tight bun at the back of her head. Her face wore its permanent frown of annoyance.

Patrick sat at the table beside her, his chair drawn back, as though he was trying to move away from her. His face wore a slightly shocked expression.

"Hello, Melissa," Thompson said, smiling, "You're looking lovely. You've done something different with your hair, haven't you?"

Priestley gave him a look of anger.

She looked at Packer.

"I have spoken to Herman," she said, with completely undisguised annoyance, "I have given him very strong advice not to speak to you and he has refused to accept that advice."

Packer was barely able to hide his surprise.

"What?" Thompson said, with an almost comical look of shock.

Priestley nodded. "I spent some time trying to persuade him otherwise, but he is, very foolishly, determined to speak to you."

She glared at Packer. "Let me be clear, Sergeant, that I will be reviewing the interview very, very closely. If there is any attempt whatsoever to pressure him or breach the rules, I will be objecting very strenuously to the interview being used in court."

"I would be disappointed if you didn't," Packer said, "Detective Senior Constable Thompson will help you find the door."

"I will remain here," Priestley said, firmly, "in case he requires further legal advice."

"Sorry," said Packer, "We need the room. You're welcome to wait in the public reception area downstairs."

She glared at Packer briefly, before picking up her handbag and marching from the interview room.

Thompson grinned at Packer, then followed her out.

"Wow," Patrick said, after they had gone, "That's one very fierce lady."

"She's lovely once you get to know her," Packer said.

***

It had been over four hours since Herman had last been provided with a meal. Packer asked for another to be provided to him in the cells before continuing the interview.

After another hour, Herman was brought up to the interview room once more. He sat beside Patrick, with Packer and Thompson facing him across the table.

"Interview recommencing at 11:14pm," Packer said, "I'm Detective Senior Sergeant Tony Packer and with me is Detective Senior Constable George Thompson. Present again is Patrick Johnson interpreting.

"Herman, I told you before that you had certain rights and I cautioned you that you did not have to speak to us. I'm going to remind you once again of those rights."

Packer did so, running over the same list that he had at the beginning of the interview earlier in the evening.

"I understand you've not had some legal advice from Melissa Priestley at Legal Aid," Packer continued, "Is that correct?"

Herman nodded.

"You're nodding to indicate, 'yes'. She told us that she advised you not to speak to us, is that correct?"

Herman spoke in Indonesian and Patrick translated.

"She said that, but I will speak to you."

"Okay," Packer said, "Before we took a break, I was asking you about the police in Indonesia. You told me that you had been in trouble with the police there."

Herman took a deep breath before letting it out slowly.

He looked down at the table as he spoke, clearly having thought this through in the holding cell. When he spoke, there was none of the guarded expression that had been on his face earlier.

"Police in Indonesia are bad people. They take bribes. They break the law. Some sell drugs or make girls have sex with them.

"In my village, it is known that the local police officers sell drugs for criminal gangs. People avoid contact with the police. One policeman was called Ahmad. He sold drugs and he beat people. He was an evil man.

"I have a sister. Her name is Duri. From the time she was a child, she was very headstrong. She always did what she wanted, even if she knew she should not. When she became a teenager, she began to drink alcohol and spend time with friends in the city. I tried to make her stop this, but she would not listen to me.

"One night, she went out. She did not return home. My family were very worried. My mother could not leave the house. Again and again, my mother said that Diru had been killed. She would not listen to anyone who said this was not true.

"My friends and I went into town to look for Duri. For eight days, we looked for her. Eventually, one of my friends found Duri in a house. It was a place where drug users lived."

Herman's voice began to trail off at the end. He rubbed at his eyes and breathed heavily for a moment before continuing.

"Duri was wearing a shirt, but no pants. She smelled of other men. She had used drugs and did not recognise my friends or me."

He paused again, his breathing heavy.

"One of the others in the house saw what had happened. He told us Duri had been using drugs. She had been in the house for a week. She let men use her to get drugs.

"I asked what men. They told me the policeman named Ahmad had brought her there and did this to her."

Herman stopped again. Now, though, he was not holding back tears.

He was holding back anger.

"I went to find this man, Ahmad, and asked him if this was true. He laughed at me. He told me Duri was his now. That she was his dirty whore.

"I do not remember exactly what happened next, but I know I beat Ahmad in anger. When I finished, he was dead."

Herman looked up at Packer. His eyes showed a grim defiance.

"That is why I left Indonesia. If I had stayed there, I would be killed by the police. If I am sent back there, I will be killed. I came to Australia to save my life."

"Do you like Siti?" Packer asked.

Herman fell silent, startled by the sudden change in direction.

"Siti's family is known to my family."

"You told us that. I asked if you like her."

"Yes, I like her."

"Is she your friend?"

"Yes, she is my friend."

"Do you ever argue with her?"

"Even friends have arguments. We argue sometimes."

"What do you argue about?"

"Money sometimes. We do not have so much and things are so expensive here. Sometimes we need to buy food or cigarettes, but Siti says we need the money to pay the rent."

"She looks after the money?"

"No, we have our own money. But she always worries about paying the rent."

"Does it annoy you when she tells you what do with your money?"

"No."

"But you said you argue about it?"

"Sometimes it annoys me. Yes."

Packer nodded. "Angers you, too?"

"Sometimes."

"Do you ever hit Siti?"

"No."

"When we went to the house, she had a black eye and a split lip," Packer said, phrasing it as a statement, rather than a question. He looked at Herman.

"I was very angry with her," Patrick translated after a moment.

"Why?"

"She talked to you when you came to the flat the first time."

"Why did that make you angry?"

"She knows why I came to Australia. She knows I will be sent back if the police find me."

Herman clicked his teeth and muttered in Indonesian.

"And now I will," Patrick translated.

"Are you in a romantic relationship with Siti?" Packer asked.

Herman shook his head. "No."

"Did you have a girlfriend in Indonesia?"

Herman shrugged. "There were some women."

"Do you have a girlfriend in Australia?"

"No."

"Have you had a girlfriend since you came to Australia?"

"No."

"You've lived here over a year. That's a long time on your own."

Herman shrugged again. "That's just how it is."

"Did you have romantic feelings towards Emily?"

"No."

"You told us you thought she was very beautiful."

"Yes, I did. But I did not think about a relationship."

"You told us you wanted to be her friend."

"Yes."

"But she did not want to be yours."

"She did not."

"Did that make you disappointed?"

"No."

"Frustrated?"

"No."

"Angry?"

"No," Herman answered in English. His voice had grown louder, and he was leaning forward in the chair.

"Do you get angry easily?" Packer asked.

"No."

"You got angry with Billy."

A stream of Indonesian.

"He got angry with Siti," Patrick translated, "I had to intervene."

"You got angry with Siti."

"I told her not to speak to the police, but she did not listen."

"You got angry with Ahmad in Indonesia."

"He gave my sister drugs and raped her."

"Did you get angry with Emily?"

"No," Herman answered in English. He was leaning forward in the seat now, visibly growing agitated, his voice much louder.

"Never?"

"No."

With his eyes locked on Herman's, Packer opened the folder and pulled a photo from it. He turned it to face Herman and flicked it across the table to land in front of him.

"Did you do that to Emily when you were angry?" he asked.

Herman looked down at the table.

An image of Emily's dead body, lying in the alleyway, was on the table in front of him. Her body lay cold and broken, her eyes staring sightlessly.

Herman jumped in the chair, shoving his body back against the backrest and trying to pull away.

There was a string of frantic Indonesian, as he looked down at the photo with wide eyes, unable to look away.

"No more questions," Patrick translated, his own voice showing clear shock, "I will answer no more questions. Stop now."

"Interview terminated at 11:42pm," Packer said.

He looked across the table at Herman.

Herman would not meet his eyes.

***

Packer sat on one of the chairs outside the interview room, his head down. He put the palms of his hands over his eyes and held them there.

He was so tired, the exhaustion so powerful that it was almost a physical sensation.

Uniformed officers took Herman down to the holding cells at the bottom of the station, taking the interpreter with them to help with the paperwork and explain the situation to Herman.

Thompson turned to Packer.

"I'll get in touch with forensics," Thompson said, "We'll have to get an FME out to take DNA swabs from Herman. I'll give them a hurry up, but I doubt we'll have a match before the end of the week. We can hold him for Immigration in the meantime, even if we can't charge him with murder yet."

Packer said nothing but rubbed gently at his eyes with his palms.

"They'll want to extradite him to Indonesia for killing the policeman," Thompson continued, "so we'll have to put them straight about that until we've finished with him."

He looked over at Packer.

"I'll see if Siti will give us a statement now. I think she'll be a bit more talkative with Herman locked up. Good circumstantial evidence, that."

"It's not him," Packer muttered from behind his hands.

"What?" Thompson asked, not quite hearing.

Packer lowered his hands and let out a tired breath.

"It's not him," he said again.

"What d'you mean it's not him? He's a violent prick who killed a police officer and beats up Siti. He knows Emily. He's got the means, and he's got no alibi."

"What's the motive?"

"I don't bloody know. He's a sick bastard. What other motive d'you want?"

Packer shook his head, wearily.

"It's not him. Herman killed the police officer in anger because he was giving drugs to the sister. Emily was bound and raped, then strangled while the killer was looking at her face. That's a killer who's cold, not a killer who's acting in anger."

"Oh, so you're a bloody profiler or something now, are you?" Thompson said, raising his voice, "You can look inside the mind of a killer? The DNA will match. And I bet we can pin him to the kill room, too, when-"

"It's not a kill room."

"- we find the van."

"It's not him, George."

"If it's not bloody Herman, then who is it? Eh? Who is it?"

Packer looked at him with tired eyes.

"Stop talking for a minute and think," Packer said, "Does it feel right to you?"

"Aye," thundered Thompson, "It does. It's feels bloody right!"

"George."

Thompson closed his mouth. For a long moment, he looked at Packer, thinking through what Packer had just said.

And then his shoulders slumped.

"Okay," Thompson said, sitting down on another chair, "It's not him."

Packer took a deep breath, then let it out slowly.

He and Thompson sat there in silence for a long moment, as they both thought over the evidence they had and what they knew about Emily's murder.

"So, if it's not Herman," Thompson said, "we're back to square one."

Packer looked at him for a long moment in silence.

Then he nodded.

Chapter 25

Packer sat with his back against the wall, the concrete cold against his bare skin. He stared out through the clear glass panels that lined the balcony of his apartment into the night.

The silent grass of Langley Park spread out below until it met Riverside Drive, deserted now, and the slow-moving waves on the river. The darkness was pierced by the dull glow of the lines of streetlights curving away into the distance along the edge of the water.

Across the river rose the dark sea of high-rise apartments that lined the other side of the still water at South Perth. Now, in the early hours of the morning, the windows were all in darkness, with only a few lights glowing faintly in the gloom.

Packer followed the curve of the river along to the Bell Tower, surrounded on two sides by luxury hotels. The streets were empty, apart from an occasional taxi.

Beyond, the river curved past the base of King's Park. The streetlights along the empty street cast their faint glow over the water.

Packer thought over the interview with Herman.

After the hostile silence at the flat and the failed attempt at escape, beating Siti for her cooperation with them, Packer had expected to get nothing from Herman.

But once Herman had realised they knew about the police officer in Indonesia, it had been like a dam bursting. Despite the Priest's firm advice not to speak to them, Herman had clearly been eager to get this off his chest.

Packer had seen the same thing before; it wasn't unusual. When the realisation came that they had reached, it was often joined by the need to confess. Herman had lived with what he had done for over a year, constantly on his guard and in fear of capture. Now the chance had come to let it go, and it had all come flooding out.

Indonesian police had sent a report on the killing through the AFP and Packer had read over it earlier. It differed markedly from Herman's account of the killing of the police officer, but that that didn't surprise him. Despite their insistence that all their officers were above reproach, the corruption of

Indonesian police was well known. Even if Herman's account had a smell of exaggeration about it, it sounded far more convincing than the official report, which described him suddenly going crazy and killing a police officer he had never met without the faintest hint of a reason.

But none of this was Packer's problem. Whatever the truth was about what had happened in Indonesia, someone else would deal with it. If Herman was deported, he would have to face Indonesian authorities for what he had done.

Packer's problem was Emily's murder.

Base would insist on Herman being charged, but Packer did not believe that Herman was Emily's killer.

They had enough now to obtain a DNA sample from Herman. This could be compared to the stain Goodge had found on Emily's underpants, and Packer was confident there would be no match. But even if there was not, that alone would not be enough to exculpate Herman from her murder. The stain on the underpants could have come from someone else at another time, rather than during the murder. Herman would remain in the frame.

If Herman named the owners of the restaurant and they confirmed he had been there on Sunday, the alibi would be enough to exclude him. He would be cleared. Herman had refused to name the owners for now, but perhaps he would change his mind when his predicament sank in. Or perhaps he would remain silent, feeling he had nothing left to lose any more.

And without an alibi, Herman remained their chief suspect, even though Packer knew he wasn't Emily's killer.

So, if it wasn't Herman, what were they left with?

There were too many pieces here and none of them fitted together.

Why had the workshop in Osbourne Park been fitted out the way it had? After the effort to organise the workshop and the garote, why was Emily dumped so carelessly in the alley? That didn't gel.

How did this fit with Claire's investigation into the client who bound and strangled a prostitute with a belt? Had Emily been working as a prostitute and come across the same client? None of the other prostitutes in the area knew her.

Billy Harrison and Tom Kirby were both on the periphery of this and there was something about both of them that bothered Packer. Neither was being completely honest, and neither was telling them everything.

And what was Frazier's connection to all of this? His name kept coming up. It couldn't be coincidence.

Something moved in the dull haze of a streetlight near the water, a nocturnal animal moving through the dark.

Packer's eyes were heavy, and he rubbed at them.

How long had it been since he had slept? Three days? Four?

Sleep came rarely to him and never while he was working an active investigation. He spent the nights turning over the details gathered during the days, trying to find the delicate network of lines that connected it all somehow together.

But he was so tired. So tired. He could fight it off during the day, but at night, it crept up on him, strong and relentless.

And even then, sleep would not come. He was exhausted but could not sleep. The pieces kept turning, shifting in and out of focus, changing shape, trying to find a connection with the rest of the puzzle.

They would fit together. Somehow. They must.

But it was just outside of his vision. Somewhere he couldn't quite see.

He stared out into the night again, the pinpoints of light breaking through the darkness.

Packer closed his eyes, and the dull glow of the city night disappeared.

Emily tugged at the bonds

The ties cut into her wrists as she strained against them. They tore at her skin. Blood began to seep down her wrists towards her hands.

A sound echoed behind her.

She whipped her head around, braids flailing, as she searched the darkness for the noise she had heard.

Footsteps.

And the sound of leather slapping against skin.

He held the belt in one hand and hit the open palm of the other with it.

Emily whimpered in terror.

Measure steps drew closer.

There was no reaction from him. No laugh, no words, no sound. Nothing.

He was cold, emotionless.

Slowly, he approached.

Holding out the belt, he wrapped it around the back of her neck.

Emily moved her head, shifting from side to side, trying to get free.

He pulled the belt tighter, threading the tongue through the buckle, and began to close it around her neck.

Holding the belt against her throat with one hand, he used the other to pull at the end.

Emily gasped, her eyes bulging as her breath was cut off.

He leaned closer, watching her in the dark.

There was a movement behind Packer, and he gave a start, his head jerking up.

He looked out over the city lights again, breathing hard as reality snapped back into place.

The door to the apartment slid open beside him.

Chandra sat on the ground beside him, making no attempt to hide her nakedness, her bare arm warm against his. She crossed her ankles, her long, brown legs arched in front of her.

"It's three in the morning," she said, "What are you doing out here?"

"Couldn't sleep."

"Really? I thought I might have at least done something to wear you out."

Packer said nothing but looked out over the city. In the distance, headlights crawled slowly along Riverside Drive, a late-night delivery truck heading for the freeway.

"Such a beautiful view," Chandra said, "It seems so peaceful by night."

"There are things you can't see," Packer said, "Things crawling below the surface."

"What's that supposed to mean?" Chandra asked, a smile in her voice.

"The city's not a safe place. There are ugly things here that nobody sees. Perth has the highest methylamphetamine use in the southern hemisphere," Packer said, "and the second highest murder rate in the country. There's evil here."

"You're a miserable bastard, aren't you?" Chandra said, "There's a naked woman sitting beside you, and all you can talk about is drugs and death."

She wrapped a hand around his wrist and tugged gently at it.

"Come back to bed," she said.

"I'll be there in a minute."

"No, you'll be there now," she said, pulling harder.

Packer allowed her to pull him to his feet.

She was tall, her head coming up his chin. She pulled his hand behind her back, wrapping his arm around her naked body, as she stood on her toes to kiss him.

Her breasts pushed against his chest, her skin warm against his, and he felt himself responding.

She led him back inside to the bedroom.

Thursday

Chapter 26

Packer sat at the bench in the kitchen, the warm glow of morning growing steadily brighter through the curtains. He was halfway through a cup of coffee when Chandra walked out of the bedroom.

Despite himself, he couldn't keep his eyes from her naked body.

Stopping in front of the bench, she picked up his coffee and began drinking it.

"Take mine," Packer said, "or I can make you a fresh one. Either or."

"Make me a fresh one," she said, then drank more of his, looking over the rim of the cup at him with her large, brown eyes, "Make yourself one while you're at it."

Packer grinned.

He stood up and walked over to the cupboard to get out another cup.

Chandra sat down at the bench and watched him while he made more coffee.

"I don't want you to think I'm complaining..." Packer began.

"Fine. I'll make my own bloody coffee."

"...but last night was," he paused, before continuing, "Unexpected."

Chandra looked across the bench at him for a long moment.

"I've wasted half my life on a miserable marriage and an ugly divorce," she said, "I'm not wasting any more of it by tiptoeing around or playing games. I wanted you. End of."

Packer couldn't stop himself from smiling again, surprised by the forthright nature of the woman and the strength of her personality.

"And just so we're clear," he said, the smile fading to something much smaller, "What exactly did you want? Was that it last night, or is it something more?"

Nish looked at him, brown eyes fixed on his. She gave a slight shrug.

"I don't know yet," she said, "Let's find out."

Packer nodded but said nothing for a long moment.

"Look," he said, eventually, "I don't want any misunderstandings. I'm not sure I'm looking for anything serious."

"You're happy to sleep with me, but you don't want to date me?" she said, bluntly.

"Last night was your idea."

"Yes, it was. And I'm glad it happened. I hope it happens again."

Nish pushed her glossy, brown hair away from her face.

"If it goes somewhere, then fine," she continued, "If not..."

She shrugged.

"We're both grown-ups, Tony."

She raised the coffee cup to her mouth, and drank, peering at him over the rim.

He watched her for a moment.

"I've never met anyone like you," he said.

"No, you haven't," she agreed, "So make the most of it."

She put the cup back down on the bench and smiled sweetly, fluttering her eyelids at him.

***

When Packer arrived at the station, Seoyoon and Thompson were already in the incident room. It was almost unheard of for any of the team to be there before Packer, and it had never happened during an active investigation, but if either of them noticed, they said nothing.

"Boss," Thompson said in a low voice, walking over to him, "The inspector's been down here this morning looking for you. He wants you to go and see him."

Packer looked at his watch.

"It's only just gone eight. He's off to an early start."

"He knows about Osbourne Park and about Herman murdering the police officer in Indonesia. He wanted to know whether we'd charged Herman. He just about blew a valve when I told him we hadn't."

Packer nodded in resignation. "Alright. Anything here I need to know about?"

"AFP rang," Seoyoon said, "They're expecting an arrest document from Indonesia this morning. They want to take custody of Herman, so they can start extradition proceedings."

"He's ours for another thirty-six hours. Where's Claire?"

"She rang earlier," Thompson said, "She thinks she's got a line on the prostitute who was bound and choked, so she's gone to check it out."

Packer nodded.

"Alright. I better go and talk to the inspector."

***

Packer walked back down the corridor from the incident room to the elevator. He took it up to the top floor of the station.

Inspector Base's office was at the end of the floor, past a series of conference rooms, and the offices which housed Base's support staff and the station's media liaison and administration officers.

Base's secretary had a desk outside Base's office. She was studiously looking at her computer screen and typing, avoiding Packer's eye.

Packer knocked on the door.

"Come," called Base from inside.

Packer opened the door and walked in.

Base's office was bigger than the incident room. It contained a row of lounge chairs grouped around a coffee table, a row of bookshelves and a wall lined with framed photographs recording the highlights of Base's career, which largely involved him being commended by politicians.

Across the back wall was Base's desk, which was completely empty apart from a computer screen and a small pile of neatly stacked papers.

"Senior Sergeant," Base said, his voice flat and cold, "Close the door."

Packer shut the door and walked across the room to Base's desk. Base's eyes followed him in silence the whole way.

Packer pulled out one of the chairs and sat down.

"I tried to contact you yesterday, Senior Sergeant. Several times."

It wasn't phrased as a question, but the intention was clear.

"I was busy," Packer said, "I think we found the place where she was killed."

"So, I've been told," Base said, "Not by you, though."

Base was clearly looking for an apology and an explanation.

Packer gave him neither.

Base let out a sharp breath in frustration.

"At any rate, you've got the man in custody now. Yet George Thompson tells me you haven't charged him."

Packer shook his head. "It's not him."

Base frowned hard, clearly surprised by this.

"Not him? Has he got an alibi?"

Packer shook his head.

"Something that points to another suspect?"

Packer shook his head again.

"Then what?"

"It doesn't feel right."

Base nearly exploded. "*Doesn't -*"

He broke off, inhaling sharply and letting his breath out slowly to get his temper under control.

He raised one hand and counted off the points on his fingers.

"He's got no alibi, he resisted arrest, he lived with the victim, he assaulted another woman living with them, and he's on the run from Indonesian police for murdering a police officer. Is that all correct?"

Packer nodded.

"Sounds pretty conclusive to me, Senior Sergeant," Base snapped, "Charge him. Stop pissing about and charge him."

"It's not him," Packer said again.

"Because you've got a bloody 'feeling' it's not him?"

"Herman's got a temper. He gets violent when he gets angry. Emily was bound and strangled while the killer was watching her die. That's not someone killing in anger."

"She was beaten before she was killed."

"Yes, but the killing wasn't done in anger. And there are other things that don't fit."

"Such as?"

"She told her flatmate that she was doing sex work for a violent pimp. There's nothing to connect Herman to the Osbourne Park unit where she was killed, or the white van that was used to move her body. Jeffrey Frazier's name keeps coming up."

"Frazier? The property developer?"

Packer nodded.

Base's expression of incredulity was almost comical. "Oh, so a millionaire property developer is going around killed prostitutes?"

"I didn't say that."

Base leaned forward in his chair, stabbing a finger at Packer.

"You charge that man downstairs, Senior Sergeant," he hissed through gritted teeth, "Go from this office and do it immediately."

"It's not him," Packer said, "There's too much that doesn't fit. If we get it wrong and another one dies, what then? How does that look? Do we tell the press that we ignored the other leads and jumped the gun?"

Base glared at him.

There was a long silence while the two men stared hard at each other, both refusing to give in.

"Look, the AFP are working on extraditing Herman to Indonesia," Packer said, "And he'll be given Legal Aid to fight it. That'll take months. He's not going anywhere. Let me chase down the other things and see how they fit. If they connect to Herman, I'll charge him."

Base glared at him for a long, dangerous moment.

Then he let out a sigh of frustration.

"What time did you arrest him?" Base asked.

"Five o'clock yesterday evening."

"You can hold him for forty-hours without charge. You have until 5:00pm tomorrow," he said, "If you haven't got someone else by then, and you haven't found evidence to exclude him, then you charge that man downstairs. That's a direct order. Is that clear?"

Packer nodded.

"Is that clear, Senior Sergeant?" Base snapped.

"Yes," Packer said, "It's clear."

Base waved a hand, dismissing Packer, and turned to his computer screen.

Packer got up and left the office. He took the elevator back down to the incident room.

Thompson and Seoyoon looked up when he entered.

"How was the inspector?" Thompson asked.

"Very supportive," Packer said, "We've got until five o'clock tomorrow. Let's make it count."

Chapter 27

Jeffrey Frazier arrived at the East Perth police station forty minutes late, just late enough to show his disdain for the police, but not so late that they would come looking for him.

He parked his bright red Ferrari in a parking space near the front door that was marked, 'Reserved'.

He was wearing trousers and an open shirt with the sleeves rolled up over his forearms.

The lawyer he brought with him had his hair combed across his bald head. He was wearing an expensive suit over his gaunt frame and carrying a designer briefcase.

When Thompson went down to the reception area to collect them, Frazier was sitting on one of the visitors' seats, with his arm over the back of the chair and one ankle on the other knee.

"How do," Frazier said, giving Thompson a confident grin.

"Morning, Mr Frazier," Thompson said, "This way, please."

Frazier casually got up and walked forwards, the lawyer at his heels.

Thompson recognised the lawyer as Don Wheeler SC. He had never met Wheeler but knew him by reputation. Wheeler wrote opinion pieces for the West Australian newspaper, attacking the police and 'oppressive' criminal laws, and appeared on radio whenever there was a media frenzy over a high-profile arrest or court case to offer his opinion on the disgrace of the justice system.

When they reached the door leading to the inside of the police station, Thompson looked at Wheeler, waiting for him to introduce himself. Wheeler didn't.

"I'm sorry, sir," Thompson said, "You are?"

Wheeler gave him a frown of annoyance.

"Don Wheeler," he said, apparently thinking this sufficient.

Thompson waited.

"He's me lawyer," Frazier said, still jovial, "Thought I'd bring him along, just in case. Any problem with that?"

"Not at all, Mr Frazier," Thompson said, ignoring Wheeler, "Come this way."

Thompson led them along the corridor towards the interview rooms on the lower level.

Packer was waiting in one of the rooms at the end.

"Hello, Sergeant," Frazier said, with a grin, when he entered, "How's it going?"

"Never better," Packer said flatly, pointing at the seat opposite.

Frazier sat down confidently.

"This is Mr Frazier's lawyer, Mr... Wheeler," Thompson said. He turned to Wheeler. "Have I got that right?"

Wheeler gave him another frown of annoyance and nodded, as he sat beside Frazier.

"Yeah, we've met," Packer said, dismissively.

"Right, now, Sergeant," Frazier said, draping his arm over the back of the chair, "What's all this about, then?"

"Just a few questions," Packer said.

"Last time we spoke, you told us that you had a number of shelf companies that own residential property throughout Perth," Thompson said, taking over.

Frazier nodded. "Yep. Heaps of them."

"Do you own commercial property, too?"

Frazier nodded again. "Yeah, got a few of them. I own a couple of car-yards in Victoria Park. I don't sell the cars, of course, just lease the yards to the blokes who do. I've got shares in Karrinyup shopping centre and Garden City. There's a couple of restaurants and eateries in Freo that I lease to the people running them."

"What about commercial units?"

Frazier nodded again. "I think so."

"You're not sure?"

"Some of the companies own workshops and warehouses and shit. I was doing a good trade in those during the mining boom back in 2008 and 2009. COVID fucked all that up, of course. Fuckin' government was paying businesses to stop trading and then when they cut off the money, everybody went broke. The units are all empty now, as far as I know."

"How many units do you have?" Thompson asked.

"Oh, geez. Couldn't tell ya," Frazier said, "I had a heap of them in Balcatta, but I managed to flog off most of those. Cut me losses on them. There's still a heap of them down in Canningvale that I finished building just before COVID hit. They're all vacant still. Fuckin' white elephants now."

"Anywhere else?"

Frazier nodded. "Yeah, there are. Look, you should have just asked on the phone when you rang. Nat could have got all the details for ya. I don't really pay much attention to this stuff."

"No?"

"Nuh. Billy looks after the rental places, flats and that. I had another bloke who used to look after the commercial tenancies, but I didn't really need him any more. Nat looks after it now, not that there's much to look after."

"Do you own anything in Osbourne Park?" Packer asked.

Frazier turned to look at him, staring silently at him for a moment.

He nodded. "Yeah. I built a lot of the warehouses out there back in the 80s. That was when I first starting out on my own. I was building for other people in those days, but I built a couple of my own, too, once I had the money. Never huge money-spinners, but they gave me the capital to move into developing apartments."

"Do you still have any there now?"

Frazier shrugged, a faint grin on his face. "Pretty sure I do, although you'd have to ask Nat for the addresses."

"Do you own any in Cuthbert Street, Osbourne Park?"

"Why do you wish to know about that specific address, officer?" Wheeler asked, speaking for the first time.

Packer kept his eyes on Frazier, who kept the faint grin in place.

"Is that one of yours?" Packer asked.

Wheeler gave a huff of annoyance. "I asked why you wish-"

"I'd have to think about it," Frazier said, cutting him off, "Like Don says, though, why you askin' about that?"

"We entered unit 3 at 96A Cuthbert Street yesterday," Packer said.

"If that property does belong to Mr Frazier," Wheeler said, "and to be clear, we are not agreeing that it does, but if that is the case, we will require a copy of the search warrant."

"A warrant wasn't required," Packer said, keeping his eyes on Frazier, who looked back at him, "We're entitled to perform an emergent search without warrant if we have reasonable grounds for belief that a crime had been committed there."

"Then we require a written outline of the reasons for that belief," Wheeler said.

"Do you?" Packer said, looking at Wheeler, "What legislation requires me to provide that to you?"

Wheeler glared at him for a moment, clearly annoyed at Packer challenging him.

"No legislation," Wheeler conceded, "Just basic courtesy."

Packer moved his eyes back to Frazier.

"The walls inside the unit were covered with soundproofing and the windows had been painted black," Packer said, "Someone didn't want anyone to know what they were doing in there."

"What were they doing in there?" Frazier asked, eyebrows rising in a look of mock surprise, "Killing someone?"

Packer looked back at him but said nothing.

"You told me the other day that your prostitute was killed in Northbridge," Frazier said, "Now you're telling me she was killed in Osbourne Park. Can't you make up your mind, mate?"

"I said she was found in Northbridge," Packer pointed out, "not that she was killed there."

"Oh, right," Frazier said, "My bad. So why would some bloke kill her in Osbourne Park and then take her into Northbridge? Sounds like a lot of trouble to go to."

"You still haven't answered my question, Mr Frazier, " Packer pointed out, "Do you own that unit at 96A Cuthbert Street?"

"Mr Frazier has already said he does not know, officer," Wheeler said.

"He said he'd have to think about it," Packer corrected, eyes still on Frazier, "Why don't you do that, Mr Frazier? Think about it."

Frazier looked around the room and took in a breath.

"Yeah, you know," he said, after a moment, "I'm not completely sure. But I do remember building a few units in Cuthbert Street back in the 90s. I think that might be one of mine."

He leaned forward on the table. "Surely you blokes could just do a property search and find out, couldn't ya? Didn't youse think of that?"

"Have you been near that unit recently? Packer asked.

"How recent is 'recently'?" Frazier asked.

"This year?"

"Do you have any evidence that Mr Frazier was near that unit?" Wheeler interrupted.

Frazier fell silent, looking at Packer.

Packer gave a slight frown and let out a breath.

"I'm surprised you felt the need to bring your lawyer along, Mr Frazier," he said, "You're not being formally interviewed, and Detective Thompson made that clear on the phone. I just wanted to ask you a few questions. But you turn up with him holding your hand and he keeps butting in."

"That is highly offensive, officer," Wheeler said, his voice rising, "Mr Frazier does not-"

"Settle down, Don," Frazier said, cutting him off, "It's okay."

"It is highly inappropriate for the police to be-"

"I told ya to settle down," Frazier said firmly, turning to look at Wheeler, "I'll let you know if I need ya help, right? Zip it."

Wheeler looked ready to argue, but instead settled back in the chair. His face had coloured and he now wore a frown. He clearly did not like being spoken down to by either the police or his own client.

Frazier looked back at Packer again. He rolled his eyes.

"Right," he said, "What's the question?"

"Have you been near the unit in Osbourne Park this year?"

"Don't think so," Frazier said, "I do a bit of business out that way, so I drive through there occasionally. I might've gone down Cuthbert Street, but I don't remember if I did."

"What sort of business do you do in Osbourne Park?"

Frazier shrugged. "Signing contracts out there sometimes. There's a lot of suppliers out there for tiles and windows and shit. I sometimes sort those out."

"You do that personally?"

"Do you know how many tiles go into a block of apartments? If you're buying five thousand square metres in one go, there's plenty of room for a discount. I usually sort that stuff out meself, rather than leave it up to the project manager."

"These are commercial suppliers that you deal with?"

"Yep."

"What sort of hours do they keep?"

"The usual ones."

"Business hours? Weekdays?"

"Yeah."

"Not Sundays?"

"No."

"You wouldn't be out there on a Sunday, then?"

Frazier paused for a moment. "Not for business, no."

"Some other reason?"

"I take me sister's kids out to Ikea sometimes. They love the meatballs."

"Ikea's not very close to Cuthbert Street."

"Yeah, well. I like to drive around a bit when I've got the kids in the car. The oldest one thinks the Lambo and the Ferrari are pretty cool, heh?"

Frazier gave Packer a wide grin, letting him know clearly that he wouldn't be outfoxed.

"Were you at Ikea last Sunday?" Packer asked.

Frazier frowned in concentration and looked around the room again.

"Hmmm. Lemme think. No. No, I wasn't. Not last Sunday. I was feeling pretty rough on Sunday, actually. Went to watch the gee-gees racing with Tom Kirby on Saturday night. He loves the horses. I just go for the piss-up."

"Were you in Osbourne Park on Sunday for some other reason?"

Frazier shook his head. "Don't think so. Not that I can-"

He broke off suddenly, then clicked his fingers.

"You know what?" he said, grinning widely, "I've just remembered. Last Sunday? I was at a business do at the Hyatt. The Chamber of Commerce was holding a big dinner and drinks there. I was one of the speakers actually. Said a few words about Perth's economic recovery after the pandemic. Why don't you check with them? Probably about six hundred people who can tell you I was there from three in the afternoon until midnight."

Frazier settled back in his chair, grinning smugly at Packer.

He turned to Wheeler.

"Grab ya briefcase, Don," he said, "I think we're finished here."

***

"I checked with the Chamber of Commerce, boss," Thompson said, "They confirmed what Frazier said. He was one of the keynote speakers. Gave a talk on the challenges facing the property industry in WA. I arrived at three o'clock for a conference with the mayor, then gave a speech in the afternoon. Stayed for dinner and drinks and was one of the last to leave. He was very friendly, by all accounts. Insisted on having his photo taken with all the high-flyers there for the newspapers."

Packer leaned back in his chair as he listened.

He nodded.

"Looks like the connection to the unit was just a coincidence," Thompson finished.

"There's still something about him that feels off," Packer said quietly.

"It wasn't him dumping the body, boss. There's dozens of photos proving he was somewhere else."

"So why bring Wheeler along to the station? Why string us along with all that other bullshit instead of telling us straightaway that he had an alibi?"

Thompson shrugged. "Because he's a prick. I don't know. He has got a rock-solid alibi, though."

Packer exhaled in frustration.

Then he nodded.

Chapter 28

Packer dialled Billy Harrison's number. He expected it to go straight to message bank and for Harrison to then ignore him.

He was surprised when Harrison answered almost immediately.

"Hello," Harrison said.

"Mr Harrison. It's Senior Sergeant Packer. I'd like another word with you if you can spare us the time."

"Pretty busy, mate, eh? I might be able to pop in next week."

"We're investigating a murder, Mr Harrison. We need to speak to you before then."

"Still looking for clues, are youse?" Harrison said, not even trying to hide his cockiness, "Alright. Tell you what. I've got some maintenance work I gotta do at one of the properties out in Dianella. I'll give you the address and you blokes can meet me there."

Hiding his irritation, Packer took down the address and agreed to meet Harrison there in an hour.

"Well?" Thompson said.

"He's in a cocky mood this morning. Frazier's been in touch with him."

"Has he? Well, probably to be expected."

Packer nodded.

He looked at Seoyoon. "Any luck with the white van?"

She shook her head. "No, boss. I've been through nearly all the property registers now. I don't think we're going to find any businesses connected to Billy Harrison at all."

Packer nodded. "Alright. It was a long shot. If it was him in the white van, then he probably wouldn't have used it at all if he knew it could be traced back to him."

"The other thing I could do is try going back through all of Frazier's companies. There's a lot of them, but the van may be registered to one of them."

Packer nodded. "Okay. Try that."

He turned to Thompson. "Let's go and talk to Harrison."

***

Dianella was only a few suburbs out from the edge of the city. It had been a working-class suburb in the sixties and was filled with endless blocks of affordable housing and cheap flats.

As the city limits had begun to expand, many of the older houses were being demolished to make room for newer developments. Blocks of high-rise apartments loomed over the train line and more expensive townhouses bordered them.

The older buildings further away from the railway had begun to fall apart through poor maintenance, and lay waiting for their eventual demolition.

Packer and Thompson found Harrison's Falcon station wagon parked on the verge outside a block of ten flats that were probably even older than the block in Girrawheen. The tailgate was up, and a ladder was tied to the roof racks.

Thompson parked the car behind Harrison's car, and they headed for the driveway.

Wearing faded work trousers and a shirt with the sleeves rolled up, Harrison came walking in the opposite direction. A few lengths of guttering and some downpipes lay across the end of the driveway.

"You found the place, then?" Harrison said, grinning, "I was startin' to worry you might have lost yourselves. You gonna give me a hand with the stuff in the car?"

"This won't take long, Mr Harrison," Thompson said, "Just a few questions to ask."

Harrison grinned widely at him. "Go on, then. Shoot."

"You used to work on building sites for Mr Frazier," Thompson said, "and then moved on to managing his rental properties. How did that come about?"

"I used to work on sites for Jeff when he was still managing them himself," Harrison said, "but he got big enough that he started using project managers on site instead of coming down himself. I kept working on site a bit longer, but then he suggested I could just look after the rentals for him instead."

"He didn't promote you to project manager?"

"Not really my thing. Plus, I wanted to get off the sites, just like Jeff did. Long hours, dangerous conditions. Collecting the rent and doing odd jobs is a lot more cushy."

"How long ago was this change in occupation?"

Harrison shrugged. "Dunno exactly. Five years? Six, maybe. Something like that."

"And you only manage residential properties for Mr Frazier?"

Harrison nodded. "Yep?"

"No commercial properties at all?"

"Nuh."

"Have you ever looked after any of Mr Frazier's commercial properties?"

Harrison nodded, a slight smirk on his face. "Yeah. Sure have."

"Whereabouts were they?"

"All over the place."

"Osbourne Park?"

"Sure."

"Whereabouts in Osbourne Park?"

"Can't remember all the addresses to be honest. Pretty sure I looked after the one that youse blokes broke into, though."

Thompson bit down on his anger.

"A young lady was murdered in that building, Mr Harrison. She was nineteen. Your daughter's not much younger than that, is she?"

Harrison's smile disappeared, replaced by a flare of anger.

He glared at Thompson.

Then he shook his head, the anger dissipating.

"Nah, she's not," Harrison said, "Alright. Yeah. Jeff rang me, told me you were askin' about the units in Osbourne Park. He told me to jerk youse around a bit, before talkin' to you. But I'll tell you what you wanna know. What is it?"

"You managed the unit in Osbourne Park?"

Harrison nodded. "Yeah, there were twelve out there. Jeff built them in the nineties, back before I started working for him. When I started looking after the properties, I used to look after the commercial places, too. Not that there was much needed doing with those. Businesses who rent them places maintain them pretty well, so they look good for the customers."

He jerked his head towards the block of flats beside him. "Not like these fuckin' places. The tenants run 'em into the ground. Jeff started selling the commercial places, though. Got rid of the Osbourne Park units a few years back."

"Why was that?"

"Big overheads on commercial places. Insurance and government taxes and stuff. Plus some businesses go broke, owing money, which is a pain in the arse. Residential places are less hassle, and the return on them's much higher. Jeff's still got a few of the newer commercial places, but not many. I don't look after those. Nat does most of it."

"When was the last time you went out to the Osbourne Park workshop?"

"Fucked if I know. Before Jeff sold it, obviously. I think I might have gone with the new owner to have a look at the units before he bought them."

"Not since then?"

Harrison shook his head. "Nuh."

"We spoke to Tom Kirby," Packer said, abruptly, "He said you leant him your van back in July."

Harrison looked at him and frowned. "What van?"

"The white van. He had some engine trouble with the bus and needed to move cleaning supplies, so he borrowed your van for the day."

"Well, he's full of shit," Harrison said, "'cause I haven't got a van. I'm pretty sure I told youse that the other day."

"He mentioned you get a bit fiery when you've had a few drinks, too," Packer said, "Is that right?"

"Nuh."

"Your ex-wife seemed to think so, too."

Harrison frowned. "That's all bullshit. I never fuckin' touched her. She just made that shit up so she could keep the kids."

"You've got a conviction for assault. Is that bullshit, too?"

"That was fuckin' twenty years ago," Harrison snapped.

"We all lose our tempers sometimes, Mr Harrison."

"Yeah, and I'm fucking losin' mine, now."

"Yes," Packer said calmly, "I can see that."

He stared blankly at Harrison.

Realising that Packer had goaded him into a response, Harrison made a visible effort to get his anger under control. He straightened his shoulders and took a few breaths.

"Anything else you want to know?" he asked, after a while.

Packer shook his head.

"So can I get back to work again?"

Packer nodded. "Thanks for your help, Mr Harrison."

Leaving Harrison in the driveway, Packer and Thompson walked back to the car. Harrison watched them leave, then went back over to the pile of guttering and began carrying it around to the back of the property.

"Still says he didn't have a white van," Thompson said, "Do you think Kirby's leading us on?"

"Maybe," Packer said, watching Harrison, "but Frazier rang Harrison before we did. He knew we were coming, and he knew what we'd be asking."

"He certainly knew about the unit in Osbourne Park."

Packer nodded. "Frazier's connected to the unit in Osbourne Park and the flat in Girrawheen. But so is Harrison."

"It changed hands five years ago, though."

"Yeah," Packer agreed, "and three days ago, someone was using it to kill Emily."

Thompson drove down onto the street, and they headed back towards the city.

***

When they returned to the incident room, Seoyoon was alone.

"Where are the others?" Thompson asked.

"Claire hasn't come back yet," Seoyoon said, "Mickey's gone out to Osbourne Park to collect some CCTV from one of the car yards there."

"Isn't he running out of places to find it?"

Seoyoon nodded. "A lot of them only keep it for 48 hours before it gets recorded over. Most of the places he rang this morning no longer have any footage from Sunday."

"Ah, well. We're probably lucky we found what we did."

"AFP contacted me, too," Seoyoon said, "They've got the arrest warrant from Indonesia. They want to pick up Herman this afternoon and move him to their cells."

Thompson looked around.

Packer was standing in front of the whiteboard.

Emily's face sat in the middle, and the margins were filled with the information that had gathered, but there was nothing to connect any of it together. The key they needed to unlock all of this was still missing.

Thompson came to stand beside him.

"What now, boss?" he asked.

"It's there, George. The answer's there somewhere."

He stood at the whiteboard for a moment longer, before returning to his office.

***

Packer spent the next few hours on the phone to AFP arguing about who got to retain custody of Herman. Given the choice, he would have been more than happy to let AFP take Herman away and avoid the pissing contest with the federal police, but right now, he needed to keep Inspector Base on side so that he could continue the investigation. If it looked like AFP were going to take Herman, Base would force Packer to charge him with Emily's murder and shut down the enquiry.

That would mean Herman being charged for a murder Packer was sure he had not committed, and it would leave a murderer free to kill again.

So instead, he wasted precious time arguing with increasingly more senior officers at AFP as his thirty-six hours continued to run out.

By mid-afternoon, he had managed to forestall things until the next day.

As he hung up the phone, he could hear Thompson's voice in the incident room. There was a clear note of urgency in his tone.

Packer got up and walked out of his office.

Thompson was standing behind Seoyoon's desk, leaning over her shoulder as he read the screen.

"Boss," said Seoyoon, her voice intense as she looked up at Packer, "You need to look at this."

Packer walked across to her desk.

Seoyoon's computer screen had a series of windows open. The one on top was a record search of the police's internal record system.

"I was thinking about Herman getting violent with Siti. I started checking all our records for the address of the flat, thinking there might have been a previous complaint or uniform might have been called out there previously. Nothing.

"But then I started thinking it the other way around. If Billy Harrison was the aggressor, instead of Herman, then he might have got involved in something at one of the other properties when he went to collect the rent. Even if he wasn't charged, a call-out would be recorded."

"Good thinking," Packer said, "And?"

"P&R Holdings owns a whole series of shelf companies which are used to hold rental properties. So, I made a list of all the addresses and started checking them against our records."

Seoyoon pushed moved her chair back and pointed at the screen.

"This just came up when I searched one of the others."

Packer began reading over the details.

It was a report dated just over eighteen months ago, involving a girl named Mariana Chou, who had been living at a unit in Balcatta.

"There was a girl who was living at one of Frazier's units," Seoyoon said, "She went out one night and never returned. She's been missing ever since."

Chapter 29

"Yeah, I remember the job," Detective Senior Constable Pete Swallows said, his voice tinny over the phone speaker, "I don't think I'm gonna be much help to you, though. We never had that much."

Swallows was no longer stationed at Balcatta and was off-duty that day, but it had only taken a moment to locate his number on the police's internal phone list and call him at home. Seoyoon put him on speaker on the phone on her desk and Packer and Thompson stood behind him.

"She was reported as a misper?" Packer said.

"Yeah," Swallows confirmed, "She lived in this shitty flat backing onto the freeway, one of those horrible blocks of 1970's brick boxes. It was a weird set up. There was this woman calling herself Patricia, who was like this 70-year-old Chinese woman dressed up to the nines with all this make-up and fake fingernails. She was kind of looking after all these girls who were coming in from China, like some kind of fairy godmother or something."

Thompson exchanged a glance with Seoyoon. This was sounding familiar already.

"The missing girl, Mariana, had been staying with her for a couple months and working in a restaurant or cafe or something like that. I'm not real sure now. This Patricia was expecting her back and she didn't turn up for a couple of days, so she rang '000' and it got put through to us.

"Patricia didn't seem to be able to tell us anything, although there was something weird about the whole set-up, like I said."

"Weird how?" Packer asked.

"Mariana had taken some of her clothes with her but had left behind other stuff. There were all these letters in someone else's name, like dozens of them, so I'm stuffed if I know what that was about. Dan Riley was on duty with me, and I remember him asking Patricia about it. She said, 'We Chinese have many names,' whatever the fuck that's supposed to mean."

"Do you remember the name on the letters?"

"No. Something Chinese, I think. I can't remember."

"Never mind."

"We did all the standard enquiries," Swallows continued, "but never found anything. Mariana owed Patricia a couple of weeks' rent money and there was drug paraphernalia in her bedroom, so we figured she'd just done a runner. There was nothing there to suggest foul play."

There was a brief pause, while Swallows thought for a moment.

"I think that's about it. How come you're asking about this? Have you found her?"

"No," Packer said, "We're investigating a murder. The dead girl was another illegal living in a flat owned by the same man, like Mariana Chou."

"Oh, I didn't think they were illegals," Swallows said, slightly surprised, "Not Patricia, anyway. She had family here who owned the restaurant the missing girl was working at, I think."

Packer frowned.

"Are you sure about that?"

"Pretty sure. Patricia was real cagey about it, though. It was a tax scam or something."

"Do you remember the name of the restaurant?"

"Golden something. Well, they're all Golden 'something', aren't they? Nah. Sorry. I'm not sure. I would have made a note of it in the case file, though. Talk to Balcatta. They'll have it in storage."

"Alright. Thanks for your help."

Seoyoon leaned over and disconnected the phone.

There was a brief silence, while they absorbed this.

Packer looked up and found Thompson looking at him.

"What?" Packer asked.

"Told you he'd done it before."

"What?"

"The unit at Osbourne Park. He used it before-"

"Oh, don't start this shit again, George. It's not a fucking kill room."

Thompson opened his mouth to speak, then closed it again. He threw his hands up in defeat and looked away.

"Leaving aside the unit at Osbourne Park, though," Seoyoon said, carefully, "We are working on the basis that this is another murder, aren't we? Mariana Chou?"

Packer looked at her for a moment.

Then he nodded.

"So, they're living in flats owned by Frazier," Seoyoon continued, "Both immigrants with few connections, needing money."

"Not Mariana Chou," Thompson said, "She had family here."

"Patricia had family here, not Mariana," Seoyoon corrected, "and Pete Swallows didn't seem all that sure about that."

"Okay," Thompson said, "Either way, the connection's Frazier."

"Or Billy Harrison," Packer pointed out, "He's been managing Frazier's properties long enough that he would have been collecting the rent from the flat Mariana Chou was living in."

"Do we know that for sure?" Seoyoon asked.

"No," said Packer, standing up, "but let's find out."

Thompson stood up, too.

"Where are we going?"

"We'll go and collect the case file from Balcatta. Then we'll have a word with Patricia."

***

While Packer drove, Thompson rang Balcatta police station and got them to dig out the file from the storage room. It was waiting for them at the front reception desk when they arrived.

It was a depressingly-thin, buff-coloured folder.

Packer asked if they had a free room, and they were shown through to an empty interview room.

Other than the standard paperwork, there was very little in the folder itself. The contact form did at least list Patricia's full name as 'Patricia Lee,' and provide the name of the restaurant Mariana Chou worked at as the Golden Swan. There was little else, though.

As Swallows had said on the phone, they had carried out the standard enquiries, but that seemed to have been about it.

"There's nothing in here," Thompson said.

"Dan Riley was in charge," Packer said, "Have you ever met him?"

"No. Have you?"

Packer nodded. "Yeah. Lazy prick. I'm not surprised nothing's been done. He would have been desperate to find a reason to avoid doing any work on it. She owed a month's rent and there was a syringe in her room. That would have been more than enough for him to say it was an addict doing a runner and close it off."

"If we find evidence Mariana Chou has been murdered, it's the end of his job. Swallows, too, probably."

Packer nodded.

He opened the door and walked back to the reception desk.

"Can you run a details search for me?" he asked the officer there, "Current address for a Patricia Lee, DOB 12-06-54."

The officer tapped away at the keyboard for a moment, then turned the screen slightly so that Packer could see it. He read the address aloud and Packer found Patricia was still living in the same flat in Balcatta.

"Alright," he said to Thompson, "Let's see what Patricia Lee has to say for herself."

***

The edge of Balcatta closest to the freeway was industrial, with a dozen blocks of factories and warehouses. Moving further west, the suburb became residential, but its proximity to the industrial area meant that it consisted largely of cheap units and social housing. It felt much like the streets in Ghirraween where Siti and Herman lived.

Thompson stopped the car outside a block of plain brick units that looked like they had been built in the seventies. The low brick fence was still standing but a deep crack ran through it, and the wheelie bins at the front were lying on the ground.

They walked up the concrete staircase at the front and along a narrow verandah towards the back of the block.

Patricia Lee's unit was at the rear end of the verandah.

Thompson knocked at the door, and they waited.

After a few moments, the door opened.

Swallows's estimate of Patricia Lee's age was correct; she must have been around seventy, and her face was heavily lined, the skin of her neck hanging loose. But she wore heavy makeup, with rouged cheeks, dark eyeliner and bright red lipstick. Her dry-looking hair was dyed black and piled up into a bun on top of her head and fixed in place with decorative pins. She was wearing an oriental-patterned kimono with, incongruously, a Nike hoodie over the top.

"Yes," she asked, eyeing Thompson.

"Police, madam," Thompson said, dropping the 'love' that he customarily used for women. Something told him he would be wise not to get too familiar with Patricia Lee. "Are you Patricia Lee?"

She turned to look at Packer, running her eyes up and down him, before turning back to Thompson again.

"I am," she said, "Won't you please come in?"

She stepped back, holding the door open, and beckoned them in them with a slow wave. Her fingernails were lacquered red and must have been a full two inches long.

The kitchen looked like the original seventies design with chipboard doors and Laminex fronts, but genuine care had been taken to make it look presentable. The benches were lined with a neat row of spice jars and a stainless-steel rack held cooking utensils next to the sink.

The light was turned on, but covered with a thick tasseled shade that filled the kitchen with a red-tinged twilight.

There was a strong smell of fragrant incense filling the room.

Patricia waved Thompson and Packer towards the table in the centre of the room.

"Please be seated," she invited, inclining her head slightly.

The table was covered in a heavy maroon tablecloth with a bowl of flower petals in the centre. It was missing the neat rows of table settings, but otherwise looked like a Chinese restaurant.

Thompson suddenly pictured Patricia producing a menu for each of them, and he had to suppress a smile.

He introduced them both and they held up their identification. Patricia looked over the cards with a faint smile on her face, then nodded, as though showing her agreement that they were, in fact, police officers, as they had claimed.

Without asking them, Patricia moved over to the sink and filled a kettle with water. She placed it on the stove top and turned on the heat.

Then she opened the top drawer beside the stove and took out a long cigarette holder. She fitted a slim cigarette into the end and lit it. The smell of smoke was swallowed by the heavy fragrance of incense.

Inhaling delicately on the cigarette, she looked expectantly at them.

"You've lived here a few years, Ms Lee," Thompson said, "Is that right?"

"I have."

"And it's a rental property, is it? Who collects the rent?"

"Billy. He collects it every week."

"Has it always been him since you moved in?"

"Yes."

"And you live here on your own?"

"I do. Sometimes, I have others stay. Not now."

"We're making some enquiries about Mariana Chou," Thompson said.

Patricia's expression did not change, but she noticeably paused for a second, her whole body going rigid. Then she tilted her head back and slowly exhaled the smoke.

She looked at Thompson once again but said nothing.

"We understand she was living here," Thompson said, "Is that right?"

Patricia nodded. "That is correct."

"Was she related to you in some way?"

"She was not."

"How did she come to be living here?"

"I was her sponsor."

"How did that come about?"

"I was asked to do so."

"Asked by who?"

"It was arranged by a friend of the family."

"Your family or Mariana's family?"

"A friend of both families."

"How was that arranged?"

"I was contacted and asked. I agreed."

Thompson was unsure whether there was a language barrier, or whether Patrica was being deliberately vague. Either way, he felt himself beginning to grow frustrated and this slow process of question and half-answer.

"What do you mean by 'sponsor' exactly?"

"I believe it is the term used by your government. Is that not correct?"

"You mean be the Department of Immigration?"

"Yes."

"Okay. So, Mariana had authority to come here, but needed a sponsor already here in the country?"

"That is correct."

"You're Australian?"

"I am not Australian. I am a permanent resident."

"Okay. So, this arrangement was made while you were living here, but before Mariana came here?"

"That is correct."

"Did you know Mariana before she came here?"

"I did not."

"But you agreed to sponsor her?"

"That is correct."

"Why?"

"We Chinese always help each other, no matter where we are. It is our way."

"How long did Mariana live here?"

Patricia pouted as she considered this, a spider's web of wrinkles appearing around her mouth. "Perhaps half a year."

"What was she doing here? I mean, was she working or what?"

"She was."

"And where was that?"

"A restaurant."

Again, the vague half-answers. Thompson was certain now that Patricia was being deliberately unhelpful. He felt his irritation rising.

"Look, Ms Lee," he said, doing his best to keep his voice level, "These are very serious matters. We're investigating the death of a young lady."

Patricia raised her eyebrows and inclined her head slightly. "You believe that Mariana might have been involved in this death?"

Thompson frowned at the oddness of the question.

"No," he said, "but we've been investigating the death of this girl. We know about this girl's living circumstances before she died, and there are certain similarities between how she was living and how Chanxin was living."

"She was also Chinese?"

"No. That's not what I meant. She had recently come here to Australia, but not from China. I can't really tell you much about those details, but it's important that you tell us everything you know about Mariana."

"I am doing so."

"Mariana was working in a restaurant named the Golden Swan," Packer said, cutting in, "We know this already. That restaurant is owned by a family member of yours. We know that, too."

Patricia remained in the same position, but her eyes swivelled to focus on Packer. She looked at him without blinking.

"When she failed to come home one night, you contacted the police. You told them that were expecting her home, but she had not arrived."

Patricia looked at him in silence.

"You were obviously worried about her then," Packer continued, "even if the officers who came here at the time were not."

He was taking a punt on that, but there was the slightest twitch at the corner of Patricia's eye that told him he was correct.

"They should have shown more interest in Mariana. I'm sorry they didn't. But we do want to find out what we can. And we need your help."

For a long moment, Patricia simply stared at him in silence, her face blank.

Then she lifted the cigarette to her mouth and took a long draw on it. She held the smoke in her mouth for a moment, then let it out slowly.

"I will help you. What do you wish to know?"

"Did you have any idea what had happened to Mariana?" Packer asked, "Any suspicions? Anything you were worried about?"

Patricia took a slow breath, then let it out again. Once more, she lifted the cigarette to her mouth and inhaled a lungful of smoke, then let it out slowly.

"We Chinese have always understood the virtue of patience. For generations, we have been content to wait. But children now have no understanding of patience. Everything must be now for them.

"Chanxin was the same. For her, nothing could come quickly enough. She could have waited for citizenship in Australia, but she would not. Instead, she must come now. She could have saved a little money, but she wanted more now. Always now."

Patricia looked at Packer.

"This made her do foolish things. She became involved in terrible things. Evil things."

"What things?" Packer asked.

"It is not my place to tell you this."

Packer felt his own frustration rising but kept a hold on his temper.

"If we could ask Mariana - Chanxin - herself, we would, but we can't. We need you to help us. What was she involved in?"

Patricia stared back at him, her face blank, but her eyes oddly defiant.

She said nothing.

"A girl's dead," Packer said, brutally, "Her name was Emily. She was nineteen. She had a future ahead of her. It was stolen from her. She was tied up. She was raped. She was strangled. Then she was dumped in an alleyway and left to rot.

"I want to find the man who did it. Help me to do that."

Patricia flinched, as though she had been slapped.

She stared back at Packer for a long moment. Then she dropped her eyes to the floor.

With a hand that was shaking now, she lifted the cigarette to her mouth and inhaled, her breath uneven. For a moment, she held the smoke in her lungs, then let it out slowly.

She looked up at Packer, her eyes milky.

"Forget about Chanxin. She is in a better place now."

"I think so, too," Packer said, "That's why I need you to tell us what you know. Help us find out how she died."

Patricia's eyes narrowed, a frown of confusion on her face.

Then she grinned, lips pulled back over nicotine-stained teeth. She gave a braying snort of laughter.

She looked at Packer and shook her head.

Holding the long cigarette holder delicately between the middle and ring fingers on one hand, she opened the top drawer again and moved things around.

She withdrew her hand, holding a plain, white envelope.

Reaching in with surprising grace, despite the lacquered red talons, she eased out a letter and unfolded it then handed it to Packer.

Packer took the letter and turned it over.

A single page was covered with row upon row of tiny, neat Chinese characters.

"What is this?" he asked.

"An apology," Patricia said, "One month after she left, I received this letter from Chanxin. She is not dead. She is living in a better place now."

Chapter 30

Claire Perry looked at her mobile phone again. No messages.

She looked through the window of the tiny coffee shop at the street outside and decided to give it another ten minutes. She had spent over an hour driving all the way down here to Mandurah, then forty minutes waiting here, and would have to spend another hour driving back to Perth afterwards.

A woman appeared at the edge of the window and peered inside. Her eyes locked on Claire's and she stared for a moment.

Claire gave her a tiny wave and a slight smile of encouragement.

The woman stared at her a moment longer without smiling.

Then she walked slowly towards the door of the coffee shop and entered.

"Georgia?" Claire asked.

The woman nodded. "Are you Claire?"

Her voice was low and carried an odd croak.

Claire nodded. "What can I get you? The cappuccino here's good."

The woman gave a slight nod. "Okay."

Careful to remain casual, Claire gave a vague wave towards the chair on the opposite side of her table and turned back towards the counter.

Georgia sat down in the chair, sitting stiffly upright and holding her handbag protectively against her stomach. She said nothing as the waitress came to the table and Claire ordered two cappuccinos.

As the waitress left, Claire turned back towards Georgia.

Georgia was probably only in her late twenties, but she looked ten years older than that. Her face had the gaunt cheeks and sunken eyes of hard living. Her shoulder-length hair needed a wash and she smelled strongly of tobacco.

Claire chatted idly while they waited for the coffees to arrive, doing her best to put Georgia at ease. Georgia gave a few half-hearted responses, but said little, remaining stiff in the chair.

Eventually, the coffees arrived and Claire took a sip. Georgia left her cup untouched.

"I'm really glad you agreed to meet me," Claire said, "Suzanne told me you might be able to help me with something."

Georgia looked down at the table and gave a slight shrug.

"I'm trying to find out about a guy in Perth who gets pretty rough with girls."

Georgia remained silent.

"Suzanne said you told her about a guy like that," Claire prompted, "You know who I mean?"

Georgia was silent for a long moment.

"I don't do that stuff any more," she said quietly, "I come down here to get away from it."

"It's good you got away from it. A lot of girls can't. It's hard. And I'm sorry to have to talk about it again, but it's really important."

There was no response from Georgia.

"The guy I want to know about likes to tie up girls. Puts something around their neck. Suzanne said you told her about that."

Still no response.

"Did that happen to you, Georgia?"

Nothing.

"I'm really sorry to have to ask you about it," Claire said gently, "but I need you to tell me whatever you can. Did it happen to you?"

Georgia looked up at her, her eyes blazing.

"I don't know nothing," she said sharply, "Suzanne's wrong, okay? I don't know nothing. Sorry."

She stood up, the legs of the chair scraping loudly across the floor, and turned to go, clutching at her handbag.

The waitress looked over at the noise.

"Georgia, wait," Claire said, standing up and putting a hand on Georgia's arm, "Please. I know this is hard, but it's really important."

Georgia tried to shrug her hand off, but Claire held on.

"A girl's dead, Georgia," Claire said, keeping her voice low, "It could have been this man."

Georgia pulled her arm away and Clair was forced to let go.

Georgia stood still, looking at the ground, but making no move towards the door.

"If we don't find this man," Claire said, "He might kill again. Nobody wants that. Please help me."

For a long moment, Georgia stood in place, her body rigid.

Then she muttered something unintelligible.

"Say again?" Claire said, "I didn't hear."

Georgia sniffed hard, sucking back a sob.

"It was nearly me," she said, voice breaking, "He nearly killed me."

***

"So, the letter has Bencubbin post mark on it," said Seoyoon, "and all this Patricia knows is that she's working as a farm hand for a Chinese family?"

Thompson nodded.

"It's not much to go on."

"Aye, lass," Thompson said, with a grin, "but we know you can work miracles."

Seoyoon raised an eyebrow at him.

"Where's Bencubbin?" Mickey called from his desk.

"Out in the wheatbelt," Thompson said, "It's like *Wolf Creek* out there. Anyway, haven't you got CCTV to check through?"

"This is the last of it," Mickey said, "Once I'm finished, that's it."

"Off you go, then," Thompson said, nodding towards Mickey's screen.

"The area's not huge," Packer said to Seoyoon, "Maybe a thousand people in the farms around there that come into town sometimes. The police out there will have some local knowledge, and so will the post office, the agricultural suppliers, whoever. It'll be a fairly big farm if they need to employ staff. It's owned by Chinese. They've got a girl working for them who is in her mid-twenties, who turned up about eighteen months ago. She was known in Perth as Mariana before she fled, then she'll be using a different name now. Maybe even her real name if she's living with a Chinese family."

"Alright," Seoyoon said, unconvinced, "I'll see what I can find."

Packer moved over to the whiteboard. In the bottom corner, he wrote, 'Mariana Chou,' together with the date of her disappearance. Below this, he wrote a series of dot points: immigrant girls, prostitution, living in Frazier's properties, Harrison collecting rent.

"It's a definite pattern," Thompson said, "but what's the connection between the two girls?"

"When we find Mariana Chou, we'll ask."

"You're sure she's still alive?"

Packer nodded. "Patricia got the letter a month after she disappeared."

"Could have been faked."

"Why?"

"To cover up the fact that Mariana Chou's dead."

"Patricia believed it was genuine. If the handwriting or the language used were off, she might not have."

"Maybe Mariana was forced to write it before she was killed," Thompson suggested, "and it was then sent later."

"It's a lot of effort to go to, George," Packer pointed out, "and there was nothing similar with Emily."

"Aye, well, Emily didn't have anyone here who would worry about her. Just Siti."

"That's true," Packer conceded, "but until we know otherwise, we have to work on the basis that she's still alive."

"Do we think Mariana was working as a prostitute?" Mickey asked, standing behind them.

"Patricia said she was involved in 'something terrible,'" Thompson said, "although she didn't actually say prostitution. What else could it be, though?"

"There's a drugs connection," Packer pointed out.

"Did Patricia confirm that?" Seoyoon asked.

Packer shook his head. "No, but the case file at Balcatta says they found a couple of syringes in Mariana's things, one used and one still in the packet."

"Could the drugs be the 'something terrible' that Patricia meant?"

"Maybe," Packer said, "but she still had to pay for the drugs somehow."

He thought for a moment.

"Actually, the drugs don't fit the pattern. Emily wasn't using."

He wrote 'drugs' on the whiteboard under Mariana Chou's name and put a circle around it.

"It goes with the lifestyle, though," Thompson said, "Maybe she just hadn't been servicing clients long enough."

Packer nodded. "Maybe."

There was a logical sense to that. Prostitution was an ugly occupation and most of the girls used drugs to take the edge off. They had to pay for the drugs, too, which meant they quickly became more heavily entrenched in prostitution to fund their habit.

"Do you think there are others?" Seoyoon asked, "Other girls missing, I mean?"

"Aye," Thompson said, quietly, "There are others."

Packer gave him a warning look.

The phone rang, breaking the tension.

"I'll get it," Seoyoon said, glad of the excuse.

She got up and hurried over to her desk.

"We've found two," Thompson insisted.

"As far as we know, Mariana Chou's not dead," Packer pointed out.

"I'll believe that when we speak to her."

"Well, you might get your chance."

They were interrupted by a clicking sound.

They both turned to look at Seoyoon.

She was half-standing up, behind her desk, her head to one side, holding the phone in place against her ear with her shoulder. She was using a pen to tap on the top of her computer screen.

As they both began to walk over to her desk, she sat down and began tapping quickly at her keyboard.

Packer and Thompson listened while Seoyoon spoke on the phone.

After a few minutes, she hung up.

"That was AFP," she said.

"Wanting Herman again?" Thompson said, looking at Packer, "I thought we'd put that off for now."

"Not about Herman," Seoyoon said.

"What then?"

"They're watching Sheffler's bank account."

Thompson looked at her in confusion. "Okay. Steady on, lass. Start at the beginning."

"Sorry," Seoyoon said, "The owner of the Osbourne Park unit sent me the bank account number where the rent is paid form. I got a warrant and sent it over to the bank earlier today, asking for the details of the account holder. The account is held here, but the account holder is Roger Scheffler, and he used an address in Indonesia."

"Indonesia?" Thompson said.

Seoyoon nodded.

"Because it was offshore, I can't trace it. But AFP can, so I rang them and left a message with their finance section while you were out, so they could make enquiries through the Indonesian police.

"But when they started running the account details, it brought up an alert on their system. The AFP have an active investigation into that bank account already. The officer in charge of that investigation just called me back."

"Why?"

"They're investigating Roger Scheffler."

"What for?" Thompson asked.

"Importing pornography. They intercepted a parcel through international document exchange with his name on it that was filled with illegal DVDs. AFP kept surveillance on the DX drop, but nobody turned up to collect the package, so they figure he got a tip-off and stayed away. They traced previous shipments through the same DX, so they think he's bringing it in from overseas in big quantities."

Packer felt something shift at the edge of his thinking. Pieces that didn't fit before were beginning to slide into place.

"Who imports porn these days?" Mickey asked, "You get it free on the internet. There's about a thousand sites with millions of free videos."

"How do you know this, son?" Thompson dead-panned, "Did a friend tell you that?"

"Everyone knows that," Mickey retorted, but he at least had the grace to blush.

"Not like the kind Roger Scheffler is bringing in," Seoyoon said, "It's highly illegal."

"Kids?" Thompson asked.

"No. But apparently, it's really nasty stuff. Involving torture, and women forced to have sex with animals."

"So, what's the connection with the Osbourne Park unit?" Thompson asked, "His distribution centre?"

"No," said Packer, quietly, "He's not importing it. He's exporting it. That's why the walls are soundproofed, and the windows are painted over. It's his studio. He's filming it here."

Chapter 31

"Took me a while, but I tracked down this girl named Georgia," Claire told the rest of the team, "She was a working girl in Northbridge two years ago. She's down in Mandurah now. She's trying to get off drugs and get herself clean.

"She knew exactly who I meant when I started asking about a guy who ties girls up and chokes them."

She got out her notebook to read back over her notes as she recounted what Georgia had told her.

"She was working the streets here for a couple of years to pay for a meth habit. She got picked up one night by a guy in a car who said his name was Roger. She told this Roger it was fifty for oral. She blew him and then he gave her the fifty, plus another two hundred. Told her that he had a way for her to make a lot more money, thousands of dollars. Georgia thought this all sounded shonky, but she owed a lot of money to her dealer, so had to take the risk.

"This Roger collected her one night, then took her to an empty shop out in the suburbs. When she got there, there was a video camera set up and big lights. Another guy filmed Roger having sex with her and they gave her five hundred for it.

"Roger told her she'd done a great job and said his customers were gonna love it. Said he wanted to film her again if she was up for it. Five hundred was more than she usually made in a whole night, so she agreed.

"The next few times, it was just straight sex," Claire continued, "but then it started to move into something stronger. Roger paid her a thousand to tie her to a post and had sex with her wearing a mask. The next time, it was two thousand, but he blindfolded her and spanked her hard enough to bruise. The money kept getting higher and he kept moving into more and more hardcore S&M stuff. Georgia needed the money, so she went along with this.

"One night, Roger bound her wrists and ankles with cable ties. Then he put a belt around her neck and started tightening it while he was forcing her to perform oral on him. She passed out, and he had to slap her around to bring her to.

"Afterwards, he paid her and told her he wanted to do another scene the following week.

"She was too scared to say no but went straight home to collect her stuff and got out of Perth the same night."

"Very wise," said Thompson, "Otherwise it might have been her in the alleyway in Northbridge."

"That's what she thought, too," Claire said.

"The place where this Roger took her to make these videos," Packer said, "Was it always the same place?"

"That's what she said, yeah," Claire said.

"Did she say where it was?"

Claire shook her head. "I don't think she knew. Roger always drove her there. She said it was a small shop in a row of others. The windows were covered up and there was padding on the walls."

"Sound like the Osbourne Park unit," Thompson said.

Packer nodded.

Thompson looked at him. "I got carried away about that place, boss. I should have listened to you."

Packer dismissed the apology with a shake of his head.

"What about this Roger?" he asked Claire, "Did she describe him?"

"Not really. White male, middle-aged, blonde or brown hair, average height, average build. No distinguishing marks."

"Can we get an artist down there to see her?" Mickey suggested, "See if she can do a sketch of this bloke?"

"Have you ever seen one of those things that looked like the actual suspect?" Claire asked him, "because I never have."

"What about the other man?" Packer asked, "The one filming it?"

"She never got a good look at him. White male. That was about it."

"The car he picked her up in?"

"White sedan with dark upholstery. That's it."

"Pretty bloody useless witness," Mickey said, "Doesn't she remember anything?"

"Well, she was high on drugs for most of it," Claire snapped, "and it was two years ago."

Mickey raised his hands in front of him.

"Well, it definitely eliminates Herman, at least," Thompson said, "No mistaking him for a middle-aged white man with blonde hair."

"The inspector's gonna explode when he hears that," Mickey said.

"Aye," Thompson agreed, "but he can take comfort from the fact that we didn't charge the wrong man by mistake."

Packer closed his eyes and rubbed them with his fingers. There was something nagging at the back of his mind, something just out of sight.

***

Seoyoon tried the Bencubbin police station, but neither of the officers stationed there knew of anyone local who might have been Mariana Chou. The post office knew of several Chinese families who farmed in the area, but none with a woman in her twenties.

The hardware store and local council were of little help either.

She had spent nearly three hours working her way through most of the local businesses when she found what she needed.

"Boss," she said, tapping on Packer's office door, "I think I've found her. There's a motor mechanic in town who was called out to a local farm about six months ago to fix a tractor that had slipped a camshaft, whatever that means. He knew the farmer, a Mr Chen, who works the property with two sons, and had done work on his truck and some other machinery before.

"When he got out to the farm, there was a young woman there working in the fields who he'd never seen before. He figured one of the sons must have got married and asked Mr Chen about this.

"Mr Chen got aggressive with him and sent the woman inside. He said Chen couldn't get him off the farm fast enough after that."

"Have you got an address for the Chen farm?" Packer asked.

Seoyoon nodded and held out a sheet torn from her notebook.

***

After the rest of the team left, Packer returned to his office to review the tiny amount of material in the case file for Mariana Chou's disappearance. He thought again over what Patrica had told him.

He tried to get a feel for the girl. In a foreign country with no family, living with the eccentric woman they had spoken to earlier in the day.

Why had she fled, leaving her possessions behind, then written the letter a month later to tell Patricia she was safe?

How did this fit with the syringes found in her things?

There were many similarities with Emily's disappearance, but things that didn't fit the pattern either.

He realised it had grown late and left the station to buy takeaway food for dinner.

He ate at his desk, tasting none of it, as he reviewed the material again, trying to make some sense of it.

He was tired, but sleep would not come, and he made more coffee.

He took a mouthful of the bitter liquid, feeling it burning down his throat as he swallowed.

Leaning back in the chair, he placed the coffee cup on his knee, holding it in place with his hand against the armrest.

Slumped back in the chair, he began to drift.

A light blazed from the darkness, blinding her with its intensity.

There was movement in the shadows behind the light, a man watching her from behind the camera. His face was hidden by the glare and impossible to make out.

Emily turned away from the glare, her wrists and ankles bound to the table and lowered her head, waiting.

Footsteps echoed across the room, their sound muffled by the insulation covering the walls.

She turned her head from side to side, trying to find their source.

A shadow cut through the glare, moving between her and the light.

She looked up at him, but his face was blank, features hidden behind the mask. Only his eyes were alive, staring at her without blinking.

He raised the belt, holding it in front of her face.

His hand jerked, and she flinched away, but the belt slapped against the palm of his other hand, the sound piercingly loud beside her ears.

As he slowly wrapped it around the back of her neck, Emily pulled back, straining against her bonds.

He held the belt in place against her throat and began to tighten.

She tried to speak, to beg, but could not.
His arm shook with the strain, as he cut off her air.

Sudden pain cut through Packer's leg as the spilled coffee seeped through the leg of his trousers, burning his skin.

"Shit," he grunted, jerking upright in the chair and lifting the coffee cup off his leg.

He placed the cup on the desk, leaving a ring of spilled coffee beneath it, and stood up quickly. There was a wet squelch from the wet patch on his thigh, and he felt the hot liquid dribbling down his leg.

He stood there for a moment, breathing hard.

Then he went to find something to clean up the spilled coffee.

It was going to be a long night.

Friday

Chapter 32

It was still dark when Packer arrived at Thompson's house.

He had spent most of the night pacing the floor at the station and checking the clock on the incident room wall.

Thompson answered his mobile after Packer's second call, groggily promising to be out shortly. Five minutes later, he emerged from the front door, wearing a shirt and trousers, and carrying a tie in one hand and his electric shaver in the other.

Thompson slumped into the passenger seat and was still pulling the door closed as Packer reversed out of the driveway.

"Christ, boss," Thompson mumbled, "It's the middle of the bloody night. It's not even five o'clock yet."

Packer ignored him, accelerating through the dark towards the freeway.

Bencubbin lay three and a half hours away from Perth.

They had a long drive ahead of them.

***

The turn-off from the freeway took them along a sealed bitumen road whose condition deteriorated the further they got from Perth.

As the sum began to rise, suburban houses were replaced with larger rural properties and eventually those too disappeared.

Thompson persuaded Packer to stop at a remote service station so that he could buy breakfast and coffee before they continued driving.

An endless road lined with cattle farms and paddocks lay before them, before these too gave way to miles of red dirt and bush.

It was bleak country with nothing around.

After several hours of driving, fenced properties began to appear beside the road once again, followed eventually by signs telling them that Bencubbin was up ahead.

It was mid-morning when they reached the town itself.

The main street looked like any other rural town in Western Australia. A road ran through the centre of town, lined on either side with tiny shops that had been here since the town was settled over a hundred years earlier, and a pub at the end of the street.

There was mobile phone reception, but it was patchy.

Packer had thought ahead, though, and had printed out the map of the area he had found during the night. Thompson followed the narrow lines on the page, directing Packer as they left the tiny township and headed along unsealed roads leading into an empty expanse of crop fields.

They drove for another thirty minutes, before seeing signs of their destination

Rouch fencing made of steel posts with wire stretched between them lined either side of the road. Eventually, they found a break in the fencing where a wide dirt track led away from the road.

Packer slowed down and turned off the road.

Years of use had turned the rough track at the front of the property into two parallel ruts that led into a wider area beside a wooden house. The porch was surrounded by piles of wood and empty plastic containers from agricultural chemicals. A huge water tank sat rusting beside the house and a Landcruiser ute with a flatbed tray was parked beside it.

Packer stopped behind the ute and they got out.

A screen door was closed, its peeling flyscreen held in place at the edges with dirty electrical tape. A couple of holes were patched with tape of a different colour.

Thompson banged on the door but got no answer.

After a few minutes, he tried calling out, but still got no response.

He tried the handle, but the door was locked, which seemed a pointless gesture, given that it was ready to fall off its hinges with the slightest amount of force.

"Let's try out the back," Packer said.

They walked past the water tank and the ute.

A row of poorly maintained hedges provided a natural fence from the front of the property.

Behind the hedge stretched rows of wheat that disappeared into the distance. The plants further away were the height of a man, but those closer to them had been cut down to only a few inches off the ground.

A couple of hundred metres away was a tractor, moving slowly across the field, pulling a wide cutter behind it. Figures in broad-brimmed hats moved on either side, stooping down as they moved behind the cutter, then straightening to load the severed plants into a trailer that lay between them.

Packer and Thompson began walking towards them.

The dirt blew up around their feet, the remains of the cut wheat catching on the legs of their trousers.

When they were a hundred metres or so away, one of the figures saw them and stopped gathering up the plants.

There was the sound of words, too far away to make out, and the others stopped and straightened up, too.

They watched in silence and Packer and Thompson walked towards them.

As they drew closer, Packer could see them better.

A Chinese man, aged somewhere between sixty and seventy stood near the front, his shoulders rounded from a lifetime of hard, manual labour. A woman of about the same age stood near him. It was her that had seen them first.

Two younger men, both Chinese were further behind them, one carrying a rake.

Further back, Packer could see a woman. Her broad-brimmed hat cast a shadow over her face, but he could make out her features. She younger, in her twenties, and Chinese too.

She was too far away to make out any more detail.

The farmers watched them in silence as they approached.

"Hello," Thompson called, producing his identification, "Police. Are you Mr and Mrs Chen?"

The older couple looked at them without a response.

"No trouble here," said the man, after a moment.

"We're looking for a young lady," Thompson said, "Chanxin Chou."

There was no response.

Packer looked past them to the young woman standing at the back. She was about fifty metres away.

"No trouble here," said the man again, "That person no' here."

Packer pointed to the young woman at the back.

"Can we have a quick word with her, please?"

"That no' who you want," the man said firmly, "That person no' here."

"Even so," Packer said.

The old man stared at him, a firm expression on his face.

The younger man holding the rake called out something in Chinese, a distinct note of hostility in his tone.

Without taking his eyes off Packer, the old man turned his head slightly to the side and yelled back a response.

He looked at Packer for a moment.

Then he lowered his head, moving his gaze to the ground. He waved Packer past.

He stood there in silence as Packer walked past him.

Packer had to pass the two younger men, who stared hard at him, but said nothing.

When Packer reached the young woman, she was standing still, her eyes on the ground.

Packer stopped two metres in front of her.

"Hello," he said, "My name's Tony Packer. I'm a police officer. You're not in trouble, Chanxin. I just need some help."

The woman stared at the ground, saying nothing.

"I cannot help," she said, her voice so low Packer could barely hear her.

"Please," he said, "It's important."

She shook her head in silence.

Packer took a deep breath, as he watched her.

"I'm investigating the murder of a girl named Emily," he said, "She was nineteen. Bound and strangled. Left naked in an alleyway. I want to find the man who did it."

The woman continued staring at the ground. She was silent.

"It could have been you," Packer said, "If I don't find him, it could be someone else."

There was a long moment of silence.

After a moment, Chanxin walked past Packer to the older man. She stood in front of him with her head down and they spoke in Chinese.

Then she turned back towards Packer.

"I will tell you what I know," she said quietly.

She began walking back towards the house. The old man glared at Packer and Thompson as they passed, following behind her.

There was a slight breeze blowing, lifting the residue of the wheat through the air. With the faintest of crackling, the wheat crops shifted in the breeze as they followed her across the field towards the house.

In the open expanse of the field, Chanxin looked so tiny.

***

When they reached the house, Chanxin took off the wide hat and placed it on a table on the porch. Her glossy, black hair was pulled into a tight ponytail behind her head.

She was wearing gloves made of a thick fabric and took these off, placing them neatly on the table beside the hat.

With a tiny hand, she opened the back door to the house and led them inside.

The door opened onto a kitchen that was old, but neatly kept. A large sack of rice leant against the wall and a pile of vegetables covered in dirt lay on the bench. In the centre was a large table, its Laminex top scarred from decades of use.

Chanxin gestured towards two chairs with a flat hand, then sat opposite.

She stared at the tabletop, her hands clasped together in her lap.

Packer and Thompson sat opposite.

Packer looked at Thompson.

"We've spoken to Patricia," Thompson said, "So we know some of what happened. We need you to tell us the rest."

Chanxin was silent.

"Patricia told us you came to live with her when you came to Australia," continued Thompson, "She was a friend of the family."

Chanxin gave no response, simply sitting with her head down.

"What made you decide to come to Australia?"

"I had no choice," Chanxin said, quietly.

"Why was that?"

Chanxin was silent for a moment.

She inhaled slowly, then breathed out.

"My father was a financier in Hong Kong," she said, her voice clear, her accent almost British, "He was a very clever man and very good at his job. But he had a mistress and a gambling habit. For many years, he hid this. And then one day, men came looking for the money he owed. My mother was heartbroken. There was only one choice left for me. I came here where I could earn money to pay for my father's debts."

She fell silent again.

"And you worked in a restaurant?" Thompson prompted, "The Gilded Swan?"

Chanxin gave a slight grimace.

"I was training to be an accountant in Hong Kong. I had nearly completed my studies when I was forced to leave.

"Here, I was plucking chickens, gutting fish. The hot oil burned my hands, scarring them. I smelled of fish always, no matter how much I washed. I was abused for my heritage, ridiculed for being from a wealthy family, yet forced to clean up offal with my hands. And I was paid a pittance. No matter how many hours I worked, I could never pay my father's debts and the interest was increasing every day.

"One evening as I left Patricia's home to go to work at the restaurant, a man approached me. His name was Roger. He told me he had seen me at the building before. He was aware of my situation. I do not know how. He told me I could make money. So much money I would never have to work in the kitchen again."

Chanxin's voice was oddly flat and emotionless.

"I am no fool. I knew what was being proposed. I considered refusing him. But I could not. If I returned to the kitchen, I would work for six hours and make only a few dollars. Being paid much more to have sex with a man did not seem so terrible.

"And at first, it was a merciful release. I could send money to my mother in sums large enough to make a difference. I told myself I was a courtesan, and I tried to excel being one."

She looked up at them, her almond-shaped eyes oddly defiant. "Does that sound terrible?"

Thompson shook his head. "Of course not, love."

"I expected Patricia to be angry when I did not return to her brother's restaurant. But she was not. She had expected that I would leave when I found a better alternative. I was evasive when she asked what I was doing, but she suspected. She was no fool either.

"After a few weeks, Roger proposed a way to make even more money. I would have sex in front of a camera. I agreed immediately. I could pay my father's debt faster and be done with this.

"After the first occasion, we watched the footage together. The girl I saw on the screen was not me. She was someone else. It made me feel I had lost a part of myself. I was sick afterwards. But always there was the debt, always there was the need for more money.

"I began using drugs. They numbed me, sent me somewhere else while the other girl on the screen had sex for money. Soon, my father's debt was forgotten. I was performing only to pay for the drugs that I needed to continue.

"Roger began to wear a mask. I realised then that he had shown the earlier films to nobody else because he would be recognised. And he wanted to be anonymous for what would follow."

Chanxin's voice remained steady, and she did not move, but a tear ran down her cheek. It was followed by another.

"He began to tie me. To whip me with rope. He urinated on my face, made me drink it. He laughed at me while I beat me. I did whatever he told me to do, and in return I could purchase the drugs I required.

"This continued for many months. I became ill, unable to think, unable to refuse. My body was a mass of bruises, my only thought was for my drugs."

"What did he look like, this man, Roger?" Thompson asked.

"Younger than you," she said, "but not much. Maybe his middle forties. He was white, blonde hair. Your height."

"Was he alone?"

"Sometimes. At other times, he brought another to operate the camera."

"What did the other man look like?"

"Older, I think. Fatter. He was unmasked, and always careful to remain where I could not see him."

"Where were these films were made?"

"Yes. A small building. A room that was blackened and insulated so no sound would escape."

"Where was this building?"

"The northern suburbs, I believe. I do not know exactly where. Roger blindfolded me at first, making a joke of this. Later, I was too affected by the drugs to know where he was taking me, and he no longer bothered to cover my eyes."

"Was it always the same place?"

Chanxin sucked in a hard breath, her voice breaking in a loud whimper.

It took her several minutes to recover.

"It was always the same building, until the very last time. Then it was another place."

She stopped again, rubbing at her eyes with tiny hands, her breathing coming out in a hiss.

"After that last time," she wept, her words almost incoherent, "I wanted to die. But I could not. I ran. For days, I slept on the street. Every second, I wanted to go back. I needed the drugs. But I knew what I must do to pay for them. And I could not.

"I do not know what happened in those weeks. But eventually, I was found. I was brought here, and I was cared for."

Chanxin wept, her tiny shoulders shaking uncontrollably. She covered her face with her hands, the fingers pressed against her skin as she wept.

They waited long minutes until she could recover.

"The last time," Packer said, "was somewhere different."

Chanxin's mouth opened wide, and she sucked in a loud breath. She gave a low whimper.

She nodded.

"Can you tell us what happened?"

For a long moment, she was silent.

When she began, her voice was oddly flat again.

"One day, Roger collected me in his car and gave me drugs. More than usual. I expected to be taken to the same warehouse. Instead, he drove near the river and took me somewhere else. When he stopped the car, he told me, 'You have a new co-star today, a real stud.'

"I was so affected by the drugs that I did understand what he meant until he took me inside.

"The place was filthy and smelled of faeces. The lights were on, and the camera was ready. The other man stood behind the lights watching. Roger made me lie across a bench in the centre of the place and tied my hands and feet down, so that I could not move."

Chanxin let out a low whimper.

"Light flooded the room as a door was open behind me. I heard the sound as the horse was pulled inside. Even through the haze of the drugs, I knew what was going to happen. What was going to be done to me.

"I screamed and tried to pull my hands free, but I could not move. They laughed at me.

"I felt the horse on top of me as they moved it into place, its legs against mine.

"There was pain, pain like I had never imagined."

Her voice trailed away, as she began to weep again.

Packer suddenly pictured the black-painted windows and the soundproofing inside the workshop in Osbourne Park.

A private place.

An isolated place.

A place cut off from any chance of being discovered.

"Where did this happen?" Packer asked.

"In the stables."

"Stables where?" Packer asked.

Chanxin shook her head.

"His own stables. Behind his house."

It fell into place

Packer's stomach tensed, like he had been punched.

"Near the stables," Packer said, quietly.

"What?" Thompson asked.

"He told us he lived in Ascot near the stables. We've got to get back to the city, George. It's Kirby."

Chapter 33

They broke several speed limits on the way back to Perth.

The police car was unmarked but was fitted with concealed sirens and flashing lights on the front and rear dashboards. Packer activated these as they neared the city, encouraging the traffic along the freeway to move out of his way as he weaved between cars.

When they turned off the freeway past the airport and entered the Great Eastern Highway, he cut off the lights and sirens and reduced his speed. Kirby's house at Ascot was only a few minutes' drive from here.

Ascot was an odd pocket of housing. Despite being prime real estate near the river, its proximity to the racetrack meant that the blocks were zoned as equestrian and could not be sub-divided or developed into the towers of luxury apartment buildings that lined the river further along.

The result was twenty blocks of dilapidated post-war houses. Most of them still had stables in the backyards, although less than half still housed horses.

Thompson found the address for Kirby's property part way along Matheson Road. The houses on either side were run-down, with overgrown front yards, fences that needed repair and peeling paint. Kirby's front yard had been paved over to avoid mowing and the fence was still standing, but there was an air of neglect about the place.

Thompson knocked on the front door, and they heard the sound echoing hollowly inside. There was no response, and he tried again after a few minutes.

Still no response.

"No car in the driveway," Thompson pointed out, "Maybe he's out."

Packer said nothing.

There was a large window next to the front door, which probably faced out from the lounge room. It had curtains drawn across it, making it impossible to see inside.

"Let's try down the back," Packer said.

There was a concrete strip between the side of the house and the fence twice the width of a car. Two wooden gates seven feet high closed it off and prevented any view into the backyard.

"Locked," Thompson said, trying the handle on the gate.

"Try the other side," Packer said.

The other side of the house had a much narrower path between the house and fence. A high, wooden gate blocked it off and was secured with a chain and padlock.

Packer put his hands on top of the gate and pulled himself off the ground, so that he could see over the top of the fence into the backyard. There was a Colorbond shed in the far corner on this side of the yard and a larger building on the other side, but he could only see the end of it from here.

He could not see any sign of movement.

"Give me a leg up," Packer said.

"I don't think he's here, boss," Thompson said.

"Let's have a look anyway."

Thompson cupped his hands together and Packer put one foot in them. Holding on to the top of the gate with his hands, Packer pulled himself up and swung one leg over the top.

He dropped down to the other side of the gate and looked back at Thompson.

"Go around to the other gate," Packer said, "I'll see if it opens from the other side."

"Right, boss."

Packer walked down the side of the house, hearing nothing.

The backyard was large. Most of the blocks in Ascot were quarter-acre blocks, which was huge by current Perth standards. The ground had large bare patches and where there was grass growing, it had not been mowed in a while.

A Hills Hoist stood in the centre, rusting away and joined to the house by a concrete path that had weeds growing around its edges.

As Packer rounded the corner, he could see the stables against the side of the yard nearest the wooden gate. Four wide doors covering the front. Dark green paint covered the surface but was now peeling.

The stables lay silent, now unoccupied.

Packer walked back along the concrete path to the wider wooden gate.

It was closed with a thick bolt at the top and a metal latch in the middle. Neither were locked, and Packer undid both.

He pushed open one of the gates and Thompson stepped through.

"Anyone home?" Thompson asked.

"Haven't seen anyone," Packer said, standing still, as he looked back towards the rear yard.

"What is it, boss?"

Packer shook his head. "I don't know. Something just feels...off."

Thompson stood beside him for a moment, listening.

"You're giving me the heebie-jeebies, too, now," he said, managing a smile. But he could feel it, too. There was something strange about the place.

Thompson pulled the gates together and closed the latch again.

They walked along the concrete towards the backyard.

"Have a look in the shed," Packer said.

Thompson headed around the clothesline over to the far corner.

Packer walked up to the stables and tried the first door.

The handle gave only a little before stopping. It was locked.

He walked along to the second and found it locked as well.

Expecting to find the third one locked, too, he was surprised when the handle turned down easily.

He pushed the door inwards.

The inside of the building was almost completely dark. There were a couple of skylights overhead, but they were filthy and covered with fallen leaves, leaving the place in darkness.

There was a smell of damp and filth about the place. And another smell, too, something sweet and chemical.

In one direction, Packer could see waist-high beams where horses had once been corralled. There was a larger shape in darkness on the other side.

Packer looked around the walls beside the door, but it was too dark to see anything.

He ran his hand along the wall at shoulder height until it came into contact with a thick cable. He followed the cable down with his fingers until it connected with the kind of round light switches used in the fifties.

There was a loud click, as Packer turned the lights on.

An unshaded bulb came on overhead, casting a cone of bright light straight down.

The ground beneath was covered in grimy concrete, stained with sump oil and mud.

Rows of wooden stables lined the back wall, with housing for eight horses. Against one wall, a rusting shovel lay against a lawnmower covered in cobwebs and half a dozen neglected garden tools lay on the ground beside them.

The light from the overhead bulb was eaten up by the darkness on either side. Packer took out his mobile phone and switched on the light, using it like a torch.

He walked along past the rows of abandoned stables.

The first was filled with newish-looking cardboard boxes stacked up to shoulder height. They were surrounded by mops, buckets and a dozen large drums of industrial cleaner.

The next one contained more cardboard boxes, but these were much older and had cobwebs hanging was some of them. A two-wheeled racing sulky sat beside them, rotting away.

Packer heard movement from the doorway and spun around.

"Just me, boss," Thompson said, stepping into the stables.

Thompson looked around. "Looks like the storage shed, eh?"

Packer said nothing but turned back the way he had been heading.

At the end of the building there was a large, square shape covered with a grey sheet that rose up almost to the ceiling.

"Give me a hand with this," he said, putting his phone back in his pocket.

Thompson walked over to join him, and they each grabbed an end of the grey sheet and pulled.

It was heavy, industrial tarpaulin and it took some effort to tug it back towards them. It slid along the top of the shape with a loud scraping sound.

Once they had pulled enough forward, the weight of the tarpaulin took over and it slid to the ground with a loud swish, falling in a heap at their feet.

The white van stood before them.

"Christ," Thompson hissed.

Packer took his phone back out of his pocket and switched it on again.

"You got any gloves on you?" he asked.

"There'll be some in the boot of the car," Thompson said, "Do you want me to get some?"

"In a minute," Packer said.

Careful not to touch the side of the van, he held his phone just in front of the passenger window. The light lit up the inside of the van. There were a couple of pens on the dashboard and empty drink cans on the floor.

Packer moved along the side of the van. There were no windows.

He moved around to the back of the van and shone the phone light in through the rear window.

The back of the van was empty, apart from a crushed Coke can, some small corners of torn cardboard and a few small pieces of rubbish.

"Look at the floor," Packer said.

Thompson leaned in beside him and Packer held the beam of the phone light steady.

The floor was covered with thick matting that had once been a light tan colour, but was dirty and covered with stains from chemicals and solvents. The edge along the step next to the side door was heavily frayed and there were torn patches where things being moved in and out of the van had ripped open the vinyl surface of the mat.

In the light from Packer's phone, tiny fibres of underlay poked through the torn patches.

"The hair on the bra," Thompson said.

Packer turned away from the van.

He stepped back towards the door to the stables.

He had taken only three steps when there was a loud, wet thump and Thompson cried out. He crashed into the back of Packer, knocking him down.

Packer pushed against the filthy concrete, trying to get up, but Thompson was lying across his legs.

He shifted to the side.

Something hard and sharp slammed against the side of his face, knocking his head back. Intense pain flared up the side of his face, making him grunt loudly.

Shaking off the sudden shock, Packer saw a dark shape run past him.

Yanking his feet out from under Thompson's heavy bulk, Packer got his knees underneath him.

"George!" he yelled, "George!"

"Aye," Thompson grunted, "I'm alright. Get the fucker."

Packer shoved himself to his feet. The movement made the stable swim wildly around him and he felt like vomiting. He could feel blood running down the side of his face.

A man moved quickly from the cone of light under the bulb and disappeared out through the door of the building.

Packer raced along the side of the stables and out through the door, black spots flaring across his vision.

As he fumbled with the latch and pushed against one of the gates, Tom Kirby turned back to look at Packer. He was holding a length of rusting steel fence post in one hand.

Realising he would not get the gate open before Packer was on top of him, Kirby stopped and took a step forward.

Packer's head was screaming, blood pouring down over one eye.

As Kirby swung the steel length at him, Packer stepped back and shifted to the side. The ground lurched dangerously beneath him.

The steel post passed by his face with little room to spare, and Packer felt the air shift as it passed by.

Kirby's arm was heading down, the force of the swing moving it away.

Packer swung a fist up into Kirby's stomach, turning at the hip to put his weight behind it.

Kirby gave a loud grunt as the wind rushed from him.

But fired up with adrenaline, he straightened up again. He swung at Packer with his free hand, thumping into the open wound in the side of Packer's face with a wet squelch.

Packer grunted loudly as agony flared along the side of his face and his vision went fuzzy.

He was knocked back by the blow and Kirby followed after him.

Barely able to see, Packer ducked low, feeling the steel beam pass close by his head once again.

He charged forward, grabbing Kirby around the chest in a tackle and lifting his feet off the ground.

He slammed Kirby against the wooden gates and heard the clang of steel on concrete as the post hit the ground.

Without pausing, Packer pulled his arm back and slammed his fist into Kirby's stomach again. Kirby clawed at the open wound, making Packer grunt with pain through clenched teeth.

He slammed his fists into Kirby's stomach, punching him again and again, until he finally felt Kirby begin to slump.

As Kirby began to slide down the gate, Packer put his hands on the gate to steady himself.

Holding himself up with one hand against the gate, and panting hard, Packer looked down at Kirby.

Kirby was lying on the ground at his feet, clutching at his stomach and whooping hard as he struggled for breath.

Packer drew his leg back and sank his foot into Kirby's stomach as hard as he could.

Thrown back against the gate, Kirby curled up, trying to protect himself. Packer stamped down on him again and again.

"Boss," Thompson yelled from across the yard, "That's enough."

With an effort, Packer stopped. He leant against the gate and looked down at Kirby's motionless body.

Thompson stood behind him, one hand on the back of his head. Blood was running down his arm and dripping over his shoulder.

Packer breathed hard.

"I told you it was your turn this time," he said.

Chapter 34

The door of the interview room opened, and Thompson entered.

He closed the door behind him, then sat down at the table beside Packer. They were both facing Kirby, who sat in the chair opposite.

"We're recording, boss," Thompson muttered.

"The date is 3 October," Packer said, looking at his watch, "and the time is 3:23pm. I'm Detective Senior Sergeant Tony Packer. With me is Detective Senior Constable George Thompson. Can you please state your full name and date of birth?"

"Thomas Francis Kirby," Kirby said, "16 July, 1980."

"We are currently in the East Perth Police Station," Packer continued, "This is a recorded interview. Before we go any further, I wish to advise you that you have certain rights. Firstly, you have a right to silence. You do not have to answer any of our questions. You may answer some, all or none of the questions we ask. It is entirely up to you. Do you understand?"

Kirby nodded.

"Can you answer by speaking, please?"

"Yes," Kirby muttered, "I understand."

"If I ask you ten questions, how many do you have to answer?"

"None," Kirby said.

"In addition to your right to silence, you also have the right to legal advice. Have you spoken to a solicitor."

"No."

"Do you wish to speak to a solicitor?"

Kirby shook his head. "No, I do not."

"You also have the right to speak to a friend or family member if you wish. Do you-"

"No."

"You also have a right to medical treatment. Do-"

"No," Kirby said, more firmly, "Can we just get on with it?"

Packer nodded. "Alright. Earlier today, at approximately twelve noon, I arrested you for the murder of Imani Mbanda, also known as Emily Mbuta. You remain under arrest for her murder."

Kirby nodded.

"Did you know Emily Mbuta?" Packer asked.

"Yes, I knew her," Kirby said.

"How did you first meet?"

"She was doing cleaning work for me."

"Tell us how the cleaning work first started."

"I had a business cleaning building sites. The overheads were huge, and I kept borrowing money to try to keep it going. But it still went broke, leaving me with about eighty grand in debts. I had the idea of doing commercial cleaning after hours, and my account suggested using contractors to avoid all the costs of having employees. There were tons of illegals living in Jeff's properties and they always needed money. None of them are supposed to be here, so they can't work normally. I just started asking some if they wanted some cheap labour, cash-in-hand, no questions asked."

"And they did?"

"Shit, yeah. They thought it was fucking Christmas. There were a few problems sometimes. A few of the blokes came here illegally because they had criminal records in their own country. They sometimes started a knuckle or stole shit, so we had to get rid of them. One of them stabbed someone once. That was a fucking nightmare, sorting that out."

Packer interrupted, before Kirby could wander too much further off track.

"When did you first meet Emily?"

"January, I think. February, maybe."

"Of which year?"

"This year."

"How did she come to be doing cleaning work for you?"

"There was another African girl living at the same flat as Emily, who was working for me at the time. Precious, I think her name was. They all contact each other somehow, like a network that lets them know where to stay before they come here. Precious knew Emily and told her to come and stay with her. She brought Emily along to work one night."

"You told us previously that Billy Harrison sent people to you for a spotter's fee."

"Yeah."

"But Emily was not one of those?"

"No. Not all of them come through Billy. The ones that are here get in touch with their friends and families in their own country and tell them how to come here and where to stay. Kind of like passing on tips to help others get around the rules and get into Australia, too. I got a lot of people that way. Word-of-mouth."

"You said Emily was there one night?"

"Yeah. They know to wait near the train station opposite Forrest Place to get picked up. Precious said Emily wanted work, so I gave it to her."

"Did you have any direct contact with Emily that first night?"

Kirby nodded, grinning. "Yeah."

Recognising that there was something else here, Packer fell silent. He watched Kirby, waiting for him to continue on his own.

"Emily was gorgeous," Kirby said, "Huge tits and a round arse. Real pretty face. So, I started talking to her, making a big deal of her. Told her at the end of the night she'd done a really great job and I wanted to her come back again.

"It's easy with the illegals. They don't usually know that many people here, and they're worried they're gonna get caught and sent home, so if someone's friendly to them, they usually jump on it right away."

"Is that what Emily did?"

Kirby nodded. "Yeah. I took her out for a drink a couple of times, bought her dinner. She wasn't stupid, though. Some of them think you're looking for a girlfriend. Emily knew I just wanted to fuck her."

"And did you?"

Kirby nodded. "Not at first."

"What then?"

"She wanted money to bring her family out here to Australia. She came in on a student visa, but they couldn't do that. Her brother was just a kid, and the father had been in jail a few times in Africa, which destroyed his chances of getting a visa. The only choice was people smugglers, and that's too expensive unless you're willing to bring in drugs with you when you come, which is fucking risky."

"Emily told you she wanted money to bring her family here?"

"Yeah. Said she wasn't earning enough from the cleaning, and wanted to know if she could get more money another way."

"What did you tell her?"

Kirby looked up at him. He let out a low breath.

"Emily wasn't stupid. I told you that," Kirby said, "She wanted me to pay to fuck her. Made it clear she wasn't going to come across just 'cause I was buying her dinner."

"How did you respond?"

Kirby gave a faint smile.

"I was pissed off about it, to tell you the truth. I fucked a lot of these girls for the price of a glass of wine or a cheap night out. Asking me for money on top was pretty fucking rude, you know?"

"Did you pay her?"

Kirby nodded. "Gave her fifty bucks for a blowie. Then next time, I gave her a hundred for a proper fuck."

He looked across the room, staring at the wall.

"Then I told her about the movies."

Kirby fell silent again.

Packer waited, saying nothing.

"Even at the time, I thought it was risky," Kirby said, eventually, "You learn how to pick the ones who can keep their mouths shut. The quiet ones. The stupid ones. Emily wasn't dumb, and it was her that asked me for money. I had a bad feeling about it, but I needed a girl, and Emily was really hot. She could be a big earner."

"What do you mean when you say the movies?" Packer asked.

Kirby took in a breath and let it out.

"Stick movies. Porn."

"You said you learned how to pick girls?"

Kirby looked at him. "Why are you asking me this? You fucking know all this."

"You tell us about it," Packer said, "Why were picking girls?"

"I was picking girls to be in the movies. Then I was filming them."

"Porn movies?"

"Yeah, but niche stuff, right? The stuff you can't get anywhere else. Special interest stuff."

"Such as?"

Kirby shrugged. "Animals. Heavy S&M. The stuff that's illegal."

"And there's a market for that?"

Kirby smirked. "Huge fucking market. You would not believe how many people want this shit. And they pay a fucking fortune for it, too. Especially if it's made to order."

"How did you first become involved in making these movies?"

"Would you believe it started with a man in a pub?" he said, grinning.

Packer remained silent.

"That really is what happened," Kirby went on, "I started talking to some bloke one night over in Northbridge who was pissed off his tits. He was telling me about these hardcore S&M DVDs he got from Thailand or the Philippines or somewhere. We ended up back at his place, watching a few of them. He told me he paid a fortune for them. The site cleaning business was still going then, but it was going broke and running up huge debts. It suddenly occurred to me that if this bloke was willing to pay $300 for a movie, then so would other people. I could hire a hooker and make my own to sell. Use the money to keep the business afloat. That's how it started."

"Where did you make these movies?"

"The site cleaning business operated from one of Jeff's sheds in Osbourne Park. Bringing the hookers there was a bit risky, but I had nowhere else to take them. There was a heap of insulation that I cleaned out from a demolition site, and I stuck that up on the wall to deaden the sound. Worked pretty well."

"And you used prostitutes for this?" Packer asked.

"To start off with, yeah," Kirby said, "but none of them would do bondage or any of that. They all reckoned it was too dangerous. So, I had to start by filming normal porn and work my way up gradually to the harder stuff. I kept increasing the money each time, so they all went along with it even when it got harder and harder. Eventually, it got to a point where they wouldn't go any further and wouldn't do it again. So, then I had to find another hooker and start again."

"How many prostitutes did you use for this?"

Kirby shrugged. "Not that many. Six or seven, probably."

He shook his head. "Then one of them got this idea that she could blackmail me. Told me she'd go to the police if I didn't pay ten grand. She would have, too, so I had to pay her. Cleaned out everything I'd earned up until that point."

"What was her name, this girl who blackmailed you?"

"I don't know. It was years ago. None of them used their real names anyway."

"She knew your name?"

Kirby shook his head. "I used a fake name. She knew the car, though."

"What happened after that?"

"That scared me off for a while. I paid her, but I was shitting myself that she was going to go to the police, anyway. I stopped for months after that. Started up the cleaning business with the illegals from Jeff's places, instead."

"You started again, though?" Packer prompted.

Kirby smiled. "Yeah. Prostitutes were risky, and I wasn't going to take that risk again. But then it occurred to me that the illegals were a safe bet. They couldn't go to the police, or tell anyone about what I was doing, because they would get deported. They needed money under the table, and they couldn't rat on me to the police."

"How many girls from Frazier's flats did you use?"

Kirby thought about it.

"Thirty maybe? I couldn't keep using the same ones, because the customers got bored. They wanted to see new faces all the time."

"Do you remember any of their names?"

"Yeah, some of them."

"Mariana Chou?"

Kirby nodded. "Yeah. I remember her."

"Tell us about her."

"Started off okay. She was good, too, loved the camera. But then she started using drugs. She was doped out half the time when we were filming, so she wasn't reacting properly. And she started to look like a druggie. Lost heaps of weight, her face got that hollow look. She disappeared one day. Probably dead, now."

"What happened before she disappeared?"

Kirby shrugged. "I can't remember now."

"Something out of the ordinary?" Packer asked.

Kirby looked hard at him. "You know about that, do you? A few people knew about the movies by then. I started getting special requests, which some blokes were willing to pay through the nose for. One bloke owned a racehorse. He wanted to see the horse mounting a girl. Mariana was so out of it by then that she'd become a liability anyway. I used her. Got thirty grand for the video. It was a nice little earner."

"What then?"

"I started hunting around Jeff's places for another girl."

"Did Frazier know you were recruiting cleaners from his places?"

"Yeah. He was pretty happy with the arrangement, because it meant they had money to pay the rent each week. Fewer tenants were missing rent payments."

"Did he get suspicious it was more than that?"

Kirby looked at him, his eyes narrowing in confusion.

"How do you mean?" he asked.

"Did Frazier ever suspect you were using the girls from the flats for the movies, too?"

Kirby blinked.

He looked to Thompson, then back to Packer again.

"I thought youse knew," Kirby said, "Jeff was the fucking camera man. He filmed most of them."

Chapter 35

"How did Frazier first become involved?" Packer asked.

"My big mouth," Kirby said, with a slight snort, "Jeff and me have been going to the races for years. He knew the site cleaning business had gone under and he knew I had big debts from it. But I was still taking some pretty big punts on the horses. He wanted to know where I was getting the money from. I was pissed off my tits and he was a mate, so I told him."

Kirby shrugged. "I thought he'd just laugh about it. Instead, he wanted in. He had money issues as well and wanted a piece of the action on the videos.

"Of course, I already knew he was having money problems, too. He never shut up about it. He'd sold off a lot of his commercial properties because he couldn't afford to keep them. He actually sold the unit I was using out at Osbourne Park, which was a pain the arse, but I got in touch with the new owner and arranged to lease it from him using a phony name. Jeff thought it was fucking hilarious when he found out what I'd been using the place for. Told me he reckoned he was owed royalties on all the videos up until then because he was the studio owner."

"Did Frazier film all of these videos after that?"

"No. I told you I had to start off doing straight sex with the girls at first. He never came for any of those, and I just hit 'record' myself. No one was ever going to see any of those anyway. But after it started moving into the stuff we were selling, he'd come along to help. Enjoyed himself, too."

"Did he ever work in front of the camera?"

"No. That was all me."

"Tell us about Emily."

"What did I get up to before?" Kirby asked.

"You were paying her for sex. Then you told her about the movies."

Kirby nodded. He was silent for a moment while he thought.

"It started the same as all the others. I took her out to the workshop and rooted her while I filmed it. Paid her five hundred that. I did that a couple of times. Then I started paying her more and going a bit further each time."

"She was a willing participant?"

Kirby grinned. "She was an *eager* participant. Kept asking what she had to do to make more money."

Kirby fell silent again.

He took in a breath and let it out.

"The first couple of times it was standard S&M stuff. Tied her up and gagged her before fucking her. I told her she could make more money if it was rougher. She just wanted to know how much more money."

He shook his head slightly. "So, she moved on to rougher stuff. Rape scenes. It was all fake, but the violence was real. I'd punch her up a bit, few kicks in the guts, then straight into it. Had to pay her a couple of grand for those because she was all bruised and shit afterwards."

"How many times did you this?"

"Four straight S&Ms and two rapes," Kirby said.

His voice fell to little more than a whisper. "Then the last one."

"Tell us about the last one."

Kirby was silent for a long time, staring down at the table.

"There was a collector who bought all the earlier videos with Emily. He was talking about wanting to meet her. Pretty fucking weird. Then he started asking if we could get her to do something even rougher."

"Did he say what?"

Kirby nodded.

"Yeah," he said, quietly, "He wanted to see her getting choked. I'd made those before and sold them to him, but he wanted more. He wanted to watch Emily getting choked until she passed out, then revived, and choked again. He never actually said it, but what he really wanted was a snuff movie. He wanted to see Emily getting choked to death."

"Did you arrange this?"

Kirby nodded again. "Took us ages to agree on a price. Got seventy grand out of him. Emily's cut was eight."

"She agreed to this?"

"Didn't even fucking hesitate. As soon as I told her she'd get eight grand for it, she wanted in."

"What happened?"

"I picked her up and took her to the workshop. That's where I filmed all of them. It started off like the other movies. I put the mask on and punched her a couple of times. Then I put her over the bench and used cable ties on her ankles and wrists, so she couldn't move. Fucked her a bit from behind while I was hitting in the back with a belt."

Kirby trailed off.

His face had gone pale, and he was staring at the table, his eyes unfocussed.

He took in a breath and let it out.

"Then I went round in front of her. I put the belt around her neck and made her suck me dick. Pulled the belt tight and hit her in the face a couple of times. Just as she started passing out, I loosened up the belt and let her get her breath back. I did this a couple more times.

"She was trying to talk. I think she was saying, 'stop,' but we'd been paid, so we had to deliver the product."

Kirby swallowed hard and shook his head.

He sat there for a moment, thinking about it before he continued.

"So, I pulled the belt tight around her neck again, then stuck my dick back in her mouth. I was shoving it down her throat for a while, and she shit herself. That happens sometimes with some of the girls. The customers like it. I didn't think much about it.

"After a while, I realised she wasn't moving at all. I pulled the belt off, but it was too late. She was gone."

Kirby's breath came out in a low sigh.

"I tried to wake her up," he said, his voice little more than a whisper now, "I fucking swear, I tried to wake her up. But I couldn't do nothing. It was too late."

He trailed off, shaking his head.

Packer sat there in silence, his face blank. He waited until Kirby could get himself under control again.

"Fucking Jeff," he spat after a moment, "As soon as he realised what had happened, he pissed off and left me to deal with it. He had some business dinner arranged, but he showed up three hours early and spent all afternoon getting his photo taken, while he left me with the fucking dead body."

Kirby fell silent again.

"I didn't know what to fucking do. I sat there for ages, just trying to work it out. Eventually, I went down to the Bunnings down the road and bought a plastic drop sheet. Then I wrapped Emily and her stuff up in it and dumped her in Northbridge. That place is a fucking shithole, so I figured you'd think she'd been killed there.

"I couldn't use my own car, but I still had the old van in the shed at home. It was worthless, so I'd never bothered trying to sell it. It took me an hour to get it started. The rego had run out and I spent the whole time worried I'd get pulled over.

"That night, I started worrying about forensics and shit, so I went back and covered the place in bleach and cleaning stuff."

He rubbed at his eyes again, then sat back in the chair. He looked exhausted, but seemed somehow relieved, too. Having finally confessed, he was finished.

He looked up at Packer, whose face remained blank.

Then he looked across at Thompson, who was staring at him, barely contained anger beneath the surface.

Kirby shrugged.

"That's it. That's all of it. I got nothing else to tell you."

Packer sat there for a moment.

He looked at his watch.

"Interview terminated at 4:42pm."

Chapter 36

Packer stood by the doorway and watched in silence.

Two of the forensics officers wearing blue gloves walked out from the office below the balcony. One of them was carrying the computer, which was now wrapped in a plastic sheet. The other had an exhibits bag in each hand.

When Frazier saw the computer going past, he started yelling again.

"That's got confidential bloody information on it," he yelled, "You can't go fuckin' lookin' at that! Put that fuckin' back, you cunts!"

His hands were cuffed behind his back, but he was trying to lurch forward. The uniformed officers on either side of him held his shoulders, pulling him back again.

Donald Wheeler was doing his best to calm Frazier down.

"They're legally allowed to take it, Jeff," Wheeler said, his hands on Frazier's chest, "The search warrant specifically covers the computer. We can't stop them."

"Then what the fuck am I payin' you for, ya useless cunt?" Frazier shouted, spittle landing on Wheeler's cheek, "Best fuckin' criminal lawyer in Perth, my fuckin' arse. You're fuckin' useless!"

Frazier turned to yell at more forensics officers, who were filing into the office.

Wheeler walked across to Packer. He had taken a handkerchief out of his pocket and was using it to wipe the spittle from his cheek.

"Was all this really necessary, Sergeant?" Wheeler asked, "All you had to do was ask my client to attend the police station, and all this could have been avoided."

Packer looked at Wheeler but said nothing. Packer had a low tolerance for criminal defence lawyers at the best of times, but there was something about Wheeler that made his skin crawl. He was not at all surprised to find that Frazier had called Wheeler when four police cars arrived at his front gate, but he wasn't going to pretend he was happy about it.

"I didn't want any evidence disappearing," Packer said.

"Oh, really now?" Wheeler said, one eyebrow raised, "This isn't Hollywood, Sergeant. This is Peppermint Grove. You can't seriously believe my client has anything to do with murder?"

Packer ignored him and looked over at Frazier, who was still shouting abuse at the forensics officers.

Frazier looked around. His gaze flicked past Packer momentarily and away.

Then it flicked back to Packer again.

"You, ya cunt!" he screamed at Packer, "You fuckin' hidin' over there in the corner while you let these other fuckin' pigs do all the work. You fuckin' scared to face me, cunt? Are ya?"

Packer watched him for a moment, his face blank, while Frazier continued screaming at him across the room, the two uniforms restraining him.

"George," Packer said, "Take Mr Frazier out and put him in the car."

"Now wait a minute," Wheeler said, raising his voice, "There are media everywhere out there on the street."

Packer knew there were. He had tipped them all off before they had come here.

"There must be five camera crews out there," Wheeler continued, "and dozens of reporters. Bring your police vehicle in here and Mr Frazier can get into it in the privacy of his front lawn, where he can't be photographed."

Packer looked at him for a moment, then back at Thompson.

He jerked his head towards the door.

"Boss," Thompson said, grinning.

"This is outrageous, Sergeant," Wheeler said, his voice growing into a whine, as it got louder, "I must insist that you stop this. My client has the right to privacy from the media."

Packer stood in silence, ignoring Wheeler's ranting, as Thompson walked across to Frazier. The two uniformed officers began to manhandle Frazier forward.

Frazier was still screaming, his face red and his lips pulled back over his teeth. Spit was flying from his mouth, as he yelled, and struggled against the two large officers who dragged him towards the door.

As he drew closer to Packer, Frazier tried to lurch towards him, pulling against the officers restraining him.

"You cunt," Frazier yelled, "Get these fuckin' cuffs off and we'll see who the real fuckin' man in the room is. Come on, ya fuckin' pussy! You got no fuckin' balls!"

The two officers dragged him towards the door, as Packer watched, blank-faced.

Frazier spat at him, but it went wide, and Wheeler had to shift hurriedly to the side to avoid getting hit again.

Thompson stopped by Packer and watched.

Frazier was pushed down the steps and along the driveway still screaming abuse.

A couple of flashbulbs went off from behind the police cordon, as he was pulled closer to the gate.

"Why are you even bothering yourself with this?" Wheeler asked, "You know as well as I do that you've got no case against my client."

Packer watched Frazier being dragged through the front gates.

"The only thing connecting my client to any of this is the sole word of a pornographer who has been arrested for murder. You seriously think any of this will get to court? This is a complete waste of everyone's time, and you know it."

"George," Packer said, quietly, staring out into the front yard, "Show Mr Wheeler to his car."

"Boss," Thompson said.

He put one hand on the shoulder of Wheeler's expensive suit, but Wheeler shrugged it off.

"Take your hands off me," he snapped.

Rubbing at the shoulder of his suit jacket with his handkerchief, he stepped away from them.

He stood there for a moment, staring angrily at them.

As Wheeler opened his mouth to speak, Packer looked across at him.

Something in Packer's eyes made Wheeler take another step back. Closing his mouth, he turned and walked out through the front door to the driveway.

"Slimy prick," Thompson muttered, "I hate Donald Wheeler."

Packer said nothing.

"You think there's anything on the computers?" Thompson asked.

Packer shook his head. "Frazier's not stupid."

"So, we're relying on Harrison?"

Packer shrugged.

Thompson let out a breath.

"Wheeler's probably right," Thompson said, "We're never gonna build a case on the word of Harrison alone. I doubt the DPP will even run with it, if that's all we've got."

Packer shook his head.

"No," he said, "I don't think they will either."

He watched the camera crews following Frazier as he was dragged along the street towards the waiting police van.

"Still," Packer said, "At least he made the headlines."

Epilogue

Macguire sniffed as he stopped at the edge of the street. With his hands pushed into the pockets of his jumper, he stood and looked along Mountain Terrace towards the railway. The glare of headlights made him squint, and he waited for the car to pass before crossing the road to the park.

A single streetlight cast a feeble glow over the footpath. The park was completely dark.

He was wired from the meth he had snorted before coming out, and full of bravado. But even in this state, he was unwilling to walk into the darkness alone.

Fortunately, he didn't have to.

A man in an Adidas hoodie stepped was waiting in the shadows a few metres away and walked towards him.

Macguire sniffed again, as he watched the man get closer.

His hand gripped the Stanley knife in his pocket.

"Hey, mate, are you Macquire?" asked the man, as he got closer.

"Yeah, bro," Macquire said, grinning, as he felt relief run through him.

"Cool," the other man nodded, stopping a couple of steps away, "I was starting to think you weren't coming."

"Sorry, bro. Got kind of caught up on other shit, you know?"

"Yeah, no worries. Thommo said you might be a bit late."

The man reached into his pocket, then held out a handful of bank notes.

"Hey, whoa," Macquire hissed, pushing his hand down, "Keep your fuckin' hand down, bro."

"Oh, shit. Sorry."

"It's cool, but just don't be too fuckin' obvious, right?"

The man nodded and stood there.

Macquire looked along the street, then back again. Seeing nobody, he reached out his hand and took the small bundle of cash.

In the dim light, he thumbed through the notes, counting out four fifties. He pushed them into his jeans pocket.

Reaching into the pocket of his jumper, Macquire closed his fingers around a tiny zip-lock bag. Keeping his hand down low, he reached down and pressed it against the man's hand.

As soon as he felt the man's fingers close around the plastic bag, Macquire turned to go.

"See ya, bro," Macquire said, "Enjoy."

"Yeah, thanks," he heard the man say.

Pushing the tiny packet of methylamphetamine into his pocket, Mickey Simmons watched Macquire disappear down the street, then turned and walked away in the opposite direction.

***

"Hey, George," called one of the uniforms outside the custody area, as George headed towards the door, "There's a call for you."

Thompson stopped and looked back at the young lad, who was half-standing up in his chair, holding the telephone receiver against his chest.

It had been a long week. He thought very hard about telling the lad to tell the caller that he'd already left for the day.

But instead, he nodded and walked back to the desk.

He took the receiver from the officer and held it to his ear.

"Senior Constable Thompson," he said.

"Oh, hello, Senior," said a voice that sounded about fifteen years old, "I'm sorry if you were leaving for the day."

"What is it, son?" Thompson asked, feeling irritated.

"I'm Probationer Constable White at Mt Lawley," said the officer.

"Right. What is it?"

"We've just arrested a man on suspicion of sex assault. He was on bail for attempted sex assault already. He got a drunk female behind one of the pubs here and got her pants down. There seems to have been a struggle, and he started hitting her to the face-"

"Why are you telling me this?" Thompson asked.

"Well, there's an alert on the system. It came up when I started processing him. It says here to call you if he gets arrested again. His name's Sadiq Mehri."

Thompson felt his tiredness disappear.

"Any witnesses?" he asked.

"Yes, sir," said Probationer Constable White, "Two males in the pub saw him pull the female away and went to see if she was okay. He was hitting her when they arrived. We think one of the neighbouring shops has CCTV of the incident, as well."

Thompson grinned.

"What did you say your name was, son?"

"Probationer Constable White, sir. Matt White."

"Well, you hurry up and process Sadiq Mehri, Probationer Constable Matt White," said Thompson, "because when you're done with that, I'm going to buy you a beer."

***

With the investigation over, the rest of the team headed home early, leaving the incident room empty.

Packer sat at his desk.

He could feel the USB drive inside his pocket and resisted the urge to take it out.

He thought back over the discussion he had had with Thompson about Frank McCain.

"He was a good copper. Had a great feel for people, understood what made them tick, and he was good at getting them to open up.

"Actually, he'd had some bad breaks. He had a daughter who died a few years back. She was barely out of her teens. Leukemia, I think. It took her a few months to go. Frank had to watch it happen, knowing there was nothing that could be done about it."

Something about that jarred with Packer.

There was something playing at the edge of his mind, just out of reach.

"She was barely out of her teens. Leukemia, I think. It took her a few months to go. Frank had to watch it happen, knowing there was nothing that could be done about it."

It was almost there.

So close.

He just couldn't quite reach it.

"Jenny couldn't handle it. She left a few months after Genevieve got sick. Didn't even come back for the funeral. Frank changed after his lass died. He got more... withdrawn, I suppose. Started playing his cards close to his chest, you know? Always seemed like he knew more than he was letting on. He wasn't much of a talker."

Packer felt his stomach tense.

He stood up and walked to the doorway of his office.

He looked around to make sure the incident room was empty and the door leading out to the corridor was closed.

Then he returned to his desk and took the USB drive out of his pocket.

Pulling the cap off, he pushed the drive into the USB port at the front of the computer.

The same window appeared on the screen once more, asking for a password.

Packer typed, 'GENEVIEVE,' and hit the 'enter' key.

The password prompt disappeared, to be replaced by a file directory.

Packer read down the list of folders, a frown appearing.

He opened the first and clicked on one of the files.

"Christ," he hissed, as an image filled the screen.

***

PACKER RETURNS IN
AN ABSENCE SO CRUEL

***

If you enjoyed this book, please leave me a rating and/or a review on Amazon and Goodreads. I really appreciate your support.

To join my mailing list and receive news on work-in-progress and new releases, please e-mail me at james.viner.author@gmail.com. I will never provide your e-mail address to any third party.

About the Author

JT Viner was a prosecutor for the *Office of the Director of Public Prosecutions* in Perth, Western Australia, for over fifteen years.

During that time, he conducted criminal trials for murder, rape, abduction, child sex offending, armed robbery and other serious offences.

He spent fifteen years learning the investigative methods of the police force and the inner workings of the criminal mind.

His books are inspired by real crimes.

Printed in Great Britain
by Amazon